D0044453

TWO OR THREE THINGS
I FORGOT TO TELL YOU

TWO OR THREE THINGS I FORGOT TO TELL YOU

Joyce Carol Oates

HARPER TEEN

An Imprint of HarperCollinsPublishers

HarperTeen is an imprint of HarperCollins Publishers.

Two or Three Things I Forgot to Tell You
Copyright © 2012 by The Ontario Review, Inc.
For information address HarperCollins Children's Books,
a division of HarperCollins Publishers,
10 East 53rd Street, New York, NY 10022.
www.epicreads.com

Library of Congress Cataloging-in-Publication Data
Oates, Joyce Carol.
Two or three things I forgot to tell you / Joyce Carol Oates.
— 1st ed.
    p.   cm.
Summary: When their best friend, Tink, dies from an appar-
ent suicide, high school seniors Merissa and Nadia are alientated
by their secrets, adrift from each other and from themselves.
ISBN 978-0-06-211047-3
[1. Secrets—Fiction.   2. Friendship—Fiction.   3. Self-
esteem—Fiction.   4. Cutting (Self-mutilation)—Fiction.
5. Preparatory schools—Fiction.   6. Schools—Fiction.]
I. Title.
PZ7.O1056Tw 2012   2012009699
[Fic]—dc23   CIP
                                                        AC

Typography by Alison Klapthor
12 13 14 15 16   LP/RRDH   10 9 8 7 6 5 4 3 2 1
❖
First Edition

for Tink and her sisters

PROLOGUE: TINK

Not going anywhere. No way.
You guys would screw up totally if I did.

I

THE PERFECT ONE

1.

GOOD NEWS!

"Merissa! Congratulations!"

Hannah's excitement was genuine. Hannah's happiness for Merissa was genuine. Merissa could see.

Merissa had been afraid—just a little, putting herself in Hannah's place—(for Hannah Heller's grades at Quaker Heights Day School were invariably just slightly lower than Merissa Carmichael's, not to mention the fact that Merissa was associate yearbook editor, Drama Club president, and cocaptain of the girls' intramural field hockey team as well; and Hannah had applied to virtually the same colleges as Merissa)—that Hannah would be hurt, and envious, and even resentful, for it is not nearly so easy to be happy for your closest friend's good news as it is to (secretly) rejoice in your closest friend's bad news.

But Hannah was genuinely happy for Merissa. If there was a tiny sliver of hurt, of fear, of self-doubt, even of self-hate in Hannah's heart, she took care not to reveal it.

"Early admission at Brown! Omigod."

Hannah had not—yet—had such good news.

"Merissa, that is *fantastic*. Your first choice!"

The girls hugged each other, laughing.

Hannah felt the sharp-notched vertebrae of Merissa's spine through her sweater, and Merissa felt the fleshiness of Hannah's back beneath the tight ridge of her bra. Quickly the girls stepped away from each other as if each had been made to know too much of the other in just that instant.

"M'rissa! Congratulations!"

There came Chloe Zimmer, flying at Merissa with a quick, breathy hug. There came Anita Chang, squeezing Merissa's arm just hard enough to hurt. There came Shelby Freedman and there came Martine Hesse and there came teary-eyed Nadia Stillinger with a clumsy hug for her friend and a funny little whimper-sob—*"Ohhhh, M'rissa!"*—meant to communicate the fact that Nadia, who hadn't a chance of getting into Brown, or any Ivy League university, felt not jealousy or envy for her dazzling friend but the simple childlike sadness of losing her.

It was their senior year at Quaker Heights Day School: already, December.

Their last year together. This year, without Tink.

"Congratulations, Merissa!"

"Wonderful news, Merissa!"

"We're all so proud of you, Merissa!"

"How do you feel, Merissa? Like you've just won the lottery?"

There was Mr. Trocchi, shaking Merissa's hand as if she were an adult. There was Mrs. Conway, a quick, teacherly hug. There was Mr. Doerr, his "minimalist" smile of approval. There was Ms. Svala, the girls' gym instructor, another brisk handshake, and a damp, toothy grin. There was Dana Crowley, "Good work, Merissa!" There was the upper-school guidance counselor, Mrs. Jameson, and there was Headmaster Nichols, beaming-proud. And there was Merissa's science teacher, Mr. Kessler, who'd been the one, in his quiet way, to really, *really* encourage her.

"It must be a relief, Merissa—to know where you're going next year. To have the suspense *over*."

Except—Tink knows!—the suspense of our lives is never really over.

2.

GOOD NEWS, CONT'D.!

This fantastic week!

First, Merissa learned that she'd been chosen by Mr. Trocchi, the school drama coach, to play the coveted role of Elizabeth Bennet in a stage adaptation of Jane Austen's *Pride and Prejudice*—"You really capture Austen's unique blend of acrid humor and moral seriousness, Merissa. Congratulations!"

(Trying not to notice, for days following, the hurt, puckered expression on Brooke Kramer's face whenever she and Brooke couldn't avoid each other—for Brooke, who'd performed in a half-dozen school productions since ninth grade, had auditioned for the role also, and was bitterly disappointed to have lost out to Merissa Carmichael, who, she believed, couldn't act nearly as well.)

Next day, math class! Where, handing back tests from the previous week, Mr. Doerr observed in his grim/wry way that Merissa Carmichael had "redeemed" her gender in the matter of math, for Merissa had earned 96 percent on the test, higher than anyone else except Virgil Nagy, who'd earned his usual 100 percent.

(Trying not to notice, when Shaun Ryan received his test

from Mr. Doerr, the look of disappointment and shame that came into Shaun's face, like a quick blush; and trying not to notice how, at the end of class, when they might have naturally walked out together, Shaun avoided Merissa to hang back and exchange sardonic wisecracks with another boy who, it seemed, hadn't done so well on the test, either.)

Next day, *Quaker Heights Year '12* staff meeting! For some reason this turned out to be the most productive yearbook meeting of the fall term: Alex Wren, editor in chief, wasn't in one of his sour/sarcastic/kick-me-I-love-it moods but was funny, flirtatious, and sweet with Merissa, despite the fact that she'd "beat him by ten points" on Doerr's math test; Dana Crowley, faculty adviser, English/journalism teacher, was present for only a while, and didn't intrude in her usual kindly/bossy manner that made everyone roll their eyes, in secret, behind her back; and the beautiful cover design on which Merissa and Chloe had worked together for many hours—colors, layout, fonts—was met with unanimous enthusiasm.

("What will they say," Merissa said to Chloe, "when we list Tink, Inc. in the acknowledgments for the cover design?" The girls laughed nervously. For, almost six months after Tink's d***h, the subject of Tink Traumer was still volatile at Quaker Heights Day School. The design their fellow staffers had so admired incorporated one of Tink's Night Sky series, a brilliantly blazing photograph of the constellation Orion, into which, as in a weaving, elongated letters—

QUAKER HEIGHTS YEAR '12

—were ingeniously threaded. The effect was dreamlike and compelling. Chloe said, lowering her voice, "Do you think Tink is there?"—meaning the night sky in the photograph; and Merissa said quickly, averting her eyes, "No. Tink is *here*.")

These were events of Monday, Tuesday, Wednesday. Also on Wednesday, the (fat) acceptance letter from Brown University admissions had come addressed to Merissa Carmichael at 18 West Brook Way, Quaker Heights, New Jersey, while Merissa was in school.

(Though Merissa had asked her mother to please, please, *please* not open any of her mail, forbidding such a "violation of my privacy," Mrs. Carmichael couldn't resist tearing the envelope open on the front step, as soon as she'd discovered it in the mailbox. For the Carmichaels had talked of very little else for months but Merissa's college applications, and Merissa's father, who'd gone to Dartmouth, wanted very badly for his daughter to be admitted to a "top" Ivy school.)

Then, Thursday: when (1) Merissa learned that an essay she'd written for Mr. Kessler's science class—"Our Environment, Ourselves"—had placed third in a high school competition sponsored by *Scientific American*, which Mr. Kessler had encouraged her to enter, and would be posted on the magazine's website; and (2) the girls' field hockey team, on which Merissa was usually only an average-to-good player, managed to win against the higher-ranked Lawrenceville girls' team, partly through Merissa's deft blocking of the Lawrenceville star player—(though Merissa made a joke of limping afterward, insisting she wasn't in pain, a result of having been slammed in the ankle by the furious Lawrenceville player's hockey stick).

Also on Thursday: In the wake of Merissa's good news about Brown, which had quickly spread through the senior class, she was congratulated by the several other seniors who'd scored early admissions at Harvard, Princeton, Yale, and Brown—not close friends of Merissa's but people she liked and admired, mostly.

(Except Merissa was uneasy hearing the others boast of being *like, an elite.*)

(Except Merissa was anxious that Shaun Ryan was avoiding her—it was unmistakable now. And not just Shaun but other guys who'd applied for early admission at Brown, too.)

Then, Friday: Merissa's presentation in her AP English class, a close reading and critical analysis of the Dostoyevsky novel *Notes from Underground*, stirred a lively debate—*Is there an "underground" being who resides inside us, who determines our "conscious" ("daylight") selves, though it is not known to us? Is there any way to discover this being?*—and earned her a grade of A-plus from Mrs. Conway.

(Except it was weird: When Merissa finished her presentation in the English seminar room, where students and teacher sat at a companionable oval table, her heart was beating rapidly and lightly like a fluttering butterfly trapped in a small space, and her armpits were itching, and she'd broken out into a cold sweat! And her friends Chloe and Hannah—and Anita Chang, who was a sometime-friend, one of those friends you don't dare turn your back on, for fear they will say something mean about you, and Gordy Squires, Virgil Nagy, and Alex Wren—were all staring at her for a long, awkward moment before someone said, "Awesome, Merissa! Wow.").

Hey! Not bad, Meris.

Tink prodded Merissa in the ribs. Not much flesh on

Merissa's ribs, so the jab hurt.

Be happy, Meris. As long as they're grading you, grades are good.

Tink's warm breath in Merissa's ear. So that the fine hairs on the back of Merissa's neck stirred.

Tink's special *smell*—like burnt cloves, singed red hair, a briny, picklish scent beneath.

Main thing is—be happy, dude. Don't let me down, 'cause I need my girlfriend.

Was Tink sincere? Or teasing?

Or was Tink in one of her spiteful mean-moods? So you couldn't tell whether she was laughing with you, or at you.

You couldn't trust Tink Traumer when she was alive, so how could you trust Tink Traumer now that she'd *passed over*?

"I heard from Tink today."

Merissa spoke quietly. So that if Hannah didn't choose to hear, she wouldn't have to acknowledge it.

But Chloe drew in her breath sharply—"Ohhh! I g-guess that I did, too."

In lowered voices, the girls spoke together. They were standing at Chloe's open locker outside Mrs. Crowley's homeroom, a little oasis of quiet/privacy amid the noise of the senior corridor. They were standing together, their backs to the corridor, in the hope that no one—not even one of their close friends—would dare to intrude.

Chloe said, "I—I—I wasn't sure if it could be Tink . . . I was coming downstairs this morning, at home, and feeling kind of—I don't know, sad—and my mother was in the kitchen sort of half screaming about something—scolding my brother,

I guess; he'd tracked mud inside on his sneakers so it looked like tiny little *turds* everywhere—and this kind of sick sensation came over me. . . ."

Merissa waited. She *knew*—exactly that sensation.

"And I wondered if I could, you know—*get through it*—the r-rest of my life, I mean—though I wasn't serious, of course," Chloe said quickly, laughing, "not like Tink was s-serious. . . . And just then there was this warm, furry sensation, like a cat's fur against my face—and that way Tink's hair smelled, or her skin—that kind of singed-burnt smell?—and Tink didn't actually *say* anything to me—I think she was just kind of laughing, but not in a mean way—laughing that I would be so silly to make so much of—of—whatever. So I felt better right away. I don't know why—nothing had changed—but still, I felt a lot better. And I think it had to be Tink." Chloe paused, wiping at her eyes. "What did Tink say to you?"

All that Merissa could remember clearly was *Be happy*.

Be happy—dude?

Merissa laughed. It was like Tink to say "dude"—parodying guy-talk, the way guys talked to one another in mimicry of the Dude in *The Big Lebowski*.

"Oh, I don't think that Tink actually *said anything* to me, either—it was just, like with you, she was close by. Then—she vanished."

Merissa was too tactful to tell her friend that Tink had spoken to her. For now that Tink had *passed over*, her friends were even more prone to jealousy over her than they'd been when Tink had been alive.

3.

F

"Sweetie! Congratulations."

Steeling herself for the inevitable even as Daddy stooped to hug her—(a clumsy Daddy hug, since Daddy wasn't so at ease hugging his seventeen-year-old daughter as he'd been years ago hugging his daughter at seven)—"I knew you'd come through, M'rissa!"

Knew you'd come through.

And how the hell did you know, Daddy?

Friday afternoon. Merissa's dazzling week was winding down.

So much good news, it was like a roller coaster ride. One of those wild, terrifying rides where you believe you will die—you will not survive—shrieking with terror that sounds, to people on the ground, like laughter.

Funny to think she belonged to an *elite*.

So Daddy loved her again, for Daddy was proud of her. *A top Ivy school—that's my girl. Brown!*

"Mom had something to do with it, too, Daddy. Don't forget poor old Mom."

"Hey, nooo! Never forget poor old Mom."

Daddy and daughter laughed together, cruelly.

She'd confided in Tink once: "There's this really weird, *funny* thing between Daddy and me—like Mom is somebody to laugh at, and she doesn't have a clue."

And Tink said, "What makes you think your mom doesn't have a clue?"

Tink smirked and scratched at her freckled arms, and fixed Merissa with her green-glassy-laser stare.

Merissa said, shamefaced, "I don't remember how it got started. It just always seemed to be there, from when I was a little girl. Daddy has always been traveling on business, he's away half the time, so when he comes home it's an *occasion*, and Mom, well—Mom is always home. Mom *is* home."

"Not like Big Moms."

(Tink's mother was a well-known—or, as Tink would say, *superannuated*—daytime TV actress. Veronica Traumer was a glamorous woman driven into a rage when Tink called her Big Moms.)

(Tink's father was no longer married to Tink's mother. Or maybe had never been married to Tink's mother. And so Tink did not like to talk about her father, whom she called sometimes the Invisible Man; or the Amazing Vanishing Man. But you could not—ever—ask Tink about either of her parents, or anything she considered *Private*.)

Merissa said, "When I was really little, Daddy would squat down beside me and we'd kind of whisper and laugh together, and Mom would try to laugh with us—she'd say, 'What are you two conspiring about?' and when we wouldn't tell her, it was all the *funnier*."

Tink laughed a flat, nasal, chortling laugh: "Ha-*ha*. Fun-*ny*!"

"I'm just worried Mom might feel hurt. And there isn't anything to it, really—just teasing. . . . Sometimes Daddy reminds me of guys at school—not nice guys, but the others."

"'Male chauvinist pigs,' fem'nists used to call them."

"Oh no—Daddy isn't like that. Daddy can be a little cruel sometimes, but definitely, he is not a *pig*."

"And you know this, how?"

Her? That pug-faced little thing all freckles and elbows? She was a child star on TV?

Mr. Carmichael had encountered Tink only a few times, and not ever any really good time. Among Merissa's friends whom she'd been bringing home in recent years, he'd seemed to like Hannah, and Chloe, and Nadia—(though knowing who Nadia's father was made a distinct impression)—but not Tink Traumer, who'd startled him when Merissa first introduced them by reaching out to shake hands with him, as an adult might have done—"H'lo, Mr. Carmichael! Nice to meet you"—with the kind of smirky-scowl of a smile that you'd have to know Tink to realize wasn't insolent, or even meant to throw off an adult's expectations, but just a playful parody of a little-girl-meeting-her-friend's-daddy-for-the-first-time smile.

"Well! 'Tink'—that's your name, is it? 'Tink'—"

Mr. Carmichael loomed over Tink awkwardly. At her tallest—and Tink could stretch herself "tall" by sucking in her breath, lifting her shoulders and head, and balancing herself on the balls of her feet like a scrappy featherweight boxer—Tink was just five feet tall; she weighed less than ninety pounds; you'd have thought she was possibly eleven, twelve years old, not, as she'd been at this time, fifteen.

Merissa recalled, wincing: those months when Tink had virtually shaved her head, and sharp little red-tinged quills were sprouting from her scalp like a bizarre form of thorny plant life. And Tink's face and forearms were covered in freckles like splatters from a paintbrush, which gave to her lopsided little smile the prankish-quirky look of a mischievous child.

"Well, nice to meet *you*, Tink. Have a great time, girls."

Mr. Carmichael had backed off. The handshake with Tink was quick.

"Sorry about my dad," Merissa said, disappointed that her father hadn't seemed to like her friend Tink more, "but he's really, really busy—we almost never see him during the week. He's—I'm not sure what my dad *does*—he's 'chief legal counsel' of—"

Tink laughed. If Merissa's father hadn't made any effort to be charming to her, as he usually did with Merissa's friends, if he had time, it didn't seem to bother Tink at all. In fact, Tink had to be the only person Merissa had ever met who was amused when others, especially adults, hurriedly left her presence.

"Your dad picks up the signal—Tink doesn't *F* with her friends' dads."

"Tink doesn't what?"

"Tink doesn't *F*."

Merissa didn't know whether to be shocked or annoyed—or offended.

"So, what's *F*?"

"Flirt—Flatter—Fawn Over."

"Merissa?"

"Y-yes, Mom?"

"What are you thinking about, honey? You seem to be lost in space and looking a little . . . sad."

Blood rushed to Merissa's face. "Oh, Mom! I hate it—you spying on me."

"Merissa, I'm not spying on you—truly. I only asked . . ."

"Well, I'm not thinking about anything, Mom, just going upstairs to start homework. And I am not *sad*."

"You certainly shouldn't be, honey. Not after this week—all the wonderful things that have happened to you. At least, the ones you've told me about."

Merissa's mother laughed. As if this was some kind of joke and not a silly, senseless remark of the kind Merissa's mother was always making lately, that made you wonder what she was talking about—if she knew more than she let on, or wanted you to think that she did.

"Don't worry, Mom—I'm not thinking about you-know-who."

"I—I didn't think you were. Not this week, with so much—good news. . . ."

Tink. Of course, I am thinking about Tink.

I am thinking about Daddy, and when I am not thinking

about Daddy, I am thinking about Tink.

And when I am not thinking about Tink or Daddy I am thinking about—something else.

"I heard your father talking to you just now—he's really thrilled, Merissa. This early acceptance at Brown is very good news for us—I mean, all of us." Merissa's mother was smiling—trying to smile—but you could see the strain in her face. Quickly Merissa looked away, not wanting to acknowledge those damp, anxious eyes.

"He's so *proud* of you, Merissa. He brags to everyone. . . ."

Just barely managing not to be impolite—Merissa felt sorry for her mother, and frightened of her, of what her mother might one day soon reveal—Merissa mumbled something more about homework and needing to text Hannah about the yearbook cover, and moved toward the stairs.

By this time she'd been home about ten minutes. That itchy-excited sensation had begun, on the most secret parts of her body, beneath her clothes, as soon as she returned from school—as soon as she stepped through the door into the back hall.

Almost! Almost where I need to be.

Waiting all day for—this.

Merissa dreaded her mother catching her by the wrist, or just touching her. Merissa's mother was one of those women who *touch, touch, touch* to make sure you're listening to them.

". . . dinner tonight, just a little later at seven thirty. Your father needs to be on the phone for a while, there's a conference call . . ."

"Sure, Mom. I'll come down and help."

"He's been under pressure lately. Which is why . . ."

"Sure, Mom! See you."

On the stairs, her heart beating quick and light and excited, and she's thinking, *Flirt. Flatter. Fawn Over.*

Thinking, *Maybe I haven't, enough. With Daddy.*

4.

(SECRET!)

Now Merissa was alone.

For the first time since early that morning, when she'd wakened in the dark before dawn and the heaviness of GOOD NEWS! GOOD NEWS! CONGRATULATIONS! sank down on her like a low-lying toxic cloud.

Quickly shutting the door. In her room, and safe.

Listening to hear if her mother might be following after her—no?

And in the little bathroom adjoining her room, with trembling hands—trembling with excitement, anticipation!—opening a drawer beside the sink, and, at the very back of the drawer, seizing the handle of a small but very sharp paring knife—bringing out the knife, and pressing its tip against the inside of her wrist, where the skin was pale and thin and the little blue veins just visible—"I can do this. Any time. Nobody can stop me."

Her voice was gloating, joyous. In all of the week of Good News, not once had Merissa spoken in such a voice.

"The Perfect One," Tink had teased Merissa Carmichael.

But not even Tink knew about this.

In the mirror above the sink, a luminous-pale face hovered. The wide-set eyes were shadowed, shining, and fierce.

At such (secret) moments Merissa could bear to see herself.

For it was not *herself* she saw but another—a stranger—with the (secret) power of life/death in her hands.

Just an ordinary paring knife, stolen from the kitchen downstairs.

Where there were so many knives—some of them gorgeous, glittering, Japanese-honed stainless-steel carving knives, very expensive—no one would miss this little knife.

This (secret) Merissa had cherished for the past eighteen months—when she'd first cut herself, clumsily, foolishly, in an act of desperation and not of sublime cerebral design.

Now Merissa was *in control*.

Even Tink hadn't known. (But maybe she had guessed?)

For the girls at Quaker Heights, maybe for the guys, too, Tink Traumer had shown the way. You didn't have to like Tink—in fact, Tink had more detractors than admirers, by far—but you had to admit, Tink Traumer had not only *taken her own life in her hands*, she'd had the guts to *throw that life away*.

This week of GOOD NEWS was making Merissa sick, finally. Just so many times you can smile and say, "Thank you!" when someone congratulates you—at a point, you want to say, "Please just leave me alone! It will never happen again."

High grades, class offices, yearbook staff, field hockey, girls' chorus, Elizabeth Bennet in *Pride and Prejudice*, every honor list you can think of, plus, now, early admission at Brown—she was feeling guilty, selfish.

Like her belly bloated with Diet Coke. Just—*disgusting*.

Still, Daddy was proud of her. And if Daddy was proud of Merissa, that meant that Merissa was all right to keep going, for a while at least.

(Secretly) lifting her shirt, to check on the most recent cut.

Just a small cross, on her upper abdomen, each stitchlike scab about an inch long. Already Merissa had forgotten why she'd cut herself there—what the particular reason was scarcely mattered—but it looked good. Healing, and not infected.

And if she prodded it with the tip of the paring knife, a quick-silver flamelike pain leapt from the tiny wound like a muted shout.

Now Merissa was happy.

"'Congratulations!'"

5.

(BAD NEWS!)

"Merissa, sweetie? I have something to tell you."

No no no no NO.

6.

(PUNISHMENT!)

At 7:20 p.m. Merissa went downstairs, finally.

Wondering why her mother hadn't called her to help with dinner.

(Hadn't that been the plan? What was going on?)

After all the good news. Merissa Carmichael among the *elite*.

After Daddy hugging her and telling her, *Knew you'd come through, Merissa! That's my girl.*

Of course, this was nothing to be upset about. Morgan Carmichael was a very busy man.

Except if Daddy loves me. Loves us.

What happened to Tink will not happen to me.

Too distracted to focus on homework, she'd been wasting time before dinner texting her friends, whom she'd seen just hours before and of whom one—Nadia Stillinger—had lately a habit of texting Merissa back within seconds, as if Nadia was very, very lonely or very, very anxious, and such obvious neediness made Merissa feel mean.

Merissa didn't want to get into *that*—whatever it was.

"Mom, why? I mean—why not? Where is Daddy?"

"I—I think he had to go back to the office, honey. He'd been on the phone almost since he came home. He said—I think he said—it was some sort of 'quarterly dividend crisis.' Or maybe—"

Merissa stopped listening. She wanted to clamp her hands over her ears.

So often this had been happening, since September. So often, Daddy was working late at the office—away all weekend on business.

A hot flush of shame came into Merissa's face.

"It's all right, Mom. It's cool. No problem."

"We can eat in the kitchen, Merissa, or if you'd like to watch TV—"

"I'm not hungry, Mom. I wasn't really hungry anyway."

As if she could eat! When punishment was needed, clearly—fasting as well as cutting.

"Daddy asked me to tell you, to be sure to explain, that he was called away 'unavoidably'—he'll make it up this weekend."

Merissa thought, *Mom is lying. Mom is scared. Just like me.*

"Why couldn't Daddy tell me himself? I was just upstairs in my room. He just saw me an hour ago."

Embarrassingly, Merissa's voice was childish, whining. Tink would be surprised—was this the Perfect One? Was this the girl everyone had been envying this week at Quaker Heights Day School?

"Well, there are these sudden emergencies, Merissa. Things happen out of our control—it's no one's fault."

Yes it is. It is your fault.

If he doesn't love you. Why should I love you?

Coolly Merissa said it was all right, really she didn't mind. She'd see Daddy on the weekend, he was taking her skating at the Meadowlands.

Merissa ran back upstairs. Shut—the—damned—*door*.

Checked her cell phone, but just one text message awaited.

CONGRATULATIONS MERISSA!

HEARD TERRIFIC NEWZ U WILL LUV BROWN

XXX COREY

Corey was one of Merissa's cousins—a niece of her mother's. So quickly Merissa's good news had traveled through the family, obviously spread by Merissa's mother.

Corey was nineteen, a sophomore at—where was it?—Sarah Lawrence. Typed at lightning speed and never looked back.

Merissa erased the message without replying. Corey wouldn't remember.

The week had been too long. It was getting to be some kind of joke. She was sick with shame; Shaun must hate her.

At Brooke's party, he'd tried to kiss Merissa—in fact, he had kissed her, for the first time ever, trying to prod Merissa's lips open with his tongue—but Merissa had (involuntarily) flinched.

After so long, after years—being "friends" at school, attracted to each other—or so Merissa had thought.

When Merissa stiffened and drew back from him, Shaun stepped back from *her*.

A flush rising into his face. He'd stammered what sounded like *Oh, hey—cool. Sorry M'ris.*

25

Merissa had insulted him, for sure. She had made an utter fool of herself.

Shaun Ryan was a nice guy—basically—and he'd seemed sincerely sorry, he'd been too aggressive with Merissa; he'd misread her smiles at him, her warm, throaty, giggly laughter. But the other guys would know, and so Shaun would be embarrassed and quickly then he would come to dislike Merissa Carmichael.

No way Merissa could text Shaun

SHAUN PLEASE TRY AGAIN. PLEASE KISS ME AGAIN. I AM SO SORRY—BUT PLEASE WILL YOU TRY AGAIN. . . .

No way. You get one chance.

Anyway, Merissa had beat out Shaun and half the guys in the senior class, getting admitted early to Brown. They'd all applied; Brown was tops on their lists.

But Alex Wren had been nice to Merissa, and Alex had applied, too. Desperately Merissa thought, *Alex likes me! Maybe Shaun will know and be jealous.*

It was all so ridiculous. Tink was correct: You know when it's time to *bail out.*

Now again the shivery sensation rose in Merissa, the itchy excitement crawling along her skin. Eagerly her fingers sought out the secret, stitchlike cuts and scabs in her flesh, more than just the little cross in her abdomen—others, diamond-shaped, heart-shaped beneath her hard little breasts, on the soft curve of her belly, the insides of her thighs.

Punished! You need to be.

Now.

"Disgusting."

Her flabby skin, Merissa meant. If you could pinch and

squeeze flesh between your fingers, you were *fat*.

All the girls at Quaker Heights felt this way. Utterly, utterly disgusting to be *fat*.

How Nadia could bear to look at herself in the mirror, Merissa couldn't imagine. Nadia's features were pretty—especially her warm brown eyes—but her face was round as a plate and she had, if you looked at her sideways, an actual *belly*.

Merissa shuddered. If she looked like Nadia, she'd slash her wrists.

A text message arrived on her phone—NADIA.

Merissa deleted it without reading it.

"What does she want with *me*? She isn't my friend."

Merissa fumbled for a pair of scissors on her desk. Just a small pair of scissors, not the knife.

Quickly pressing the sharp point of the scissors against the inside of her left forearm, at the elbow. (Higher on Merissa's arm were several small, scabby wounds like tattoos.) Just a swift gesture, piercing the skin to relieve pressure in her lungs so that she could breathe.

The cut was shallow—a few drops of blood. Soaked up in a wadded tissue and the tissue flushed away in the toilet.

Not much punishment. But Merissa felt better.

7.

(THE UNSPOKEN)

Daddy is moving out for a while. You know that he has not always been happy lately and that he has been away traveling lately, and now he is moving out—for a while. Daddy wanted me to tell you first, because he will be telling you too, but when he tells you, he has requested—oh Merissa, this is important for both of us, for you, and for me, honey—that you do not CRY.

For Merissa's daddy, like many daddies—like many men, in fact, and boys—did not like to witness tears.

Especially, many men—and boys—do not like to witness tears for which they are responsible.

Tears are blackmail, says Merissa's daddy.

And how UGLY even a beautiful girl's face, contorted by tears! Snot-nose, runny eyes, twisty fish-mouth—Daddy will frown and back away when Merissa—("The Perfect One")—tries her tricks.

8.

"NOTHING TO DO WITH YOU"

"Merissa, honey—the important thing is, please don't think that this has anything to do with *you*."

But Merissa did! Merissa *knew*.

Back in early September, when it began, Merissa *knew*.

(She hadn't told anyone. Not one of her friends. Not even Tink—and anyway, Tink had abandoned *her*.)

Carefully, bravely, Merissa's mother held Merissa's limp hand.

Mother and daughter sitting together at the kitchen table in stark morning sunshine and the household quiet—(Daddy had not returned the night before)—and outside on West Brook Way the dull grinding of the Waste Management truck and a clatter of trash cans like jeering laughter.

"—he says that *there is no one else*—or if there was, for a while last year, remember when Daddy was working so hard on that Northridge account—" Merissa's mother stopped short, as if suddenly realizing she was saying too much. The skin around her eyes was puffy and bruised-looking, and there was a sourish smell to her breath that Merissa realized had become a familiar smell evident when her mother drew close to her. (Had to be some medication she was taking, to help her sleep. Or for "anxiety.") "Your father swears there *is not*—I want to believe him. 'Just a trial separation,' he says. He'll be living on the other side of town in that new condominium village on the river—he 'feels confined' with us, he says—he loves us, he says—but—"

Merissa saw her mother's mouth move, but Merissa was not hearing all that her mother said. This was so ridiculous! So embarrassing! Like a scene in Tink's TV soap opera *Gramercy Park*—(Tink had played a DVD of an episode for her girlfriends once, from a long-ago time when, in the story line of the saga, Tink had played a little girl of nine and her mother, Veronica, had played a neurotic rich man's wife, unrelated to Tink—the girls had laughed at the hokey melodrama, underscored by mood music, such sad, silly women whose lives were a tangle of disappointed marriages and love affairs)—except this was Merissa's *real life*.

Hopeless, Merissa thought. *Both of us.*

All Merissa's good news—even the early acceptance at Brown—what did it mean now?

Not a thing. Not a thing.

Whatever Daddy said about being proud of his little girl, loving her—not a thing.

Except, years ago, Merissa was sure he'd felt differently. As he had felt differently about Merissa's mother, and being married and a father.

And a long time ago, before she'd become the person she was now, when she'd been smaller, and *so cute*. When she'd been

Daddy's little girl and he'd stared at her with love—pulling her onto his lap, whispering to her.

Who's my little girl? Beautiful baby girl.

This was before Morgan Carmichael had become so successful. Before he'd begun being *away* so many nights. Sometimes weekends. *Traveling—on business.*

Because Merissa was not a baby now. She was thin—(thank God!)—meaning that you could see her ribs through her pale skin, and you could feel the vertebrae of her spine if you touched her spine—(which Merissa would not allow, if she could avoid it)—but she was definitely female: breasts, curly little hairs sprouting in her armpits, at her crotch, and on her legs.

And tall: too tall. For there were boys who were scarcely Merissa's height, who would never ask her out for that reason. Even with Merissa slouching—just a bit—there was no disguising this fact.

Last time Merissa's height was measured, she was five feet seven and a half inches tall. Her weight was 104 pounds.

That hadn't been for a while, though—now Merissa could not be examined for fear of the little wounds and scabs being discovered.

Don't touch! My body is my own secret.

She'd learned from Tink: Don't let the Enemy near.

Only friends—who have "proven themselves loyal"—can come near. But even friends shouldn't be entrusted with some secrets—

A secret can be too toxic to expose to a friend.

So, no one had known what Tink was planning.

That way, no one could stop her. No one could scream,

scream, scream at her, *Goddamn you, Tink, we love you!*

No one could betray her by telling Big Moms. Better yet, one of Tink's teachers at school.

It was obvious that what Tink had done to herself had been planned with care. Everything that Tink did, her creative efforts particularly, was planned with care and very little left to chance.

The fact was: Tink had been pronounced d**d—(Merissa could not think, still less say aloud, this terrible word)—on her seventeenth birthday, which had been June 11, 2011.

Pronounced d**d on a morning when her mother, Veronica Traumer, "Big Moms," was thousands of miles away in Los Angeles.

Pronounced d**d at the Quaker Heights Medical Center to which she'd been rushed by ambulance, having been discovered, in her bed, not breathing and unresponsive, by Mrs. Traumer's housekeeper.

"Stop! Just stop."

Merissa spoke aloud, frightened.

"Don't think of Tink *now*."

It was just too sad to think of Tink. And it was just too frustrating to think of Tink. And you couldn't, frankly, think of Tink—if you'd been Tink's friend—without being very angry with her.

Merissa's father had not ever liked Tink. Though he hadn't said anything really negative or critical, you could tell—the way a man can smile sneering at the mention of a girl's or a woman's name so you know he isn't impressed.

Not even pretty. What kind of "TV actress" could that homely red-haired girl have been?

To her shame, Merissa had laughed with Daddy. As if what Daddy said, like some cruel, crude remark tossed out by a sneering guy, was funny.

You want them to like you—love you. You laugh at their jokes that aren't funny; you smile when they break your heart.

For it was certainly true, Merissa's father *did not like her to cry.* Merissa's father *did not like her to be "emotional."*

Years ago when Merissa had been little, of course she'd cried—fretted, fussed, threw little red-faced tantrums—but only when her mother was close by.

If she'd dared to *act up* when her father was close by, he would make a cutting remark and walk out of the room.

Mom had joked, when Merissa was an infant, that any hint of *nursing, diapers, diaper changing* had been enough to make Daddy uncomfortable.

And Daddy had not ever liked the *infant smell*—baby formula, soaked diapers, baby talcum powder.

Who's Daddy's little button-nose? Daddy used to tease when Merissa was freshly bathed, dressed, and *cute.*

But that was years ago. When Daddy seemed to have more time to be at home with his little family, and to *care.*

Merissa tried to remember when Daddy first began to seem not so much to *care.*

When Merissa had been in middle school, maybe. Eighth grade.

Already, she'd been too tall. Towering over some of the shorter boys.

Being pretty—(Merissa had always been "pretty")—didn't matter so much if you were self-conscious, insecure. There were less attractive girls, like Brooke Kramer, who behaved as if they were good-looking and entitled to attention.

If Merissa had earned only "good" grades at school—B-plus, A-minus—her father wouldn't have been impressed. It took really Good News—top achievements—to get his interest. And even so, he rarely asked Merissa about her classes, her teachers, what she was actually doing/learning—he hadn't yet had time to read "Our Environment, Ourselves" as posted on the *Scientific American* website.

At Class Day the previous June, when Merissa Carmichael had been called to the stage as one of just five Quaker Heights "Outstanding Students" of the year, her father hadn't even been in the audience.

Of course, Merissa's mother had been there.

Virtually everyone's mother had been there.

Merissa's birthday was September 5. Not an ideal time for a birthday, so close to Labor Day.

Merissa had always felt deprived of attention, anyway of enough attention—too much happening at once at the start of the school year.

Her girlfriends helped her celebrate. And Mom always made a fuss over her birthday.

This year, Daddy had been *damned sorry* he had to be away—traveling on business to Chicago, then Atlanta. But he'd remembered to call Merissa on her cell phone just before dinner that night to wish her "Happy seventeenth birthday."

"Thanks, Dad! I'm flattered you got my age right."

There was a moment's startled silence at the other end of the line.

(Was Daddy's girl being *sarcastic*?)

"Just kidding, Dad. I'm really glad to hear from you . . . and miss you like crazy."

Merissa's mother was disappointed, too. And maybe just a little surprised.

But determined to be cheerful and uncomplaining—understanding, upbeat.

"Daddy is really, really sorry, Merissa—you could hear it in his voice. It just breaks his heart to miss so many—to miss special times with his family."

Merissa's mother suggested that Merissa invite her closest friends from school to have dinner with them that night, but Merissa said no thanks!

Her friends had already treated her to a really nice lunch at a restaurant in town, and they'd given her presents, and Merissa had told them that her birthday dinner was that night, just her mom and dad.

Merissa's mother persisted. "Well, maybe just call Hannah? She's such a sweet girl. . . ."

You don't know Hannah any more than you knew Tink. Or me.

"It's late notice, of course, but I'm sure that Hannah would love to come over for a while at least. There's plenty of food; we can eat in the family room, you could watch a DVD. . . . We could even invite Hannah's mother—she might be free, if her husband isn't home."

"Mom, thanks! Sounds great, except I really don't want to 'double date'—Hannah and me, and you and Mrs. Heller." Merissa spoke lightly, but inside she was trembling with rage.

Wanting to tell her mother, *If Daddy doesn't love me, nobody else matters. What do I care about anybody else?*

That night Merissa worked herself into an anxious state, unable to sleep. The little (secret) wounds on her body were smarting and hurting, and she was just slightly frightened that one or two of them were becoming infected—this was scary.

All kinds of crazy thoughts flew through her mind, and there came Tink to tease her—*What did you expect, Perfect One? Your birthday is soooo important to Daddy?*

Tink was just jealous, Merissa thought. Tink hadn't any actual father anyone had ever seen, and Tink's mother, Big Moms, would have "sacrificed" any kid of hers to her "third-rate career"—as Tink had liked to say.

Sometimes, in front of her mother, Tink would make this wisecrack. And Veronica Traumer would say, hurt, "Trina, that is so *unfair*. It is so *untrue*. I want you to apologize immediately!"

"You mean, your career isn't third-rate? That's what I got wrong?"

Insulted, Veronica might stalk out of the room. The air would quaver in her wake and smell of a strong perfume. You would get the impression that Tink and her bosomy, brassy-haired mother were flinging TV dialogue at each other, not spontaneous and sincere words, and so it was okay to laugh.

In fact, you couldn't not laugh at most of what Tink said.

But Merissa didn't want to think about Tink right now. She was worried that her mother might do something ridiculous—like conspire to give a surprise birthday party for Merissa a day late and call Merissa's friends behind her back after all.

It was a crazy worry, but at two a.m. Merissa couldn't sleep, switched on a light beside her bed, and texted Hannah.

LET ME KNOW IF MY MOM CALLS YOU ABOUT A SURPRISE
BIRTHDAY PARTY. I WILL KILL MYSELF IF THERE IS ANY
SURPRISE PARTY FOR ME.

Of course, Hannah didn't text back until morning—after Merissa spent a miserable night.

HI MERS—WHAT SURPRISE PARTY? WHOSE?

Merissa was stunned; she'd been such an idiot. Texting such a message to Hannah! Revealing too much of her private life and actually saying *I will kill myself,* which was a really stupid and gauche thing to say, after Tink.

She'd have to tell Hannah that *of course* she was only kidding. Wasn't serious.

At Quaker Heights there was a kind of red alert: *If anyone you know speaks of suicide, please do not keep this information to yourself but tell a parent, a teacher, or your guidance counselor.*

How embarrassed and ashamed Merissa would be, if her careless words got her into trouble!

If her father found out. Oh God.

Of course, Merissa's father had promised he'd make up for missing her birthday—he'd bought her a silver bracelet with MERISSA engraved on it.

(Merissa suspected that her mother had bought the bracelet, right here in Quaker Heights. Though the box was a fancy Tiffany box.)

Tonight she'd caught a glimpse of herself downstairs in the kitchen in the shiny copper bottoms of frying pans hanging from hooks in the kitchen.

Ugly! A twisted-looking face with bug eyes, little slit for a mouth.

One little turn of the dial, a beautiful face can turn ugly.

At last, the Unspoken was Spoken.

For it happened that Morgan Carmichael was "moving out"—"temporarily"—from the house on West Brook Way.

Moving out? Daddy, but why?

He tried to explain to Merissa—his decision had certainly had nothing to do with *her*.

He tried to explain to Merissa—this was a "joint decision" of his and her mother's.

(But where was Mom? Why wasn't Mom here, to make this easier?)

"Sometimes it's a good, healthy thing to put a little distance between ourselves. To get a new perspective. To see where improvements can be made in a relationship."

Merissa listened, stunned.

She could not bring herself to ask, *Is there another woman, Daddy? Is that what you are trying to tell me but don't have the nerve?*

". . . terrific new condominium village by the river. As soon as I get settled, you'll come to visit, okay?"

Merissa's mouth was numb. Her tongue felt as if it had been shot with Novocain.

". . . really convenient, just a mile from the train depot. An hour from the airport and New York City."

Still, Merissa was silent. For what she wanted to ask, she could not dare ask. A flicker of impatience came into her father's face.

"We'll talk more, Merissa. A lot more. Okay? And you'll come visit—soon as I get settled?"

Now, in the days following, Merissa heard her mother on the phone, often.

Not talking with her father, though. But talking.

(To her women friends? To those friends who, like her, had husbands who'd "moved out—temporarily"?)

Laughing, or maybe crying. Breathless and dazed-sounding and trying even so to be amusing.

"One of his closets was almost empty, and I was so shocked, I said to him, 'Morgan, what? What is this? Are you moving out of our house without telling me?' and Morgan laughs in that way of his like I've said something ridiculous and tells me straight-faced, 'My clothes are at the dry cleaner's, Stacy—I've been forgetting to pick them up.' And I was so pathetic, wanting to believe him, I said, 'Oh, I'll pick your clothes up at the cleaner's, I'm going into town tomorrow morning,' and Morgan says, like it's all he can do to force himself to look at me, 'Stacy, I don't have the receipt—I'm not sure which dry cleaner it is.' And I say, just so naive, 'But why isn't it Kraft's? We've been using Kraft's for years.' And I said, 'There are only two dry cleaners in Quaker Heights, or maybe three—if you count the one out on Route 27—but you wouldn't have gone to that one, would you?' And Morgan says, 'I'll take care of it, Stacy,' and shuts the closet door."

Merissa thought, This does not sound like a joint decision. Merissa thought, *Pathetic!*

More coolly, calmly: *He wouldn't do this to us, really.*

• • •

Text messages flew. So many, within an hour. Merissa's thumbs ached. Her head ached. Within minutes of sending a text message—within seconds of receiving one—Merissa forgot what the message was, to whom and from whom.

TINK—HEY. GUESS WHAT. YOU NEVER LIKED MY FATHER—

(IT'S COOL, IT'S OK, HE NEVER LIKED YOU EITHER, DUDE!)—

SO YOU WON'T BE SURPRISED. I GUESS HE'S IN LOVE WITH

SOME YOUNG BEAUTIFUL MODEL LIKE A TV HAIR SHAMPOO

MODEL ALL GLOSSY SWINGING HAIR AND PERFECT SKIN.

AND BOOBS! YOU BET.

LOVE FROM

THE PERFECT ONE

Merissa reread her message to Tink. Laughed and wiped at her eyes. No address for Tink! No choice but to delete.

More calmly, Merissa thought really, *really* this could not be so. Hadn't her father said it was a joint decision? He would not have lied to Merissa's face, would he?

Tink had told many tales of the Enemy: the Male Sex.

But you couldn't believe Tink much of the time. She'd been a TV child actor, and you'd think she'd been a stand-up comic, the extravagant and shameless way she exaggerated things.

All men are beasts. But not all beasts are men.

Definitely—they will bite the tits that feed them.

(Was this funny? Or vulgar? Merissa had laughed at the time, but she'd been just a little put-off by Tink, then the "new girl" in their circle who talked, talked, talked rapidly when she was—as she didn't hesitate to inform them—in her manic bipolar state.)

Oh but it was sad: pathetic. Here in the Carmichael household.

Nothing funny here. Even Tink would agree.

Merissa's poor mother, Stacy Carmichael, was that age—forty-five? Older?—like one of those still-attractive-but-fading middle-aged women you saw in TV advertisements promising miracle medication to combat migraines, hot flashes, insomnia, and depression.

In one of the scarier TV ads, a ghost-cloud of gloom hovers about the head of the afflicted woman—OBSESSIVE THOUGHTS, SUICIDAL IDEATION, INSOMNIA. Merissa never watched the advertisement beyond the first two or three seconds, quickly switching channels.

She was sure: Her mother was taking some sort of prescription medication.

But this was not *new*—was it?

Even on lovely, sunny days the ghost-cloud hovers. It is not suggested that there is a reason for the ghost-cloud—depression—for the ghost-cloud just *is*.

Merissa had not heard of SUICIDAL IDEATION before—she was sure. She supposed that Tink had.

All this made Merissa feel so sick and sad—and sort of disgusted—with her mother.

And with *herself*.

9.

"NO ONE WILL EVER KNOW"

It had begun by accident—almost.

Distracted, coming down a flight of stairs at school the previous year—just after chemistry class, in which midterm tests had been handed back and Merissa's grade was a disappointing 91—that is, an A-minus—though she'd studied hard and had expected she'd done better, and the thought came to her swift as a razor blade. *Who's "perfect" now? Who's stupid and ugly and worthless now? Who gives a damn if you live or die?*—and somehow she missed a step, fell hard, and struck her forehead on the railing, then fell several steps more to the floor; and there was blood on her face, on her hands—so quickly had it happened, Merissa felt more surprise than pain, and embarrassment—for people were staring at her, and several had stopped to help her—

"Hey—is it M'rissa? You okay?"

"Wow. You're bleeding. . . ."

Merissa insisted she was fine. She was deeply embarrassed to be dripping blood in the school corridor as people gawked.

At a little distance, guys were watching. Merissa didn't want to know who they were. A girl whom she scarcely knew, one of the popular seniors at Quaker Heights, was pressing a wad of tissue against the cut in Merissa's forehead, saying in a concerned voice that they'd better take her to the school nurse, but Merissa stiffened—"No. No thank you. I'm r-really all right—I don't want to miss my next class."

"C'mon, we'll take you! You're *bleeding*."

The girl, Molly O'Hagan, was taller than Merissa and known for being strong-willed; in fact, Molly was a senior class officer, but Merissa insisted that she was perfectly all right—she'd just missed a step and fallen.

It was thrilling—in a strange, edgy way—to be pushing away from Molly O'Hagan, gently but firmly. To be the center of this sudden and unexpected attention, to see such *sympathy* in the eyes of Molly O'Hagan and others. To say, with a resolute little smile, even as she held the wadded tissue to her bruising face, "Thanks so much, but *no*."

The cut bled for a while but wasn't deep at all—hardly more than scraped-away skin. In a field hockey game Merissa could expect to be more bruised, on another part of her body; but still, it was nice to be fussed over, and by a girl and her friends whom Merissa didn't really know—nice to be *touched*.

Otherwise, being *touched* made Merissa feel anxious.

And how thrilling—to feel the blood-trickle down the side of her face that was so startling and unexpected, and drew the sympathy of others.

And not long afterward, feeling a bump the size of a quail egg on her forehead, throbbing with pain.

But a quick, sharp, visible pain. A pain that didn't *really hurt*.

Back in the junior corridor, Merissa got plenty of attention from her friends. By this time she was laughing lightly—"Oh, hey, guys, it's *nothing*. C'mon!"

It hadn't been just the chemistry test that Merissa had been obsessing over but—oh, who knows what?—each day, each hour, it had begun to seem that there was more, more, more. "Think of your résumé for college applications, Merissa! Your résumé, *résumé, RÉSUMÉ*"—not only Mrs. Jameson, whose job it was to get Quaker Heights seniors into the very best, the very most competitive universities, but Merissa's parents also; not only her father, who was C O M P E T I T I V E as hell, but lately Merissa's mother as well.

We need you to do really, really well, sweetie. Daddy is counting on you, and so am I.

Which was why, for the sake of Merissa's college application résumé, she was taking as many honors courses as she could and was involved in as many extracurricular activities as she could be, plus JV (Junior Volunteer) projects that took her, by chartered bus, on alternate Saturday mornings, to devastated urban areas in Newark and New Brunswick, where prep-school students like Merissa assisted adult volunteers in tutoring (black, Hispanic) teenagers who were said to be "functionally illiterate."

Merissa had complained to Tink, "You'd think my mother is entering me in some kind of *horse race*, and *little horsie* had better do well or the *horsie owner*, that's to say my father, will fire us both."

Tink snorted with laughter. Not that she thought this was funny.

"Dude, you got it. So what're you going to do?"

Just run the horsie race. And hope I don't stumble and break my neck.

And Merissa felt anxiety not just about the college application résumé but anxiety about boys: the boys who asked Merissa Carmichael out whom she didn't really much like, and the boys who didn't ask her out whom she liked a lot more, or thought she did—at this time, sixteen, Merissa hadn't really been out with any boy, only just with a group of friends, and no one actually "with" anyone else.

Since ninth grade, she'd been in love with Shaun Ryan.

And it was clear, at least most of the time, that Shaun liked Merissa, too. In any gathering, the two just naturally gravitated toward each other. Nobody made Merissa laugh quite the way Shaun did when he was in a funny mood.

In the life of a popular girl, there are always boys who like her—in some cases, *a lot*—whom she doesn't like but doesn't want to offend, either.

For instance, Gordy Squires.

For instance, Virgil Nagy.

These were nice—brainy, boring—guys. Every time Merissa seemed to turn around, there was Gordy, or there was Virgil—awkwardly smiling at her.

Merissa murmured *Hi!* with an excuse about being really, really in a rush, and escaped.

Even Alex Wren, whom Merissa sort of liked. But felt self-conscious when Alex fell in step with her, walking with her and trying to talk about—whatever it was Alex was always trying to talk about with Merissa.

The poor guy's crazy about you. Face it, M'riss! Tink had jabbed her in the ribs.

Merissa had laughed. Not wanting to be cruel, but for God's sake, what could she do about it? Half the guys in Merissa's grade school (for instance) had had crushes on her, even the short boys whom she'd towered over.

If only Shaun felt that way about her. Or if only she felt that way about Alex Wren.

Her father had said, "You are not to go out with any boy until I have checked him over—and not before your thirtieth birthday. *Comprendez?*"

But Daddy had been joking. Of course.

For Daddy wanted Merissa to be popular, too.

It just did not make sense—(Merissa wanted to protest)— that her father wanted her to be beautiful, and popular, and (she guessed) "sexy"—but at the same time, he didn't want her to go out with boys.

The way he'd been jealous of her mother, Merissa's mom had told her, when they'd first been married; though he'd encouraged her to wear "sexy" clothes, paint her finger- and toenails, and wear high-heeled shoes she'd hated.

All these things, Merissa had been thinking about when she'd fallen on the stairs. Thoughts like angry hornets buzzing inside her head.

So, falling and hurting herself so publicly and, for the rest of the day, feeling her head pound, touching the bump on her forehead and the little scratch that had ceased bleeding but felt like fine stitching in her skin, had been, unexpectedly—*pleasurable*.

And the attention! Not for scoring high on a test, which

makes everyone hate you, but for *bleeding, being hurt*, which makes people feel sorry for you and want to help you.

And you can say, with a little stoic smile, *Thanks, but I'm fine. I really am! It's nothing.*

It was punishment for being an essentially worthless, ridiculous, and not even very good-looking person, but at the same time, it was a reward.

"M'rissa? Hey—I heard you hurt yourself. . . ."

"Shaun, hi! No, it's like—really nothing. . . . It didn't even bleed much."

"What happened? Somebody said—you were pushed on the stairs?"

"No! I was not pushed! Who told you that?"

Shaun shrugged. Just something he'd heard.

"Of course no one pushed me. Why would anyone push *me*?"

"Maybe jealous of you? There's lots of . . ."

Shaun was joking, of course, but his voice trailed off as if he thought better of what he was saying.

. . . lots of people who hate you.

Shaun peered at Merissa's bruised forehead. There was an anxious moment when Merissa thought—half thought—Shaun might lean forward and kiss it.

If he had—(but Merissa knew he wouldn't: She and Shaun didn't have that sort of relationship)—she thought she might *faint*.

"Wow! Does it hurt?"

"I told you, Shaun—no. It's nothing compared to being battered out on the hockey field."

Later, Merissa would regret having spoken so assertively.

Shaun had shrugged, laughed, and backed off. Merissa had wanted to call after him—*Oh, Shaun, wait! It does hurt. I think I'm going to faint.*

But she went away in a state of near euphoria, thinking, *Shaun does like me! He cares.*

This was a surprise—wasn't it?

Come off it, M'riss. Shaun is crazy about you too, except the poor guy is scared of you—the Perfect One.

And at home there was Merissa's mother, near hysterical at seeing such a "lurid" bump on her precious daughter's forehead. And there was Merissa's father, home for dinner that night, blinking and staring at her forehead before asking, in a faltering voice, what had happened. And when Merissa told him, insisting that it was really nothing and didn't hurt—(which was more or less true: the little injury looked worse than it was)—Daddy cried, "Hey! Let Daddy kiss it and make it well."

Which Daddy did.

Daddy loves me. He does!
That was proof.

Soon after, Merissa began the cutting.

Why? Because she couldn't fall down the school stairs every day and hurt herself.

And she needed to be *hurt*. She needed to be *punished*.

She needed to *bleed*. And she needed to *cease bleeding—to heal*.

She needed *a secret world. A world to hide in.*

She needed to *seize control, to defy others' control of her.*

She'd heard of girls who *cut* themselves in secret, as she'd heard of girls who starved themselves, or stuffed themselves and forced themselves to vomit; and there was the example of Tink Traumer, who spoke openly of her several *suicide attempts*—but with such an air of gaiety and drollery, you were led to conclude that of course she wasn't serious!

(So, when news came that Tink had at last k****d herself, that Tink was at last d**d, the first thought that came to her friends was, *Oh Tink, come* on! *You're not funny.*)

Merissa had heard of these girls and had always thought they must be mentally ill, or neurotic—to *cut themselves* with something sharp! It had seemed just too weird, like pulling out your hair a single strand at a time—why would anyone want to do such a thing?

Eating disorders were so common, no one was particularly surprised or judgmental. In Merissa's circle of friends whom she'd known since middle school, there were several girls, including Chloe, who had a tendency to be anorexic, and others who overate and induced vomiting. (Merissa wondered about Hannah, sometimes. And Nadia Stillinger, who looked so, well—*soft.*)

Merissa could go without eating for hours—she never ate breakfast and often felt too restless to sit still to eat a meal, especially when it was just her mother and herself. Merissa's metabolism burnt up calories in a sort of nervous combustion, and she supposed she was—just slightly—anorexic, or would be, except *cutting* was so much more thrilling, because it was so much more dangerous, and forbidden.

It happened several days after she'd fallen down the stairs at school.

It happened when the swollen bruise on her forehead was faded, and the little cut that had trickled blood down the side of her face had healed.

It happened when Merissa was feeling so high-strung and tense—like the string of a bow pulled back, and back, and back, the arrow about to fly—and she knew she'd never be able to sleep.

Preparing for midterm tests. Or maybe it was preparing to get the tests back, next day at school.

She was in her bathroom, her hair wrapped in a towel. She'd just had a shower, and the room was fragrant with steam.

And maybe she'd been thinking about Shaun Ryan—or maybe she'd been thinking about her father.

Her father and her mother. Who seemed to have little in common any longer except *her*.

As if a devil had nudged her, Merissa did a strange—unexpected—thing: She drew the inside of her wrist against the sharp edge of the medicine cabinet.

As if she'd wanted to cut her wrist, and to cut into the little blue artery. But the edge of the cabinet wasn't sharp enough and made only a red mark in her skin.

Pulses were beating in Merissa's head, in her ears—a terrible pressure was building up. In a drawer she rummaged for the little scissors she used to cut her finger- and toenails, and before she could think what she was doing, she drew the sharp points of the scissors along the tender inside of her left arm. At once a thin vein of blood emerged, delicate as a cobweb.

"Oh!"—the shock of it, the sensation of *relief*.

The cuts were not deep, just scratches. But fascinating to

Merissa, how rapidly she could alter her physical state.

She'd been nervous, and she'd been fretful, and she'd been frustrated, and she'd been bored. But suddenly all that had vanished—now she felt *pain*.

The strange sensation called *pain*. Since Merissa had caused it, and controlled it, and since it was secret, and no one could know—it made her very happy, in that instant.

I can do this any time I want. And no one can stop me.

Merissa, my God! What have you done to yourself?

Merissa! How could you?

Merissa smiled, imagining her parents' shock.

"But you'll never know. No one will ever know."

10.

"PERFECT ONE"

"Merissa? Can you help us out?"

Help out—who? Fourth-period science, and Mr. Kessler was smiling at Merissa in his quizzical-teasing way, for evidently he'd asked a question that another student had failed to answer adequately—and so Mr. Kessler was calling on Merissa Carmichael, who could usually be relied on to supply correct answers.

Merissa's face pounded with blood. This was embarrassing!

Guiltily Merissa confessed. She could see that Adrian Kessler was trying not to be disappointed in her.

"I—I didn't hear the question, Mr. Kessler."

(Was this happening more often lately? Since Merissa's fantastic week, since so much Good News had happened at almost the same time, she was aware of things not going so well: going *down*.)

(Her first rehearsal of *Pride and Prejudice*, for instance. Though Merissa had stayed up late several nights in a row to memorize the role of Elizabeth Bennet, she'd stumbled reading her dialogue, and at one point, after an embarrassed pause, Mr. Trocchi said,

"Merissa! Elizabeth Bennet is one of the great witty females of English literature—she wouldn't put us to sleep, you know.")

Mr. Kessler repeated the question, which was related to the homework assignment of the previous night—*What is the distinction between planets and dwarf planets? Give examples.* The question wasn't difficult, really, and Merissa gave a reasonable answer.

"Thank you, Merissa! That's exactly—almost exactly— perfect."

Perfect! Merissa was troubled to think that her teacher might be mocking her.

(But how would Mr. Kessler have known? "The Perfect One" was just a joke of Tink's—no one called Merissa that any longer; at least, not to her face.)

With adults, you never knew if they were speaking sincerely or sardonically. Adult men, especially.

But Mr. Kessler was speaking sincerely, it seemed. Merissa tried to concentrate.

"Until just recently, Pluto was a planet—the ninth planet— but in 2006 more powerful telescopes revealed that Pluto is just an object, nothing more than rock and ice, and very small—no more than one-fifth the size of our Earth's moon—like the state of Rhode Island, comparatively. So 'dwarf planet' is the new classification." Mr. Kessler paused. A sly look came into his face, you could see him preparing to *be funny.* "Like being dropped from varsity to JV status. Like being a *dork* when you thought you'd been a *jock.*"

The class laughed. Heartless, heedless.

As if, Merissa thought, most of them weren't *dwarf planets.*

Mr. Kessler persisted: "A *loser*, when you'd thought you were a *winner*. And you'd gotten away with it so long, you almost believed it yourself."

More laughter. Even Merissa smiled.

Why is it so funny, being a *loser*? Is it a law of nature?

Is it—fate?

Like a death sentence?

Adrian Kessler was one of the younger teachers at Quaker Heights Day School. It was known that he had all but a PhD degree from Columbia University in ecological studies—plus a master's degree in education. You had to wonder if he thought of himself as a *winner*, in fact. Or was he a *loser* hoping to be mistaken for a *winner*?

He wasn't conventionally attractive—his face was narrow, his eyes set too close together. He was lanky and long-limbed and often restless, moving about the classroom as he taught. He liked to toss chalk into the air and catch it; he liked to scrawl on the blackboard in sudden swoops of inspiration. Like all male teachers at the school, he wore a dress shirt and tie, but with these Mr. Kessler was likely to wear a corduroy jacket, khakis, and running shoes. He oversaw his students' lab work closely and was usually patient—or patient-seeming. He had a way of turning criticism into a joke—usually. His hair was often disheveled from his habit of drawing his fingers through it in a gesture of comical exasperation.

Once, Mr. Kessler had surprised Merissa's class by saying, as he'd handed back a test in which many had performed poorly, "Because you're at Quaker Heights, you believe you are 'entitled.' But don't be deceived."

So Kessler could be hard-edged—when he chose.

Mr. Nice Guy, packing heat.

And he wasn't an easy grader, though he wanted you to like him.

Many of Merissa's classmates resented such remarks of Mr. Kessler's—which they didn't quite understand but knew to be judgmental. As they resented receiving grades lower than A-minus.

Secretly, Merissa thought that Mr. Kessler was absolutely right. Even those classmates whom she liked, in many cases, imagined themselves *entitled*—to get high grades, to get into the best colleges, to take their places in their parents' worlds, in upscale towns like Quaker Heights, New Jersey. They would work—to a degree. But they expected to be rewarded, and could be mean and spiteful when they were not.

The fact was that Quaker Heights Day School, though it had been founded in the late 1960s, in an era of idealism, as a place in which "high-quality education" was administered in "egalitarian surroundings," was dominated by a hierarchical social structure that most teachers pretended to know nothing about, even as, in the classroom, they deferred to its rankings. For here was a social pyramid firmly in place, as in any suburban public school: popular kids at the top; misfits and losers at the base; in the middle the majority of the student population, anxious not to sink further, ever-hopeful of rising by a notch or two.

Merissa and her friends—the girls of Tink, Inc.—were somewhere near the top. While Tink had been their friend, and Tink had had an outsider reputation—famous (in another lifetime, as a child actress) even as she was controversial (that's to say, Tink had numerous detractors)—Merissa and the others had been envied for their nearness to Tink; now that Tink had departed, some residue of her reputation lingered, like a slow-fading ghost.

And now that Merissa was going to a "top Ivy" school, her status remained high.

And she was good-looking: pale blond hair worn straight past her shoulders, delicate features, large gray-blue eyes, and—when she could force herself—a "sweet" smile.

Merissa *looked* like perfection. She *looked* as if she must be very, very happy.

She'd been told there were guys who were afraid to approach her. Without knowing what she did, Merissa sent a disdainful signal that seemed to say, *Don't come near. If you like me, I can't possibly like you.*

Still, Merissa Carmichael was what you'd call a "top" senior.

Though how easy it would be to sink—as it would be easy to sink in quicksand. *Just let go.*

How had Tink *let go?* The rumor was, she'd drunk half a bottle of her mother's most expensive French wine, taken an overdose of her mother's barbiturates, and just gone to bed, in her usual grungy black leggings, her long-sleeved GUERRILLA GIRL T-shirt, barefoot and her freckled face scrubbed clean, her teeth freshly brushed and flossed.

Tink had a thing about *flossing.* Tink cheerfully described herself as OCD—(obsessive-compulsive disorder)—in minor, weird ways.

Tink must have known about *cutting.* For she had had several little tattoos on her shoulders and upper arms, and you could say that *cutting* was a form of self-tattooing.

Tink, I miss you so!

Why did you leave us, Tink?

We loved you. Why wasn't that enough?

"Hey. Merissa?"

It was Shelby Freedman, who sat just behind Merissa. Poking Merissa's shoulder, as if to wake her—but she hadn't been asleep, had she?

Shelby was an old friend from middle school. Never a close friend, but Merissa liked Shelby, and would have liked to be a closer friend—except there wasn't room for Shelby in Merissa's life.

She was not a girl in Tink, Inc.

(Did Shelby know this? If she did, she didn't seem to hold it against Merissa.)

"You okay, Merissa? What're you doing?"

What had Merissa been doing? In the midst of Mr. Kessler's science class—trying to talk to Tink?

Trying to hear Tink's faint, teasing voice?

Sure I love you, M'ris.

But first, love yourself.

Shelby had nudged Merissa, alarmed at what Merissa was doing: She'd seized a strand of her hair between her fingers, at the back of her head, and was tugging at it, without seeming to know what she was doing, as if she'd have liked to tear it from her scalp.

"M'riss? Doesn't that hurt, for God's sake?"

Merissa, embarrassed, relaxed her fingers.

Now her scalp hurt—hurt like hell—but a moment before, she hadn't seemed to feel a thing.

11.

"MAKING THINGS RIGHT"

Kiss and make well. Kissie-kiss!

Which was what Daddy had said. The last time Daddy had really taken notice of his daughter.

Because she'd fallen and struck her head. Because her "perfect" face had been injured, and Daddy had been shocked and concerned.

Exactly the way the owner of a beautiful Thoroughbred filly would feel if she'd fallen and injured herself on the track.

Each night in the secrecy of her room before she went to bed—at about eleven p.m.—Merissa took up the little nail scissors and drew the sharp points along her skin, which was sensitive and seemed to come alive at the touch of the scissors' tips, alive with a kind of anticipatory excitement.

The cuts were made carefully—not deep, but shallow—like handwriting in her flesh. She admired her handiwork. Took pictures on her cell phone.

On her computer, the pictures shimmered with a fantastical sort of beauty.

No one to send them to except Tink.

Tink, I want to be with you. Tink, please give a sign.

But there was just silence from Tink now. For quite a while now—silence.

Tink! Help me.

There is no one but you to help me.

Quickly then Merissa soaked up the blood in tissues, to be flushed down the toilet; she covered the secret wounds with Band-Aids so that her pajamas wouldn't get stained.

Sometimes, in the night, one of the cuts would begin to throb with a stinging pain, and Merissa would scratch at it and pull off the Band-Aid—"Oh! Damn." She had a dread of bloodstains on her sheets, which her mother might notice.

Soon she'd exchanged the little scissors for a small but razor-sharp paring knife from the kitchen. This was a stainless-steel knife with a chic wooden handle, one of a dozen matched knives, clearly expensive.

Essential to cut carefully, like a kind of kiss. As if a creature with a rough mouth but sharp teeth were kissing her. *Kiss and make well. Kiss-kiss.*

She was tattooing a secret language in her flesh. An elaborate pattern of cuts on her small, hard, waxen-pale breasts, midriff, stomach, lower belly where fuzzy hairs were sprouting. And on the soft insides of her thighs.

A complicated code, executed over a period of weeks.

"Oh! *Oh.*"

In the mirror, a dozen thin little curving cuts, some of which could be induced to bleed again, if Merissa scratched at them.

Such a strange—unexpected—sensation of relief. As soon

as the blood appeared in tiny droplets, Merissa shivered, and smiled.

This is punishment. You deserve it.

This makes things right.

It was the first time in her life that something made sense, Merissa thought. And no one could tell her—she'd figured it out for herself.

12.

"GUESS I'M NOT ELIZABETH BENNET"

"Merissa, are you sure?"

"Yes, Mr. Trocchi. I—I think I'm sure."

Here was a surprise: Merissa Carmichael, who'd auditioned so vivaciously for the coveted role of Elizabeth Bennet in the stage adaptation of Jane Austen's *Pride and Prejudice*, and who'd been chosen by the drama instructor over the more experienced Brooke Kramer, was having second thoughts about continuing with the play.

All the cast was astounded. And Mr. Trocchi was astounded.

"We've only just begun rehearsals, Merissa! No one knows their lines yet—it's natural for even professional actors to flounder about a little, to grope and find their way in the rehearsal process. You can't expect to *be* Elizabeth Bennet; you have to learn how to *act* Elizabeth Bennet." Mr. Trocchi was a short, broad-shouldered man of middle age, rumored to have once been an actor in off-off-Broadway productions; he was one of the more popular Quaker Heights teachers, with an urgent and intense way of speaking. He'd chosen Merissa to perform in several plays since ninth grade, but always in supporting or minor roles; Elizabeth Bennet was to have been her breakthrough role.

"I—I was thinking, Mr. Trocchi. You should have chosen Brooke. Brooke can *act*."

"Merissa, rehearsals are a learning process. You're a student—a young actor—you must *learn to act*."

Merissa hadn't thought of this. She had supposed that either you could *act*—or you could not.

And Merissa hadn't been prepared for disliking the play.

Elizabeth Bennet was a young woman of twenty-one who was very clever, and very beautiful and proud—but Merissa was surprised that Elizabeth Bennet was so uncritical in her thinking. *Pride and Prejudice* was a classic of English literature, but it was essentially just a romance—witty, comedic—with sympathetic characters not so very different from those on superior TV comedies. Merissa couldn't *respect* Elizabeth Bennet as she was supposed to.

"Austen's novels are comedies of manners—brilliant social satires. The author uses the convention of romance to reveal truths of her era—the relationships between men and women, and between the generations." Mr. Trocchi sounded as if he'd memorized a passage from the internet on Jane Austen.

Merissa objected, "But what else is *Pride and Prejudice* about, except romance? Just unmarried women desperate to get married, to men who have money. That is, 'gentlemen.' Because these 'gentlemen' don't *work*—that would be beneath them. Only their servants *work*. The play is witty and funny, but it's all kind of silly, who marries who. I think it's depressing."

"Depressing! No one has ever said that Jane Austen is depressing, I'm sure."

Mr. Trocchi stroked his mustache gravely. His thinning hair and his mustache were a faint coppery hue, which looked too young for his lined, heavy face. He was staring at Merissa as if he'd never really seen her before and wasn't sure he liked what he saw.

Merissa said, "Well, isn't it depressing if all a woman can hope for is to get married? To someone with money? In those days, a woman couldn't work except as a servant or a governess—a 'good' woman, that is. Women were all *trapped*."

Mr. Trocchi laughed dismissively.

"You don't think that Mr. Darcy is a 'good catch' for Elizabeth Bennet? You don't think that female readers, reading *Pride and Prejudice*, would love to be in her place?"

"I don't know! I don't care what other people think."

"But you'll be married, Merissa—don't worry. You might not think so now, but you will be."

Other cast members, standing about with scripts in hand, heard this exchange and laughed.

It was hard for Merissa not to think that they were laughing at *her*.

"Here, Mr. Trocchi. Brooke will be much better than I could ever be."

Merissa handed the drama teacher her script. Mr. Trocchi was too surprised not to take it from her.

"But Merissa—why don't you think this over? Tonight? And in the morning come and see me, and we'll make a decision then? All right?"

Merissa was thinking, *Oh, stop! Stop pretending! You know you're relieved that I'm quitting. You can't wait to call Brooke and ask her to take over the role.*

"I'm not going to change my mind, Mr. Trocchi. I owe it to the cast, and to you, and to Brooke, to quit. I guess I'm not Elizabeth Bennet after all. So good-bye."

A rush of euphoria came over her, how disappointed Daddy would be.

At least, Merissa thought so. If she troubled to tell him.

It was easy, Tink. You'd understand.
Like grasping a razor between your fingers firmly.
And bringing it down on your skin, and in, cutting.
And when the pain starts, not letting go.

13.

"NBD"

Strange. How easy.

Quitting the play, which had meant so much to her.

And by quitting, erasing its significance.

So that what had once meant too much, now meant nothing.

And so it happened more frequently; the stresses of her senior year at Quaker Heights no longer had the power to distract her.

Grades, tests, weekend parties, and the spillover talk in the wake of parties—rumors of crude, cruel text messages sent and copied dozens of times—nothing to do with *her*.

Now it was Merissa who ignored Shaun Ryan—coolly smiling at him on the sidewalk behind school but not pausing as she passed him, though Shaun hesitated as if hoping to walk with her.

"M'rissa? Hi . . ."

"Oh, hi, Shaun. Nice to see you."

How easy this was! And not a backward glance to see Shaun staring after her, perplexed and hurt.

See, I don't need you. Any of you.

For the first time in her life, Merissa didn't hand a paper in on time—what an exquisite sensation!

Better, even, than cutting herself. Because so *public*.

The look on Mrs. Conway's face—poor Mrs. Conway!

"Merissa? I don't see your paper here."

Merissa mumbled a vague excuse. Wanting to hide her mouth, which yearned to twitch into a smile.

Because it isn't there. Because I didn't finish the silly assignment on time. Who cares!

You'd better change your opinion of me—downward.

And when tests came back—in math, for instance—with disappointing grades, there was Merissa Carmichael doing what others did, crumpling the shameful papers in her fist, shoving them into her backpack unread.

Just so tired. So bored.

Field hockey season had ended. Just an average season, though people tried to pretend the team was *terrific*.

Next, basketball. But Merissa didn't show up for first-day practice—she'd been one of the better players, a guard, the previous year.

Ms. Svala, the girls' gym instructor, contacted Merissa to ask why, why wasn't she planning to play basketball this year, which was her senior year, her last year, and the team really needed her.

Merissa said nobody needed *her*, that was silly.

Of course the team needed her! Ms. Svala seemed surprised, and concerned.

Coolly Merissa said no—that was a misunderstanding.

The team needed the very best players, yes. But nobody needed *her*.

"If I'd never been born, you wouldn't 'need' me—would you? There're other girls just as good. And they want to be on the team."

On the team. How strange this sounded, like a bad joke.

Ms. Svala had more to say to Merissa, but Merissa just walked away.

Without a backward glance.

There came Anita Chang, staring at Merissa.

Anita, who was/wasn't a close friend, because you couldn't trust her—(could you?)—not to talk behind your back.

Anita, with her flat, round, flawless face, bright black eyes alert with quicksilver intelligence, fun, and malice—came to touch Merissa's arm in a familiar way that made Merissa stiffen.

This was weird. Anita Chang seemed *sincere.*

"Merissa, what's this about you quitting the play? Are you serious?"

Merissa shrugged and drew back from Anita.

"You *can't* quit—your audition was just wonderful, and we all loved you."

Anita spoke with such disappointment, Merissa almost regretted her decision.

(Had she been "wonderful" at the audition? But what had happened in the interim, to so discourage her?)

"Well—I've quit."

"So Brooke Kramer will play Elizabeth Bennet? Shit."

You had to love Anita sometimes: the way she flared up in defense of her friends and was comically unsubtle in putting down her enemies.

(Of course, you had to know that Brooke was Anita's enemy because of a senior boy named Kevin Drake. If you knew this, Anita's ferocity made complete sense.)

"Brooke is a *bitch*. Know what she's going around saying?"

Merissa didn't know. Nor did she care.

"She's saying, 'Merissa Carmichael has stage fright. She's quit the play and says that I can act better than she can—*and she's right.*'"

Merissa felt a jab of annoyance, but only laughed.

"You think that's funny? That bitch is lying about my girl-friend?"

Anita's nostrils flared in indignation. Anita had more to say, but Merissa slammed her locker door and turned to depart.

Anita dared to call after her, "Tink wouldn't like it, M'riss—her girlfriend quitting so that that bitch can be a star!"

This hurt. This was true Anita Chang style—a stab in the back when you turned your back.

Merissa wanted to say, *You have no right to speak for Tink. You don't know a damn thing about Tink*, but she continued walking away without a backward glance, leaving Anita to stare after her.

Brooke can think what she thinks. Say what she says. Why should I care?

Strange how you can lose interest in your friends.

You still like them—"love" them—but just don't want to see them.

Merissa had to wonder if Tink had felt that way. Just didn't want to see her friends anymore.

Not minding that she was leaving them and would not ever see them again.

She'd said to Merissa hesitantly, "Maybe—I have a favor to ask you, M'riss."

Merissa had said, sure. What was it?

And a funny look came into Tink's face—wistful, regretful. But stubborn, too.

"Maybe—I'll ask you some other time."

Merissa had said, why not now?

But of course, being Tink, she didn't explain. It was like Tink to tantalize you with some hinted-at confidence—then draw back, as if she'd thought better of it.

Well, Tink had been acting weird around that time. Or, you might say, weirder than usual for Tink.

With no warning, she'd shaved her head. *Totally bored* with her hair (she'd said) and so one day she cut most of it off with a scissors, after which—(this was Tink's gleeful account)—poor Big Moms had had to take her to an emergency session with a hairstylist for damage control.

Now she seemed embarrassed to have brought up the subject of a *favor*.

"No big deal, M'rissa. Some other time."

But that was the last time: June 8, 2011.

Merissa never saw Tink again: Three days later, Tink was d**d.

It was something to do with—what she did.
Something to do with what caused her to do it.
And now I will never know.

• • •

To each of her closest friends, Tink had sent a single, final text message at 10:08 p.m. on June 10.

These were: Merissa, Chloe, Hannah, Nadia.

If they hadn't known how special they were to Tink, they would know now. But it was a painful specialness of which they could not speak to outsiders.

HEY GUYS, GUESS I WON'T BE SEEING YOU FOR A WHILE.

LOVE YOU GUYS BUT FEELING KINDA BURNT OUT. NBD.

TINK

Not seeing friends you'd been seeing almost every day for almost all your life that matters is like not breathing.

Except you can't live without breathing. But you can live without your friends.

Merissa was letting her cell phone burn out. Forgot to charge it.

On it were numerous text messages she hadn't bothered to open.

Hannah had texted Merissa a half-dozen times, and Merissa failed to reply.

Chloe had texted Merissa a half-dozen times, and Merissa failed to reply.

Easier just to delete. Tink knew: No Big Deal.

(Merissa had never learned what the favor was that Tink had wanted to ask of her.)

(Merissa had never learned if Tink had asked her other friends for a favor, too.)

Hannah and Chloe approached Merissa at school, with hurt,

accusing eyes. "Merissa, what's wrong? Why are you avoiding us?"

Merissa smiled her bright, indifferent smile.

"I've been busy."

"Is something wrong?"

"*Is* something wrong? With who?" Merissa's eyes were evasive.

Merissa wore a long-sleeved jersey, not unlike a Tink jersey. Floppy sleeves over her wrists to hide whatever little scabs and scars circled her wrists like barbed wire.

(Did Hannah see? Was Chloe suspicious?)

But it seemed they wanted to talk to Merissa about their friend Nadia. For it seemed that people were saying things about Nadia that couldn't be true—a rash of texts and posts calling Nadia S. a *slut*.

"A slut? *Nadia?*"

Merissa was shocked. Then Merissa was disgusted.

"Who would call Nadia a *slut*? That's crazy."

"Some guys."

"Who?"

Hannah and Chloe named several senior boys. Merissa was grateful that Shaun Ryan hadn't been named, though she was determined not to care.

"Why would they call Nadia a *slut*? They don't even know her."

Hannah said hesitantly that maybe Nadia had gone out once with one of these boys—Colin Brunner.

"Brunner! Oh, I hate him. He's *crude*."

Colin Brunner was a big, swaggering boy who played varsity football and basketball—the kind of Stereotype Jock you are always surprised actually exists outside TV sitcoms and movies like *Animal House II*.

"How'd Nadia get mixed up with that jackass? When was this?"

Evidently, the previous weekend. Nadia hadn't said a word to them but . . . people were talking.

"That isn't like Nadia. Nadia wouldn't."

Merissa spoke vehemently. She felt a wave of indignation, thinking, *Anyone who insults my girlfriend insults me.*

But the feeling didn't last. She was just too tired. The (secret) little cuts and scratches inside her clothes were hurting her.

I don't want to hear it. I can't help anyone. Couldn't help Tink and can't help myself.

"Merissa?"

Reluctantly Merissa lingered to speak with Mr. Kessler after class.

She could see the concern in the teacher's eyes. She felt a stab of resentment and chagrin.

"Is something wrong, Merissa? You've seemed distracted in class lately."

Merissa felt blood rush into her face. She felt a wild impulse to run out of the room.

She hated it that other students would notice—were noticing. How Mr. Kessler was asking Merissa Carmichael to speak with him after class as he sometimes asked students who'd performed poorly or in some way required help—or discipline—while others left blithely, without a backward glance.

Mr. Kessler was tactful, and considerate—speaking quietly so that no one else could hear. She knew that Virgil Nagy, who was always glancing at her, smiling at her, and trying to get her attention, was alert to their teacher's interest in Merissa this afternoon, and was slow to leave the classroom.

"The work you've been doing lately—the past two weeks or so—just isn't up to your usual high standards, Merissa. Not to mention last Friday's test. Are you aware of this?"

Merissa shrugged. It was very hard to meet Mr. Kessler's gaze. "I—I guess so."

What an inane remark! Merissa felt her lips twitch, the impulse to smile was so strong.

Mr. Kessler said he'd been checking with Merissa's other teachers—Mrs. Conway, Mr. Doerr, Mr. Trocchi—and they'd all reported that Merissa had seemed distracted in class lately; and Mr. Trocchi had said how surprised he'd been that Merissa had dropped out of the senior play after the first week of rehearsals.

"Please tell me—or us—if anything is wrong."

Merissa stood silent. How she resented these strangers, conferring about her! The secret little wounds, scratches thin as pencil lines but rough to the touch like stitches in the flesh, pulsed with heat, inside her clothes.

She felt a thrill of elation. *He can't know. None of them can know.*

"We all realize, seniors are under tremendous strain. You do so many things—activities—there seems to be no letup, sometimes. And your personal lives, we know, can be very intense. . . ."

Where was this going? Merissa wondered. *Personal lives!*

Did Mr. Kessler know of rumors about Merissa Carmichael's "separated" parents?

Were there rumors, or was Merissa only just imagining that there might be?

Like rumors about Nadia Stillinger.

(Merissa hadn't seen any text messages or posts about Nadia, but then, she hadn't wanted to look.)

"Maybe I'm just tired of the obstacle course. Like the equestrian competitions you see on TV—poor horses made to jump over ever-higher obstacles, until they trip and fall and break their legs—and have to be put down."

Merissa spoke bitterly but with a smile. Mr. Kessler stared at her in astonishment.

"Why, Merissa—is that how you feel? Is that why you dropped out of the play?"

"I didn't 'drop out' of the stupid senior play! I resigned the role of Elizabeth Bennet because I don't respect the character, and because I'm not really an *actress*. People who can *act*, and who would do a better job than I could, should be in the play—not me."

Merissa snatched up her backpack and turned to walk away.

She was trembling with indignation and hated it that tears had sprung into her eyes.

Wanting to call back over her shoulder the phrase that had caught in her brain like litter blown against a chain-link fence—*No big deal!*

She knew she'd made things worse. Mr. Kessler would talk of her with her other teachers—at Quaker Heights, it was joked that the staff *obsessed* about students, since each student paid so high a tuition; the ratio of faculty to students was approximately one to twelve, unlike public schools in the vicinity, where the ratio might be more than twice that figure.

Mr. Kessler called after Merissa, "If you want to discuss this further, Merissa, just see me. Will you?"

Merissa hurried out of the room without seeming to have heard.

No, no, no, no, no! Damn you, just leave me alone.

Leaving Mr. Kessler staring after her: Merissa Carmichael, who'd always been, in his classes, both smart and *sweet*.

Merissa Carmichael, who'd been, as Mr. Kessler recalled, a friend of the girl who'd killed herself the previous June, just before the end of classes—the red-haired ex–child actress who'd called herself Tink.

So that in his bewilderment Mr. Kessler was led to wonder— (but of course he rejected thinking anything so ridiculous)—if the rebellious and self-destructive spirit of Tink Traumer had somehow entered the exemplary Merissa.

Ugly rumors spread fastest.

Rumors that Merissa Carmichael's father had left Merissa and her mother and was living just a few miles away from them, in the new condominium village on the river.

Like small flames, a wildfire was spreading among people who knew Merissa Carmichael and people who half knew Merissa Carmichael and people who didn't know Merissa Carmichael at all.

Merissa didn't want to know. She tossed her cell phone into a drawer, not caring if the damn thing broke.

Merissa had been thinking she was becoming immune to *him*.

If he didn't call her when he'd promised—No Big Deal.

If he failed even to invent reasonable excuses for these failings, as he'd once done—No Big Deal.

"It's just a—phase. A stage. He's overworked, he isn't thinking clearly. . . ."

Merissa's mother spoke pleadingly. She was increasingly distracted. You could see that something terrible was happening to her, Merissa thought.

Like erosion, from the inside out.

Merissa shrank from her mother. Those eyes!

Except when her mother didn't come into Merissa's room in the evening, as she'd used to do—to question her in that intimate, prying way that so annoyed her but to which she'd become accustomed—Merissa missed her.

"Oh, hey—Mom?"

And there was Mom on her bed, the bed that had been her and Merissa's father's bed, partially dressed, one shoe on and one shoe off as if she'd been flung from an accident scene, hair disheveled and mouth as flaccid as a fish's mouth, breathing in a hoarse, rasping way, terrible to hear.

"Mom? Are you—drunk?"

Merissa wanted to think yes, her mother was drunk. Not drugged, not sick, not desperate, not comatose. If she was just drunk, Merissa could despise her.

"Good night, Mom!"

Merissa dragged a cover over her mother's inert body, switched off the overhead light, and shut the door.

Poor Mom! Poor loser.

I don't need you. Either of you.

That night, lying in the bathtub, soothed by warm, sudsy water—(Merissa rarely took baths, only showers)—drawing the razor-sharp paring knife lightly, experimentally, across her abdomen where beneath, one day, if Merissa didn't prevent it from happening, there might be a *fetus*, an *embryo*, the thought of which filled her with a kind of panicked dismay; and she must have drawn the blade a little too forcibly, for suddenly skeins of bright blood streamed out, fearful to see.

For this was more blood than she'd seen. This was more than her usual small, shallow cuts.

Panicked, thinking, *Not yet! There will be a sign.*

14.

(BLADE RUNNER)

Merissa knew: The male of the species Homo sapiens is a sexual being, by nature polygamous. The instinct of the male is to have sexual intercourse with as many fertile females as possible to propagate his DNA and, in this way, to propagate the species.

There was marriage—family—morality. There was *Thou shalt not commit adultery.*

"Bullshit."

Startling to say this word aloud. But it felt good.

A word that Morgan Carmichael was heard to say, often. A word with which Morgan Carmichael seemed to be on familiar terms.

Which Merissa Carmichael rarely said. In fact, never.

There were Quaker Heights girls who used such words frequently, and easily—almost as frequently and easily as the boys.

Shit. Fuck. Go to hell—bitch!

Slut. Hate you.

"Hate you both."

Merissa laughed, like a child saying forbidden words aloud for the first time.

DEATH ANGEL BLACK SWAN BLADE RUNNER

Holding her breath, Merissa clicked on BladeRunner.com.

Immediately there popped up on her laptop screen the most amazing image Merissa had ever seen. Blade Runner was a girl of about Merissa's age, you could tell by the smooth, taut skin of her exposed neck, though she was wearing a sexy black-satin half mask so you couldn't see much of her face, and her hair—(platinum blond, like Merissa's)—was pulled back tight, tight enough to hurt her scalp, like the hair of a ballerina, and Blade Runner's narrow, slender chest was bare, her small hard-looking breasts with taut nipples like berries, and in Blade Runner's smooth, pale skin were constellations of cuts, some freshly bleeding, some scabbed over, some healed and some scarred. Merissa stared and stared, feeling faint, forgetting to breathe.

Then the camera moved lower on Blade Runner, so that you could see yet more cuts, an embroidery of cuts, in the thin flesh of her midriff, in her abdomen, and in the feathery-pale hairs at the pit of her belly.

"Oh! Oh God."

Merissa had never seen anything so—*beautiful*.

It was crazy, of course—Blade Runner was crazy—sick—but smiling calmly and provocatively at the camera, lifting her arms so you could see her underarms, where, too, there were small cryptic wounds—and—

"Merissa? May I come in?"

Merissa was stunned: Her mother had rapped on the door to her room and was opening it before Merissa could draw breath to reply.

Asking Merissa, in a bright voice, what she was doing "hidden away" in her room alone so much, with the door closed—"Seems like I scarcely see you anymore."

Merissa was sprawled on her bed, in jeans and her long-sleeved GUERRILLA GIRL jersey, which she wore sometimes as a pajama top. Textbooks and papers were spread about her like camouflage, and on her laptop screen was a Quaker Heights Day School webpage, photos of microorganisms Mr. Kessler had posted for an assignment.

"You rush through dinner and don't even watch television any longer. I miss you!"

This was pathetic—Merissa hadn't watched television with her mother in recent memory. Occasionally she'd watched with her father—the World Series last fall, History Channel documentaries on World War II, special news broadcasts, reruns of *The Simpsons*. Next to the internet, the newly discovered website blogs of Blade Runner, Black Swan, Death Angel, and others devoted to cutting, piercing, tattooing of the most amazing kinds, TV was mostly just *boring*.

"I'm working, Mom. I have tons of homework before I even get to calculus—which is really, really hard."

"But why are you working *all the time*? Does everyone at your school work so—frantically?"

Merissa shrugged. It was ridiculous, the way her mother was peering at the computer screen—at the highly magnified pictures of unicellular creatures—as if, if she stared hard enough, she would know what on earth they were. (Protozoa?)

Merissa herself scarcely knew. She'd been neglecting Mr. Kessler's assignments as she'd been neglecting Mr. Doerr's calculus assignments. She did other things with her computer and then, near eleven p.m., when she was supposed to go to bed, she became panicked and tried to compensate for wasted time: too late.

She wasn't even texting her friends any longer. All that—that total waste of time—she'd eliminated. Yet still, she hadn't time for homework, studying for tests, planning special projects.

"I can't believe that everyone at school works as hard as you do, Merissa. I've talked with the mothers of some of your friends—like Hannah—and they say—"

"Talked with who? What do you mean—'talked with'? About me? Are you talking about *me*?"

Merissa was edgy, irritable. She had tried to eat as little as possible that night at dinner, preferring to escape upstairs to her room as quickly as she could.

(Maybe, after Mom went to bed, Merissa would go downstairs—quietly!—and into the kitchen, to get a smoothie from the refrigerator to bring back upstairs with her.)

"Well—no. Of course not. But I've been worried—wondering . . . Where is Hannah? I haven't seen her here in a while."

Merissa's mother tried to speak lightly and without reproach—she was a very nice woman, Merissa knew, not at all bossy or bitchy like certain of her friends' mothers, and nothing at all like Tink's monster-mother, Big Moms—still, Merissa was tired of being spied on.

"Hannah is busy, Mom. Just like me."

"You used to study together. Has something happened between you?"

"You'd have to ask Hannah, Mom. Or Hannah's mother."

"Oh, Merissa! Please don't be sarcastic; it doesn't become you."

Still, Merissa's mother was trying to speak casually, even teasingly. When Merissa happened to overhear her on the phone speaking with Merissa's father, this was the tone she used: a desperate sort of lightness, interrupted by nervous laughter.

Merissa knew: Her mother was determined to seem cheerful around the house so that Merissa couldn't guess how anxious she really was.

(For Merissa eavesdropped shamelessly now. And cynically. At first it had been accidental, and before that—years and years before—she hadn't cared in the slightest what her mother talked about with her women friends on the phone, or even with her father. Now all conversations had to be monitored. Their contents had to be decoded, assessed. If Merissa overheard her mother saying, "Oh God—money! Will I need to be worried about that, too?" she knew that her mother was worried about separation, and divorce. Really there was only one subject in the household any longer—Merissa's father—whether he would return to them, or leave permanently.)

Merissa said, "Hannah has her own friends. A boyfriend."

"She does?"

"Everybody does. No big deal."

No big deal. NBD. What Tink had said, in her last text message.

"But—"

"But what about *me*?" Merissa laughed. "I don't want a

boyfriend. I don't want to do the things you have to do, to have a boyfriend."

Merissa's mother was silent. As if Merissa had reached over and punched her in the thigh.

"Well, I—I don't know—how does Hannah have a boyfriend then? I thought you all went out together—you met boys at the mall, and went to the movies. . . ."

Merissa felt her face heat, just a little. The lie about Hannah had sprung from her lips like a poison toad in a child's fairy tale.

"Maybe it's Nadia, I mean. Nadia Stillinger."

"Nadia? I haven't seen her in a while, either."

Because Nadia is a slut. Even a rich girl has to be a slut if she's fat. You don't have a clue, Mom!

"I'm just wishing that we could spend a little more time together, Merissa. Now that your father is . . . Now that it's just us here, for a while at least. Since you've been accepted at Brown, I don't see why you have to work so hard. . . ."

"Mom, don't be silly. The admission to Brown isn't *absolute*. I still have to finish my senior year, and I have to keep my GPA up, of course."

"And I don't see why you dropped out of the senior play, that would have been enjoyable, and fun—you'd always wanted to have a lead in a school play, and your father was so impressed. Now—I don't even want to tell him."

"Fine! Nobody has to tell him."

Merissa was furious. How badly she wished her mother would leave her room, so that she could click onto Blade Runner. Badly she wanted to send a message to Blade Runner, except she worried—if her father discovered what she was doing—what a nightmare that would be!

He would never love her again, then.

"Anyway, Mom, I didn't 'drop out' of the play. I told you—I don't respect the Jane Austen world, it's just silly, and depressing. It isn't funny—but people laugh. Women with no opportunities in life, no *lives*, except marrying some stupid man with an 'income'—meaning interest on some property. Poor people had to work for these 'property holders,' which means they were like slaves. They didn't have any choice but to work for them, like the women didn't have any choice but to get married. It's *not funny*. I didn't want to be damn old smarty-pants Elizabeth Bennet, whom everybody envies because the richest man proposes to her."

But was this the entire truth? Merissa had to concede she just wasn't an actress. She just didn't care about wearing costumes and makeup and reciting lines on stage, to impress an audience and bask in their applause.

Tink had said, *Acting is for people who don't have actual lives.*

If only Mom would leave! Merissa would connect with Blade Runner and the others and—maybe—she would take the razor-sharp paring knife out of the drawer where it was hidden, and contemplate where next she might cut herself.

Blade Runner had made the big step—to Merissa, almost unthinkable. She'd cut her breasts, both breasts. . . .

Maybe that was next: the soft, sensitive skin of Merissa's breasts.

For now there was punishment needed, for lying about Hannah—Merissa had to be seriously *hurt*.

But—oh God!—Merissa's mother *sat down*.

On the edge of Merissa's bed. (Uninvited.)

Merissa saw that her mother's ashy-blond graying hair was matted as if she'd been sleeping, one side of her head against a pillow. Her eyes were both oddly bright and not quite in focus.

Merissa had never seen her mother actually drinking except at mealtimes—but she knew.

Sometimes, entering the kitchen, on her way to purloin a smoothie from the refrigerator, Merissa smelled wine.

Merissa hated *weakness*! Seeing her mother through her father's critical eyes.

It was unfortunate, Merissa's mother hadn't gone to law school as she'd wanted to. Or graduate school. There were many mothers in Quaker Heights who worked, and who had good jobs: Anita Chang's mother commuted all the way to Manhattan to work as an investment banker; Chloe Zimmer's mother was a real-estate agent in Quaker Heights and worked "crazy long" hours, Chloe said, but she had no choice: She was divorced. Hannah's mother had taught college—community college?—and could work again, maybe, if she had to.

How pained Merissa had been, hearing her mother confide in people, *Well, Morgan and I were together for three years before we got married. And then Merissa came along.*

There'd been a kind of girlish boastfulness in her tone. "Were together" meant—what? *Sleeping together. Living together.*

And maybe Merissa's mother had been pregnant with Merissa before getting married to Merissa's father—was that the implication?

If so, it was backfiring on Stacy Carmichael now. For maybe Morgan Carmichael wouldn't have married her, except for the pregnancy.

Disgusting!

In any case, lately Merissa's mother had stopped any sort of boasting about her marriage.

"Mom, I really have to work. If you were Dad, you could help me with calculus—but you can't. So—I just can't *talk*."

Merissa's mother smiled pleadingly. How Merissa hated to see *pleading* in her mother's eyes.

"I know, Merissa. I know you have work to do. But I wanted to tell you—assure you—that things are not so terrible right now, with your father, I mean. We were talking this evening after dinner—on the phone. He's said he is certain that it's best for both of us to take time for 'sorting things out'—'discovering priorities.' He hasn't once mentioned divorce. So I think—if we get through the next few weeks . . ."

Merissa's heart beat painfully. She wanted to believe what her mother was telling her.

"And there isn't any 'other woman'—I'm sure of that now. He wants, he says, to live alone for a few months at least—and he has a business trip coming up, to China of all places. He wants to be alone to 'discover who he is.' We were married too young, he says—both of us."

Merissa shifted miserably on her bed. Every little wound in her body stung as if someone had rubbed in salt.

Why was her mother telling her such things? How she wished her mother had more *dignity*.

And had her father been so *young*? He'd been thirty-one. And Merissa's mother had been twenty-five. Hardly *young*.

"Well. Just thought I'd tell you, Merissa. Do you have any questions?"

Plenty of questions. But you can't answer them.

"Thanks for telling me, Mom. That's good news. I mean, that's cool—about Dad."

Patiently waiting for her poor, sad mother to sigh, rise to her feet, and leave—ideally, go to bed: darken the house.

Usually, her mother went to bed at about eleven p.m. She might watch TV for a while before falling asleep.

It was only 10:10 p.m. now. Early!

Which meant—plenty of time to contemplate. To anticipate.

"Well, honey—good night."

Merissa's mother startled her by leaning over and kissing her on the forehead.

Saying from the doorway, "Any time you want to—talk, I mean. I'm here, Merissa."

As soon as the door was shut, and Merissa was reasonably sure that her mother was gone for the night, she clicked back on to the internet and Blade Runner, and the astonishing picture of the girl in the black-satin half mask with the scab-and-scar-ridden body reemerged as if it had never been more than an eyeblink away.

15.

"TRY NOT TO CRY"

So maybe. Maybe he won't. Maybe it's like Mom says.

Merissa felt so hopeful, she decided not to cut herself that night after all.

Though she'd told a cruel lie about Hannah—or hinted at one.

Though Blade Runner curled in her arms in the night, in Merissa's sweaty-smelling bed.

Daddy was coming to dinner!

The first time since Daddy had *moved out*.

Of course: This would be a *special dinner*.

A special dinner Merissa helped her mother prepare: Daddy's favorite steak, which was plank steak, rare, with oyster mushrooms, whipped potatoes, glazed ginger carrots.

Merissa had come to hate red meat, especially *rare* and *bloody*. Not just that Tink had said how disgusting it was, eating "fellow mammals," and Mr. Kessler strongly hinted that eating meat was "wasteful of the earth's resources"—but Merissa had developed an actual, visceral disdain for the *chewiness* of meat.

Merissa's mother suggested that she just eat the vegetables. "You know how he feels about vegans and people who go on and on about global warming."

"Mom, I am not a vegan. I just don't like red meat."

"Well, your father does. Men do. Especially rare."

"And what does it have to do with global warming? Global warming is a scientific fact."

"Not with the terrible winters we've been having here in New Jersey. Don't get your father started on that subject, please!"

Stacy Carmichael was so excited, you'd have thought this was a first date.

And she was looking less haggard than she'd been looking in weeks: Her skin glowed (with expertly applied makeup), even eyeliner and mascara; the shadowy rings beneath her eyes seemed to have vanished. She wore lipstick. She'd filed and polished her fingernails. She wore a lavender cashmere sweater and black woolen slacks and around her neck a jade medallion Merissa's father had brought back from a trip to Japan a few years ago. (Merissa had a similar jade medallion from the same trip: She wondered if she should be wearing it, too. What sort of a distress signal would that be for Daddy to decode?)

Merissa's father had been vague about when he'd probably arrive—around seven p.m. But it was past seven thirty p.m., and it was past eight p.m., and Daddy had not yet arrived, nor had he called on his cell phone.

Merissa's mother hovered near both the landline and her own cell phone, awaiting a call.

Merissa, lightly fingering the (secret) panoply of little, healing cuts on her skin, (secret) beneath her clothes, drifted between the kitchen and the dining room, where the table had been set, by Merissa, as if for a special occasion.

And then, at 8:23 p.m., the glaring headlights of his vehicle— a sturdy steel-colored SUV—turned into the drive. Morgan Carmichael bounded into the house—*his* house—with a quick hug for both Merissa and her mother and an apology: he'd been "stuck in traffic"—some kind of "construction" on the turnpike.

Daddy's face was ruddy, and his breath held that smell— (Merissa was beginning to discern this smell at a distance of several feet)—that suggested he'd had a drink, or two, en route to *his house*.

And Daddy, at dinner, seemed not to have much of an appetite. His manner was edgy and alert and distracted: "Hey, sorry, I had a late lunch. Couldn't avoid it."

And so Daddy ate just a small portion of the bloody-rare steak.

Merissa thought, *Some poor, helpless animal had to die. For what?*

The injustice of the world—the stupid injustice of the world!—tugged at her, like Tink tugging at her elbow.

He is one of the cruel persons of the world. Your beloved Dad-dy.

Still, Merissa smiled at her father. There was no point in pretending that she wasn't happy to see him and that his gaze, however casually, even carelessly, it rested on her, didn't thrill her in a way no Blade Runner could ever touch.

And there was no point in provoking him, as her mother had wisely said.

Daddy had brought a "special wine" for dinner, which he

opened, with some difficulty, cursing as the cork splintered. Both he and Merissa's mother drank the wine at dinner—all of it.

And then Merissa's mother sent her to bring another bottle of red wine to the table, and Daddy opened that one also.

Was this a special, festive occasion, Merissa wondered, or were her parents *self-medicating*?

How superior Merissa felt! She would not ever *self-medicate* with alcohol or drugs.

Conversation at dinner was awkward. Like three people squeezed into a canoe and each trying to paddle. Mostly you'd be concerned with the canoe not tipping over, without much thought of where exactly you were going, or why.

Merissa's father brought up the subject—(the happy subject)—of Merissa's early-admission acceptance at Brown—and asked her who else at her school had gotten into "top Ivy" schools; and Merissa told him, so far as she knew.

"You really got the drop on your classmates, eh? Poor kids will be sweating it out, waiting for acceptances—or rejections." Morgan Carmichael swallowed a large mouthful of wine, as if the thought gave him pleasure. "Well, we knew—your mother and me—with that résumé of yours, you *couldn't* lose."

Merissa smiled stiffly. *Sure I could lose, Daddy. I can lose.*

And would you love me—if I did?

Merissa's father apologized—another time!—for not having taken her skating at the Meadowlands a few weeks ago. "But you're a little too old to be going out with your daddy, aren't you? Most girls your age would be, like, mortified to be seen with their *dad*."

Trying hard to be funny, using the word *like* as if in emulation of something Merissa might say. Except of course none of this was anything that Merissa might say.

"Merissa was selected as the lead in the play," Merissa's mother said, "which was quite an honor! But she's had to give it up, she has too much serious schoolwork to do. We're disappointed—of course. But—"

"Gave it up? Why?"

Daddy squinted at Merissa, holding his wineglass as if about to drink. His plank steak lay in a pool of reddish liquid on his plate, only a few bites eaten.

"I didn't give it up, I resigned." Merissa was very tired of explaining her action, which seemed to her now, in retrospect, impulsive and self-defeating—surrendering the coveted role to a girl who envied and disliked her and had been known to say things about her behind Merissa's back. Yet now, feeling defensive, she said irritably, "And I *hate Jane Austen*. I'm the only person, ever—the only female, anyway—to disapprove of her."

Tink would disapprove, Merissa knew.

Oh, how she missed Tink! She could never forgive Tink for *k*****g* herself.

"You say you resigned? Why?"

"Because, as Mom says, I am too busy with serious things."

So you're spared coming to the play. Come on, Dad—this is good news for you.

Merissa's father went on to ask about her classes at school, particularly her science course—"I haven't read your essay yet, sweetie, but it's on my calendar to read soon"—but seemed only half listening as Merissa replied.

(Was Daddy waiting for a call, or a text message? Several times at dinner he checked his shiny smartphone, which he'd had the tact to silence at the dinner table.)

And Merissa's mother chattered in her bright, nervous, breathy way—no one seemed to be listening to her at all.

Merissa shifted restlessly in her chair. She didn't know if she felt sorry for her mother, or exasperated with her. *Trying too hard. For God's sake, Mom.*

The single time Merissa had met Tink's (notorious) Big Moms—Veronica Traumer—she'd been surprised that the woman had been so *attractive*. Beneath the glamorous makeup and chic hairstyle, Ms. Traumer had looked like the kind of woman men would gaze after in the street—yet, according to Tink, Big Moms's "track record" with men had been "in the low single digits."

On TV, the several times Merissa had seen Veronica Traumer, she almost hadn't recognized her: makeup, hair, costuming.

Tink had said, *Acting is just a fraction of what you see. The expendable fraction.*

Merissa wondered if her father was acting right now—playing the role of the husband, the father who was *separated* from his family and *trying to figure out* whether he was going to return or not.

Or when.

Merissa's father was wearing a white cotton shirt open at the throat, sleeves rolled up as if for business. (But the sleeves had small buttons—you could button the rolled-up cuffs!) As soon as he'd removed his overcoat, he'd shrugged off his beautiful cashmere-wool sport coat and tugged off his necktie. His heavy jaws looked as if he hadn't shaved for a while, and he smelled just slightly—beyond the tart smell of red wine that Merissa had noticed—of something fragrant and flowery, which could not have been shaving lotion.

He is trying to decide between us and her.

But he is here with us now. He loves us!

Merissa, who'd eaten very little of the delicious dinner she'd helped to prepare, asked to be excused from the table. Carrying away plates to scrape unwanted food into the garbage disposal.

The bloody-rare steak, her father had scarcely touched! In the garbage disposal the rejected meat seemed to be twisting, groaning in pain like a live creature.

Still, Merissa was hopeful. She didn't really—not *really*—believe that her father would leave her and her mother; she didn't really believe that there could be . . .

(The very words were so hokey: *another woman*.)

(Like some made-for-TV movie on the Lifetime channel.)

Merissa lingered in the kitchen. She'd had a sense that her parents wanted to be alone, to talk about urgent, personal matters.

Helping in the kitchen was something easy and familiar, which Merissa had been avoiding lately. She was feeling guilty at not having been so nice to her mother in recent weeks—she couldn't comprehend why.

Thinking of the way Anita Chang had looked at her. And Brooke Kramer. And others, at school. *Merissa Carmichael is getting to be such a bitch.*

She knew they were texting each other this.

But they couldn't know that she'd been nasty to her own

mother. And she couldn't even remember why.

When she went upstairs tonight, Merissa thought, she'd text her friends Hannah and Chloe, maybe Nadia. . . . She felt a thrill of panic; she'd been mean to the very girls who were her friends.

For maybe now she was bargaining: If her father returned to the family, she would be a good, devoted friend.

Remembering how wistful and depressed Chloe had been in ninth grade, when her father had moved out of their house. At first Chloe had talked about the situation with Merissa and her friends—nervously and compulsively; then she'd stopped talking about it.

Except she'd said to Merissa one day, *You think it can't happen, that it isn't real. Then . . . it's like the only thing that is real.*

For a while, in ninth grade, Merissa remembered now with self-disgust, she hadn't really wanted to spend time with Chloe. No one did.

For Chloe was so—*needy, sad. Pathetic.*

The girls had made plans without Chloe—shopping at the mall, going to movies, sleepovers. This was before Tink Traumer had come into their lives, when they'd seemed so *young*.

Merissa had been planning a sleepover at her house to which she was inviting seven or eight girls, and she hadn't intended to invite Chloe Zimmer until her mother had asked her why not, and Merissa had felt so ashamed, she'd decided to invite Chloe—which had turned out to be a very good thing to do.

Chloe adored Merissa, as a consequence. For being just a good friend, at a time when Chloe had needed a friend.

Eventually, Chloe recovered something of her former personality. Her parents had joint custody of Chloe and her younger brother, and shuttling between two households, as Chloe described it, *You either sink or swim.*

Yet Merissa didn't want to confide in Chloe about her father moving out of the house. It was too shameful!

In the dining room Merissa's parents were speaking earnestly. Merissa was correct—they'd wanted to be alone but had not wanted to ask Merissa to leave.

Stacy's thin, uplifted voice. Morgan's deeper, hesitant voice.

Through a roaring in her ears, Merissa could not hear distinct words.

Half-blindly she was placing dishes in the dishwasher. She'd rinsed the plates carefully—as if being a good girl at such a time, helping out her mom with cleanup, would make a difference in this crisis.

She swallowed hard. She had a quick flash of a blond girl— anorexic-thin as a ballerina—her face hidden by a black half mask and her bare, scarred chest exposed for all the world to see. The (secret) little cuts on her own body, hidden beneath her clothes, had begun to sting. Compared to the desperation of Blade Runner, Merissa was relatively untouched—so far. But she had a dread of one of the deeper, more recent cuts starting to bleed and seeping through her clothing without her knowing it.

Merissa's mother came into the kitchen. There seemed to be something wrong with her—she was walking strangely, as if she'd lost her balance. She was trying to smile, reaching out to Merissa, who shrank away, instinctively.

"I—I'm afraid—your father has something to say to you. It's—it's a surprise—I mean—" Merissa's mother's eyes welled with tears. Her mouth quivered, but she spoke bravely. "He wants to talk to you and he's asked me to ask you—if you possibly can, honey—that you try not to cry."

Try not to cry!
So I knew, Tink.
Wish I could be with you—wherever you are.

Merissa's father led her into the living room, which was elegantly furnished—silk wallpaper, hardwood floors covered with bright Chinese rugs, the small grand piano at which Merissa had practiced her lessons since the age of seven, that *ten years of piano instruction* might be noted on her college applications.

Not that Merissa was naturally talented, as a pianist. You could say that she was average to good—when she practiced.

But in recent weeks, she'd ceased practicing. She'd stopped taking lessons. Neither her mother nor her father seemed to have noticed.

The living room was darkened, and Merissa's father switched on a lamp. The intention seemed to be that father and daughter would sit down in this somewhat formal space—"Let's get comfortable, Merissa. Dinner was fantastic. . . ." Merissa's father's voice trailed off guiltily.

Merissa stood, stricken. So frequently had she rehearsed a scene like this, she'd thought that it would be familiar to her, and in her control; yet as soon as her father began speaking, in this low, urgent, guilty-sounding voice, she began to tremble. For Daddy was smiling at her anxiously as one might smile at a small child—a small, terribly ill child.

Merissa wasn't seventeen, but seven. In an instant her poise had melted away.

She would remember what Tink had said—*Things happen to us. We don't happen to them.*

Something seemed to have been decided in the dining room just now. Between Merissa's parents.

Something her father had said to her mother. Something definite at last.

Why? Why? It was stunning to Merissa to realize that possibly her father couldn't control what was happening, either. That something was happening to him and not just to Merissa and her mother.

Like stinging insects, his words flew at her. Even as Merissa stood staring at her father's flushed, awkwardly smiling face. She was very cold suddenly, shivering.

—know that I love you, Merissa—right?

—would never want to hurt you—

—nothing will be changed between us—you and me—

—will see you as much—almost as much—

—been a while since your mother and I have made each other happy—

—wouldn't understand, honey—you're too young . . .

—didn't intend for this to happen but—

—met someone—

—not intentional, I swear—

—you will like her very much—and she will like you—

—she has seen your picture and says how beautiful you are—

—how much she wants to meet you—sometime—

—your mother doesn't have to know—details . . .

—wanted to alert you, honey—

—think it's best if I make this decision now—not later—

—start things in motion—

—your mother will have an excellent attorney—

—remember: nothing to do with you, honey—

—love you, Merissa—

—I promise—

Merissa was listening, yet she seemed scarcely to know what these strange hurtling words meant. For wasn't Daddy her friend, and why would a friend hurt *her*?

And there was Daddy smiling at her, and he was opening his arms to her—as if about to hug her. And so she was thinking—(wanting to think)—maybe she hadn't heard correctly; maybe she was just confused. And the sound of someone crying—(sobbing?)—in the other room was distracting to her and confusing—

Then Merissa's father's smartphone rang, in his pocket.

Such a look came into Daddy's face! Merissa would long remember.

He'd meant to turn off the phone—hadn't he? But somehow, he had not turned off the phone.

And so the phone rang, and he snatched it out of his pocket, saw the caller ID, and at once he was helpless, stammering an apology—

"Excuse me, honey—important call."

He did look stricken. He did look regretful. But he didn't turn off the phone. Quickly he turned away to take the call, gripping the shiny little phone to his ear and walking away, speaking in a lowered voice so that Merissa couldn't hear.

Later she would recall—after her initial shock—how unhesitatingly her father had turned away from her, how quickly he'd walked away without a backward glance. Merissa could hear how excited his voice was, how eager and urgent. For whoever was calling Morgan Carmichael, in his home—whoever had intruded on his evening with his wife and daughter—was so crucial to him, nothing else mattered.

Merissa didn't follow her father—of course. Merissa didn't seek out her mother. Instead, like a sleepwalker, Merissa made her way to the stairs.

Then she ran stumbling up to her room.

Calmly thinking, *There is nothing more I can do. Nothing more Mom can do.*

Merissa shut the door to her room. She was moving blindly, instinctively.

In the bathroom, her trembling fingers opened the drawer beside the sink, seeking the little paring knife. Yes—there it was.

Part hidden, at the back of the drawer.

The blade had been stained several times with her blood. Each time, Merissa had carefully washed it with very hot water and dried it.

Like a surgical instrument, it was. And still very sharp.

Nothing more. Nothing we can do.

Except.

At the foot of the stairs Merissa's mother was calling to her plaintively. Probably Daddy would be leaving now—whoever had called him had summoned him away. And Merissa's mother would come upstairs to her in another minute, she supposed. Wanting to embrace her daughter and cry with her—but

Merissa wasn't going to cry.

Calmly she closed the drawer.

Calmly she prepared herself.

For when her father had departed to his mysterious new life and her mother was in bed, sleeping her heavy, stuporous, medicated sleep—this would be soon, and Merissa could wait.

16.

"NOT GOING ANYWHERE"

This time, she would not be a coward.

Taking up the little knife. But her hand shook so, she had to steady it with her left hand. A pulse began to beat hard in her throat.

Oh, oh, oh, oh, oh.

The touch of the cold steel against her feverish skin. A touch that did not feel razor-sharp so much as consoling.

Never again to sleep, not a natural sleep. Pulses beating in her head, which would have to be silenced.

Terrible thoughts like furious hornets.

Excuse me, honey—important call.

Excuse me, honey—important call.

Hearing again the cell phone in her father's pocket ringing. Hearing again her father's apologetic words.

Excuse me, honey—important call.

Seeing the look on his face. His eyes.

Seeing how quickly he walked away.

And her mother calling to her—*Merissa! Merissa!*

But that was finished. Hours ago.

Now the house was darkened upstairs and down and it was a relief to her, the father had gone from her life; and the mother had medicated herself with wine and barbiturates and would sleep while the daughter's life bled away in silence.

Not a coward! They would see.

But her hand shook so, pressing the knife blade against her throat. The carotid artery, beneath her jaw—she knew what this was. Not even Blade Runner had dared to cut in such a place, but Merissa Carmichael would cut in such a place if only her hand didn't tremble so badly.

Instead she pressed the knife blade against the inside of her left forearm, where another blue artery beat beneath the soft, pale skin. On the internet she'd learned that the most effective way to slash one's wrists is not perpendicular to the wrist but parallel to the wrist and the forearm; and so she pressed the knife blade a little harder, badly trembling now but biting her lower lip, determined not to fail—*Knew you'd come through! That's my girl.*

There came a sudden stream of blood, though the knife blade had scarcely penetrated Merissa's skin—quickly she blotted the wound with a wad of tissues, before any of the blood could drip onto the floor.

She should lie in the bathtub, she knew. In warm bathwater.

This would be soothing, she would not be so frightened. She would not be so *tremulous*.

But the prospect of removing her clothes, making herself naked and exposed to strangers' eyes, lying in bathwater—and the bathwater discolored by her own blood!—this was ugly.

This did not appeal to her, for Merissa was a fastidious girl and could not bear the thought of being such a spectacle.

Maybe better to lie in her bed, as Tink had done. But Tink had swallowed her mother's barbiturates—or so it was said.

Merissa was sitting on the edge of her bed, partly dressed. She was feeling faint—light-headed—and her heart was beating strangely.

She wanted to hurt herself—as she deserved to be hurt.

She wanted to punish herself—as she deserved to be punished.

She wanted to die—as she deserved to die.

Gripping the little knife more tightly, and bringing the tip of the blade against her forearm again, which was now bleeding, slippery with blood, she swallowed hard, and there came a sound of something scratching—angrily?—at a nearby window, and Merissa turned to stare at—what was it?—at the windowpane beyond her bed in which, since the room was lighted, there was nothing to discern except the blurred reflection of the room, and Merissa's blurry figure within it.

No one, nothing there—of course.

Dry-mouthed, Merissa directed the knife blade another time, and another time there came the sharp, angry scratching sound at the window. Hairs stirred on the nape of Merissa's neck.

"T-Tink? Are you here?"

It seemed that Tink was near—a hot, furious presence—for Tink's skin often felt hot, and her carroty-red hair looked as if it had been singed with fire—and her green-glassy laser eyes that were capable of exuding such contempt.

Merissa stared toward the window but saw nothing except the

reflection. She felt someone touch her—tug lightly at her hair—but when she turned, there was no one there—of course. . . .

"Tink? Tink? Where are you?"

It was the first time that Tink had appeared to Merissa since the week of Good News, which had to be almost two months ago. So long Merissa had been lonely, yearning for Tink, and so long Tink had kept her distance, and Merissa wondered now if Tink had been disgusted with her, and no longer loved her as a friend; and that was why Tink had not spoken to her in so long.

"Tink? I—I'm not sure what to do. I think that I—should—should do this—but—" Merissa's voice faltered, like a child's voice. She was so ashamed that Tink should see her like this, lacking Tink's courage.

Another time Merissa felt someone touch her, now on the right shoulder; and when she turned, there came a touch—playful, teasing—on Merissa's left shoulder.

"T-Tink? I wish you could h-help me. . . ."

Merissa's eyes were widened, but her vision seemed to be narrowing, like a tunnel. Her teeth were chattering, though her skin was scalding to the touch. The little paring knife was gripped between her fingers so hard, the flesh of her fingers had begun to turn white, but suddenly, to Merissa's astonishment, the little knife was pried out of her fingers and fell clattering to the floor. And she felt a warm breath against the nape of her neck, and heard soft laughter.

"Tink! Don't t-tease. . . ."

Now Merissa could smell her friend's singed-orange-peel smell, which was unmistakable. And a scent of cloves and cinnamon.

She would have snatched up the knife—(which was stained and ugly-looking)—except there came a sharp little nudge in her ribs like a painful tickle, and she gave a cry of astonishment, glancing everywhere around her—but Tink, though obviously present, was not *visible*.

And as Mr. Kessler frequently said, so much of the universe was present but not visible to ordinary human eyes, from the smallest molecules and unicellular creatures to the vast emptiness of space, a no-color that defied human perception.

And in this universe, as much as 90 percent of matter was invisible—*black holes*.

"Tink? Don't be mean, Tink—talk to me. . . . Help me, tell me what to d-do. . . ."

At Merissa's feet, the little stained knife appeared to be kicked—by an invisible foot—sent skittering beneath her bed.

Merissa laughed, this was so—astonishing.

Even the girls of Tink, Inc., would not believe this.

Merissa's heart was pounding so rapidly, she could barely catch her breath. Since taking up the knife a few minutes before, she was becoming increasingly light-headed, and now her eyelids fluttered, her eyelids were drooping and heavy, she was lying on her side on the rumpled bed, not entirely awake, yet not unconscious or sleeping; she was sure she was not sleeping; and there stood Tink at the foot of the bed, hands on her hips and elbows pointed outward; and Tink shook her long, wavy red hair, which fell about her small face in ringlets, and she was wearing the grungy black leggings that had become too tight for even her small body, and the loose-fitting GUERRILLA GIRL jersey with the stretched, just discernibly soiled neck; and she squinched up her face, saying, *M'ris! Don't emulate me! Killing myself was, like, the dumbest mistake of my life.*

Tink laughed as if she'd said something witty. Merissa stared at her through tightly shut eyes, wishing badly that Tink would not vanish from her even as she knew that Tink would vanish as soon as she opened her eyes.

Time for bed, M'rissa! Fuck 'em.

Tink laughed and climbed into Merissa's bed, curling up like a big, awkwardly graceful cat. Merissa remembered how Tink had made them laugh, describing her mother's efforts to turn her into a baby ballerina—lessons that began when Tink was three years old—what a bore it was having to be *graceful*.

Like there's nobody in actual life who would be such an asshole to walk around "en pointe"—so your toes break, and bleed, and get all crippled.

Merissa was laughing, and she was shivering so badly that her teeth chattered. She knew not to open her eyes, that Tink would vanish when she opened her eyes, and so she fumbled to pull the comforter over Tink, or part of Tink, and over herself, for she was so very tired, so sleepy now, and feeling relaxed now that Tink had come to be with her at this terrible time.

Merissa groped to switch off the light on her bedside table.

Tink sighed, shivered, and curled against Merissa's foot.

I'm here. I love you, dude. I'm not going anywhere.

17.

"JUST THERE"

When Merissa woke in the morning, dazed and groggy and her bloodstained arm aching, there was no one in bed with her, no one in the room—of course.

But Tink's scent remained. And beneath Merissa's bed, kicked at least a foot under the bed, was the bloodstained little paring knife, which Merissa quickly retrieved, washed thoroughly in her bathroom, and returned to the kitchen drawer downstairs, where its absence had never been noted.

Each night following, Merissa had only to shut her eyes and Tink appeared.

Merissa had only to switch off her bedside lamp, climb into bed, and pull the comforter over her, and Tink appeared; and the healing sensation of sleep rippled over Merissa like warm water.

Remember, dude: Tink is here.

Tink is not going to go away.

• • •

It was too private; Merissa couldn't tell her friends.

Except mentioning to them, casually, "Guess what? Tink was in a dream last night—she hasn't changed much at all."

(But was this true? Tink had seemed just a little different— the hair in ringlets was a change, and what she'd said about k*****g herself—this was a remark unlike any Merissa had ever heard from her friend when she'd been alive.)

Chloe said, with a strange look, "Oh God! Last night? I think—I think Tink was in my dream, too. She didn't talk to me, though—did she talk to you, Merissa?"

Merissa shook her head no.

Hannah said, "Oh, Tink never talks to me, either! Which is weird because, in life, she talked all the time."

"Tink doesn't need to talk, does she? She just—is there."

They agreed, Tink was just—*there*.

18.

"HELP"

Merissa's mother took Merissa's hand in both her hands and held it.

Her mother said, with a brave little smile, "It's definite, Merissa. Your father and I are getting—divorced."

Merissa swallowed hard.

She said, "I guess I know, Mom."

Thinking how good it was, the way in which her mother phrased this news: *Your father and I are getting—divorced.* And not instead: *Your father wants a divorce.*

Merissa didn't shrink away when her mother hugged her and began to cry. And Merissa cried with her.

"I'll help you, Mom. It will be all right."

II

TINK TINK TINK TINK TINK TINK TINK TINK

A Scrapbook

1.

HOW TINK CAME INTO OUR LIVES: SEPTEMBER 2010

Rumor was, somebody "famous" was transferring from a revered old prep school in Manhattan into the junior class at Quaker Heights Day School.

Rumor was, this somebody was (A) a model, (B) a movie actress, (C) a New York City stage actress, (D) a TV actress.

Rumor was, she was the daughter of a famous actress-mother and a "really rich" father (who owned a sports team?) and they'd just moved into one of the new showy custom-designed houses in the exclusive gated community of Quaker River Heights.

It was the third week of the fall term. The most outrageous rumor—well, it had to be a fact—was that the new transfer had been granted special permission by our headmaster, Mr. Nichols, to miss the start of term, for "professional" reasons: She'd been in Paris on a *shoot*.

"Look!" Martine Hesse happened to be standing at a window in Mrs. Conway's classroom, just before the start of third-period English class; there, second-floor windows overlooked the front driveway.

"A limousine!"

It was a shiny black Lincoln. You couldn't have seen through the tinted windows even if you'd been down on the sidewalk past which the limousine was gliding.

And where the town car parked, you couldn't see from the second-floor windows who got out and entered the school building.

Later it would be claimed by Martine and several others in Mrs. Conway's class that they'd actually seen Tink Traumer climb out of the back of the limousine and enter through the front entrance, on her way to the headmaster's office.

In no version of the original story was it claimed that Tink's mother or any adult had accompanied her. Invariably, Tink had been alone.

But later it would be claimed by numerous others that they'd seen Tink arrive via limousine for her first day at Quaker Heights Day School and they'd seen the "uniformed chauffeur" get out of the vehicle to open Tink's door for her.

As Tink would say, with a snort of derision: "Bullshit! Nobody opens any bloody car door for *me*."

There came the short, fiery-haired girl into Mr. Doerr's third-period geometry class. Her face was pale and plain, as if it had been scrubbed, and even her freckles looked bleached; but her singed-looking hair sprang out from her head with a look of quivering indignation.

The girl had been escorted to Mr. Doerr's classroom by one of Headmaster Nichols's assistants, who gave the math teacher an admission card from which, in a bemused voice, Mr. Doerr read:

"'Katrina Traumer.' Hel-*lo*."

Mr. Doerr was being pleasantly welcoming to the new girl—but you knew, if you knew Mr. Doerr, that he was also just slightly exasperated at being interrupted at his favorite class-time activity, which was scrawling figures and equations on the board. This Mr. Doerr did each class period in a kind of fevered trance, after which he'd step back, gripping chalk in his fingers, and call out exuberantly to the class: "Who can help me out on this one?" You could see how pleased he was at what he'd been scribbling, as if it were a secret code only a few very special students could decipher.

But the knock at the door, and the arrival of the new transfer with the springy rust-red hair, had interrupted Mr. Doerr's ritual.

"Katrina Traumer—welcome! Though you are twelve days late for school, I'm sure there is a more than adequate explanation for your tardiness. And so, Katrina, if you would please take a seat in the—"

"Tink."

"Excuse me? What did you say?"

"The name is Tink."

Mr. Doerr regarded the new girl with an expression of startled puzzlement. He was at least twelve inches taller than she, and one hundred pounds heavier. Yet as she stared at him with uncanny glassy-green eyes, Mr. Doerr lost some of his composure.

"Did you say 'Tink'?"

"It's the name people call me," Tink said, "if they want me to grant them my attention." Yet the red-haired girl spoke so disdainfully, you wouldn't expect that even being called by this strange name would guarantee her attention.

We had time now to stare at her clothes. Like no other clothes any girl at Quaker Heights was likely to wear to class.

We were into Levi's straight-leg jeans and tight little Gap tops, mostly worn beneath looser-fitting shirts or sweaters. We were seriously into a "chic-preppy" look that suited us, we thought.

Here was the new red-haired transfer student from Manhattan who was wearing a dancer's leggings—black tights—beneath a pullover of some strange crinkly fabric that looked more like soft filaments of metal than cloth.

And on her feet—child feet, size four—little red leather sneakers with black laces.

"'Tink'! What kind of a name is 'Tink'?"

Mr. Doerr had just two modes of speech: Teacher Mode, which was as brisk and staccato as a nutcracker might talk if it could talk, and his Ironic Mode, which was droll and dry and intended to be *funny*. During class Mr. Doerr spent most of his time in Teacher Mode, but now and then shifted to Ironic Mode; he maintained a deadpan expression but shifted his eyebrows to signal, *Okay, kids, now you can laugh*. So we'd laugh to humor him, for you don't want to hurt the feelings of any adult who grades you or will write letters for your college applications. But with Tink in our class, already you could see that he'd have to be careful or the wiry little red-haired stranger with the green eyes glancing out over the class—gliding over our rapt faces, without lingering, like a ray of light—would make a fool of him.

Tink never smiled, either. She would confide in us, later, that the secret of humor was not smiling, so your listeners didn't know whether you knew you were funny—they had to guess, and guessing kept them alert.

"Tink is the logical diminutive of Tinkle, Mr. Door." The red-haired girl's voice was unexpectedly scratchy, like fingernails on slate.

"Excuse me—the name is Doerr."

"That's what I said, sir: Dour."

"No! Not Dour—Doerr."

"Doooer."

"Do-err. The accent is just slightly on the first syllable."

"Tinkle. The accent is just slightly on the first syllable."

"But Tinkle isn't your name, is it?" Mr. Doerr was becoming red-faced now, and not smiling; just as the red-haired girl with the glittery green eyes was not smiling but looking at him with an affronted air. "Your name is—"

"Correct. The name on the card is 'Katrina.' You can see that no one would wish to be called 'Katrina' who wasn't fifty years old, with fifty-inch hips."

Some of us in the class laughed, this was so funny. But others sat staring at the new girl and at befuddled Mr. Doerr, for whom we were now feeling embarrassment.

"I don't see that 'Tinkle' is an improvement over 'Katrina,' frankly," Mr. Doerr said, with a sudden glare. "Why 'Tinkle'?"

"Because when I was a little girl, I would go *tinkle* in the potty, just like you, Mr. Dorr."

Laugh! Everyone in our class erupted into laughter, and it was five or maybe ten minutes before poor, blushing Mr. Doerr could quiet us down, assign the new girl a seat in the fourth row, and continue with the shambles of his class.

Tinkle in the potty, just like you.

Immediately, these words were taken up at Quaker Heights Day School, from the tenth grade, which was an unusually close-knit class of fewer than one hundred students, through the eleventh and twelfth grades; even the most popular and self-absorbed seniors who had no idea who "Tink" Traumer was tossed the phrase about as if they understood the joke. *Tinkle in the potty! Just like you.*

2.

"BRATTY BITCH"

Almost immediate and near unanimous was the judgment on Tink Traumer: *bratty bitch*.

She was too small, scrappy, and young-looking to be an actual *bitch*—a *bitch* meant some measure of sexual-female maturity. But she was way too mature to be a *brat*, which meant just a young kid.

"She's mean! She's nasty! I tried to be nice to her—asked her how she liked Quaker Heights so far—and she didn't even look at me, just sort of snarled, 'There are no Quakers here, and no Heights—what's there to like?'"

"Maybe she was being funny?"

"Funny! She was *nasty*. She didn't even ask my name, or— anything."

Even worse, in Mrs. Conway's homeroom, when Mrs. Conway asked Tink where she'd transferred from, Tink said, "UWS."

"'UWS'? I'm not sure what that means."

"Upper West Side."

"Oh! Manhattan, I guess?"

By this time Tink had opened her laptop and was typing into it, as if her exchange with Mrs. Conway had concluded.

(Hannah Heller, whose desk was close by Tink's in homeroom, tried to see what Tink had logged in to—her laptop screen seemed to be showing a sequence of photographs of the nighttime sky.)

It was so: The "new girl" wasn't friendly, at least not in any normal way. If you tried to talk to her—to ask her questions— her pale, freckled little face seemed to freeze, and her green-glassy eyes quivered like a combustible liquid; but if you just smiled at her, or glanced at her without any expectations, Tink might surprise you by saying, "Howdy."

Howdy. So hokey, it was *cool.*

We were shocked by how disdainful Tink was when Mr. Trocchi tried to ask her about her *professional career.*

(Mr. Trocchi remembered having seen her TV series, *Gramercy Park*, years ago. Tink had been in the cast from the age of six to eleven, playing the daughter of an alcoholic divorcée while her mother, Veronica Traumer, played another, unrelated character. According to Mr. Trocchi, Veronica Traumer was a "competent" TV actress, but Tink had been "just terrific— you'd never think the little girl was acting at all, she was just being herself." All this Mr. Trocchi told us, and much more. He was *thrilled* to have a professional actress to work with in student productions.)

What a surprise then, and a disappointment, when Mr. Trocchi tried to question her in class.

"Tell us what it was like, Katrina—I mean, *Trink*—being a celebrity at the age of six."

Tink, seated tensely in her desk, which seemed too big for her small-boned body, stared at Mr. Trocchi coolly. "Excuse me: My name is bloody Tink—not bloody Trink."

Bloody! No one had ever heard this colorful adjective before, in such a context. Mr. Trocchi considered how to react and then—laughed.

"'Bloody' is a British expression, should any of you be interested in colloquialisms," Mr. Trocchi said, in his mock-teacherly way, to the class, "though I think it is considered just a bit *too colloquial* for polite British society. You've traveled to Britain, Tink? Or—you've lived there?"

"Some."

This ambiguous answer, reluctantly muttered, Mr. Trocchi seemed to accept as a positive reply.

Again he asked her how it had felt to be a celebrity at the age of six, and Tink stiffened and with a pained little grimace said that she'd never been a *celebrity*—"That's ridiculous."

Mr. Trocchi plucked at his mustache, protesting, "But in professional circles, you certainly were! You had a career, Tink, and you made money, while other little girls your age were in grade school and playing with dolls." Mr. Trocchi smirked at the very thought of little girls in grade school playing with dolls—he'd forgotten that the rest of his female students must have been in this category. "You and your mother, Veronica Traumer—both! What was it like?"

"My character did the acting. Not me."

"Mmm! How interesting! 'My character did the acting—not me.' I think you must mean a kind of Method acting, Tink? Could you explain to the class, Tink, what Method acting involves?"

Mr. Trocchi had no difficulty calling Tink by a diminutive. If anything, he seemed to relish the intimacy, as if he'd known Tink Traumer for a long time. When he'd been told of Tink's witty exchange with his colleague Doerr, he'd laughed as if he'd never heard anything so funny. *He* was no prissy old conformist like Doerr.

Tink murmured, "Some other time, maybe. Method acting is complicated."

"Why yes, it is! There's a philosophy of acting—and of the theater—behind it. Stanislavsky . . . Chekhov . . ." Mr. Trocchi was excited, as we'd rarely seen him.

"Well. I hope you will want to audition for our fall play— *Our Town.* You would make an unusual, I think very effective Emily—one of the great roles for a girl in the American theater."

Tink shook her head vehemently. No!

"What do you mean—no? You don't want to audition for Thornton Wilder's Emily?"

You could see—if you were sitting near Tink, as Chloe Zimmer was—that her fingernails were badly bitten. The black leggings she wore virtually every day to school looked as if they hadn't been laundered in some time, and her springy, singed-red hair looked as if it hadn't been combed or brushed, let alone shampooed, in days.

You could also see—if you stared hard enough—that when Tink's long, loose sleeve fell back from her left wrist, there was a tight, flesh-colored adhesive bandage around the wrist.

Mr. Trocchi persisted, "You mean—it's something of a professional insult, to ask you to audition? Of course—I understand. I wasn't thinking. Let me offer you the role, then—without an audition. Or we could read through the play together, after school one day this week, and see if the role appeals to you."

"I don't think so, Mr. Trochee."

"Trocchi—not 'Trochee.'"

"Trock-y."

"Trocchi."

"*Troc-cee.*"

(Did Tink mean to be funny? She was so deadpan—so serious! And Mr. Trocchi was so serious.)

"But the point is—will you play Emily in *Our Town*? I'm sure the local media will want to cover the production, and I can contact the New Jersey section of the *New York Times*. Think of the publicity for our school, and for the drama program! Merissa, you're the new president of the Drama Club. What do you think?"

Merissa frowned. Though she had played several minor roles in school productions, she hadn't yet been cast by Mr. Trocchi in anything like a leading role; it had crossed her mind that maybe Emily in *Our Town* might be her "breakthrough" role. So she was reluctant to support Mr. Trocchi in this casting suggestion.

Also, she had been watching squirmy red-haired Tink Traumer and had definitely registered the girl's stiffened expression even as Mr. Trocchi chattered enthusiastically.

"What do I *think*? I think that you should have auditions, Mr. Trocchi—as always."

Merissa tried to exchange a glance, a smile, with Tink Traumer, but Tink ignored her.

Ignored Merissa Carmichael! Beautiful, poised Merissa Carmichael with pale-blond hair, flawless skin, and ceramic-doll features.

Mr. Trocchi objected, "In professional theater, and certainly in the movies, auditions are not required for accomplished actors. We've always had auditions here, of course—all our actors are *amateurs*."

Merissa said, "But our productions are *amateur productions*, Mr. Trocchi! It isn't fair to not have auditions—open auditions, for everyone."

"But here we have Tink Traumer—a *professional*—in our midst!"

"If Tink is interested in playing the role of Emily, she can audition—like the rest of us."

Mr. Trocchi frowned, plucking at his mustache. For the fear was, of course, that Tink would not audition for the role—or any role. And he would lose the opportunity to showcase her.

"I understand your point, Merissa. And—the rest of you—I see that you agree with Merissa?—but—if we want a truly first-rate production of this great American classic, *Our Town*, we will have to cast the very best 'Emily' at our disposal. . . ."

Tink objected, "Mr. Tucchi—*Trucci*—I've tried to tell you that I'm not a bloody actor now, I've been retired since the age of twelve. I've become an *amateur*."

It was only a moment—just a blink of an eye—but you could see, in that moment, a look on Tink Traumer's face that was *frightened*.

Then, immediately, Tink's face froze again. Shut up as tight as a clenched little fist.

One thing was certain: Tink wasn't a *model*.

"A model has to be tall—Tink is practically a midget. And

a model has to be beautiful—she has to have high cheekbones. Tink has a face like a little pug dog, or a monkey. She's *homely*."

Chloe Zimmer objected. (Chloe, the sweetest of girls, never failed to defend a girl who was being criticized behind her back, even if, as in this case, the girl wasn't her friend.)

"Tink Traumer is not *homely*. Her face is just—just—her own unique face."

"Unique! Everybody's face is unique—so what?"

It was easier to think of Tink Traumer as a *bratty bitch*.

3.

"THAT CHAIR IS TINK'S"

This happened just yesterday.

Six months, two weeks, and three days since Tink left us.

We were at our table in the dining hall at school. Merissa—Hannah—Chloe—Nadia.

But also, though they weren't in the (secret) innermost circle of Tink, Inc.: Anita Chang—Martine Hesse—Shelby Freedman.

Lunchtime in the high-ceilinged dining hall, which was reputedly modeled, on a smaller scale, after a revered old dining hall in Oxford.

Lunchtime: and people were watching us.

Tink had always been easy with people staring at her. She'd pretended to be annoyed, but really, she'd enjoyed the attention. (To a degree.) When Tink had been with us, we'd often laugh so loudly that everyone in the dining hall would look at us—(yearningly?)—but we never exchanged glances with them.

Now they had their revenge. For Tink was absent from our table: Her chair, between Hannah and Merissa, was empty.

No one had planned it that way. Somehow, it had just happened.

"Hi—Merissa? Hannah?"

The yearbook art director, Devra Holman, stopped to speak with Merissa and Hannah, carrying her cafeteria tray. Devra was a nice girl whom we all liked, and so it would have been a polite gesture—it would have been a natural gesture—to invite Devra to sit between Merissa and Hannah to eat her lunch, as the three conferred about the yearbook cover; but no one, not even Merissa and Hannah, thought to invite her.

If Devra had pulled out the vacant chair at the end of the table, the girls of Tink, Inc., would have exclaimed, *Nooo! You can't. That chair is Tink's.*

Maybe Devra sensed this. Maybe she felt the presence of Tink Traumer at the table, as others did.

And so, Devra didn't pull out a chair to sit with us. And no one invited her. And after a few minutes' consultation with Merissa and Hannah, Devra continued on her way to sit with friends at another table.

4.

"PROMISE!"

If ever you feel that you are sad and confused and tempted to imitate your friend, please see me: Will you promise?

This was Mrs. Jameson, our school guidance counselor/psychologist. But it could have been anyone who knew us—any adult.

Parents, relatives. Teachers.

Soon after Tink d**d.

Soon after Tink did that thing to herself.

Will you promise? Please?

Sure! We promise.

Always tell an adult what she/he wants to hear. Especially if it's an adult with authority over you, like Mrs. Jameson.

This was Tink's philosophy: *Promise them any damn thing, then do whatever damn thing you were going to do anyway.*

We guessed that was what Tink did. Whatever damn thing she'd wanted to do anyway.

Except without telling us, either.

There are some secrets so toxic you can't share. Especially if you love who it is you'd have to share with.

5.

"TOXIC SECRET"

For a long time Merissa said nothing to any of her friends—Tink's friends. Then, one day in the late winter of senior year, when they were alone together, studying French in Merissa's room, she said to Hannah Heller, "Before Tink went away—a few days before—she said to me, 'I have a favor to ask of you.' And I said, 'Sure, what?' But then Tink changed her mind, and looked embarrassed, and said no, it was nothing. She said there were some things that were best kept secrets, because secrets could be 'toxic' between friends. . . . And I never found out what it was."

Merissa brought the subject up as hesitantly as she'd brought up the subject of whether, in their dreams, Tink spoke to them as she'd spoken to Merissa—because she didn't want their friends to feel hurt, believing that Tink favored Merissa.

Of course, Merissa believed that Tink did favor her. *Tink likes me best! Tink saved my life.*

(It was ridiculous, of course. For Tink was no longer among us.)

(Yet such petty jealousies among friends survive even d**th.)

Hannah said no. She didn't remember Tink bringing any-thing like this up with her.

"When was this, exactly? Just before . . ."

Hannah bit her lip. It was very hard to say, *Just before Tink d**d.*

"Yes. Just before."

Hannah said definitely *no*. As far as she could remember, Tink had never suggested any sort of favor.

Not a favor from you. But a favor from me! Merissa thought.

Merissa asked her friends one by one, in private. She had to speak to us singly; she could not text message such a delicate question.

Each of them said no. No, Tink had not ever asked them for a favor, or even suggested such a possibility—"Are you sure you're remembering right?" Martine asked. "I don't think that Tink ever asked anyone for favors."

Quickly Merissa said, "Probably I misunderstood. You're right—Tink never asked us for anything."

But why not? What would have been so hard about that, to ask someone who loved you to do something for you?

Maybe you'd be alive right now, Tink—if you had.

6.

"ETERNITY PUSHING THROUGH TIME"

It was about six weeks after Tink first appeared at Quaker Heights Day School that, one day at noon, in the school dining room, the idea came to all of us virtually at the same moment: "Let's invite Tink to sit with us!"

Tink had just entered the dining room, alone.

Usually, Tink was alone. In the school corridor, on the sidewalks outside school, in classes, or at assembly—Tink was alone.

Which isn't to say that Tink seemed *lonely*. But Tink was definitely *alone*.

People looked at her. Stared at her. Whispered about her. And Tink was both aware of them and indifferent to them, which made her appear, amid the clamor and bustle of the school dining room, all the more *alone*.

"You go ask her, Merissa. She'll say yes to you."

"Ohhh no! *You* ask her."

"C'mon—we can all ask her."

So we did. And Tink looked at us in that blank, deadpan way of hers that seemed to signal, *Who the hell are you?*—but in the next instant relented and smiled, saying instead, "Hell, yes—I was hoping you'd ask me."

Ever after that, Tink was our friend. And ever after that, everyone at Quaker Heights Day School envied us.

It wasn't that Tink Traumer ceased being a *bratty bitch*. But people began to discover that she was other things, too—smart, funny, witty, unpredictable, original.

In classes she daydreamed a lot. She'd slouch in her seat and in a protective crook of her arm she'd be reading a paperback book—Virginia Woolf's *Orlando*, George Orwell's *1984*, William Faulkner's *As I Lay Dying*. Yet often she could answer an irritated teacher's question, as if, with a part of her mind, she'd been listening attentively all along.

"Tink? Let's hear what you think."

And Tink would uncurl her legs in the grungy black leggings, shake her head as if to clear it, and give a reasonably intelligent answer.

Tink didn't audition for the part of Emily in Thornton Wilder's *Our Town*, to Mr. Trocchi's extreme disappointment, but she showed up now and then on the set to help with lighting, costumes, directing—she'd seemed to want to *help* but not to be *relied on*.

(Mr. Trocchi asked Tink's advice repeatedly—you'd have thought she was a young teacher and not a student. And then, near the end of rehearsals, Tink just vanished—didn't even come to opening night—but that was another story.)

In Mrs. Conway's English class, Tink procrastinated writing her term paper so that, finally, she received a grade of F for the paper—but startled us one day by reciting, in her low, scratchy, dramatic voice, an Emily Dickinson poem that embodied a theme the class had been discussing about identity and anonymity:

> *I'm nobody! Who are you?*
> *Are you nobody, too?*
> *Then there's a pair of us . . .*

In Mr. Kessler's class, Tink impressed us by describing the Darwinian theory of *natural selection*—"It's, like, a hundred million seeds are tossed up into the air, and a few of them are blown to somewhere safe, and take root, and grow—and the same thing happens with their seeds—the stronger seeds survive, and the weaker seeds become extinct—they pass on their characteristics to the next generation through their genes—it's kind of cruel, and stupid, but there's a logic to it, I guess."

Tink jammed her fists into her eyes as if she was about to cry—(this made us uncomfortable)—but let her fists fall, and laughed; and from what Mr. Kessler said, you could see that Tink was almost correct—he'd had to expand her remarks, but essentially, Tink had described the complicated process of *natural selection* accurately.

What was weird, and what definitely made us feel uncomfortable, was that, for Tink, the scientific theory was somehow *personal*.

"Tink—what's your interpretation of congruence?"

After a few weeks Mr. Doerr had come to pronounce the name "Tink" with a particular relish, like one who prods a sore tooth for the pleasure of making it ache, but he'd come around also to liking Tink, it seemed, at least some of the time.

About congruence Tink spoke earnestly: "It's like—like figures that are equal to each other—like, two triangles are congruent if their sides are equal in length and their angles are equal—like people are congruent, like twins, if the same kind of thing has happened to them—it makes them different from other people but *like* each other—*congruent*."

Mr. Doerr crinkled his forehead as if he'd never heard such an original definition of congruence—but he nodded yes, this was more or less the idea, he would have to amplify by going to the blackboard and drawing figures.

It was surprising how often Tink came up with the right answer to Mr. Doerr's math homework problems, though usually she had no clear idea why the answer was correct, nor had she the patience to elucidate the steps leading to the solution.

Tink's grades in math, as in most of her classes, were erratic. One day F, another day B-plus, and another day D—you had the impression that Tink was like one of the hundred million seeds she'd described, tossed up into the air and swirling crazily around.

Tink argued that math was like music—"Either you have perfect pitch or you don't."

Mr. Doerr denied this: "No, no, *no*. Math is rational, and can be learned. Music you must have a gift for, but math you can *learn*."

"But what if you can't learn? If you know the answer but can't learn how to get it?"

"Of course you can learn. It's a step-by-step procedure. Some young people are just impatient. Answers by themselves are not enough—you must have proof."

This was Tink's dilemma: Even when she had the correct answers, so long as she lacked proof to the answers, she never got grades above B-plus, and often much lower.

And since she daydreamed in class and, though it was forbidden in the classroom, compulsively monitored her cell phone text messages, as well as cut classes for no legitimate reason, she was always on the List—not the Honors List but the Other List.

"They won't expel me here, at least not for a while," Tink said, "since Big Moms paid full tuition through next June. The past two schools I got kicked out of, she'd only just paid the term tuition—that was a mistake. They hate to *refund*."

Senior boys who'd joked about Tink's looks when she'd first arrived in our school, how unsexy she was, like somebody's kid brother, found themselves drawn to her, trading wisecracks with her, even asking her out—but Tink told them her mother wouldn't allow her to go out until she was eighteen years old.

"Is that true, Tink? *Eighteen?*"

We commiserated with her, but Tink just laughed.

"I'm not going out with any guy, maybe ever. I know from my mother's sad, sordid love life that getting mixed up with men is about the stupidest thing you can do."

Tink could say such things about herself, but of course you could not ask Tink about herself. She'd flare up like a cat whose tail has been stepped on—"Excuse me: Is this a conversation, or a bloody *interview?*"

Especially, you dared not ask Tink about (A) her (ex-) acting career or (B) her family.

(Poor Chloe, who'd blundered asking Tink about her father—"He's the owner of a football team? Or is it a baseball team?" and

Tink turned on her with a look of fury, asking, "Do you know something I don't know?" and Chloe stammered, "I—I don't know what you mean," and Tink said, "You're asking me about my 'father' like you know that I have a father—which, in fact, *I don't.*"

For it would turn out that Tink's mother had not been married when Tink was born and that her father's identity had never been revealed even to Tink; though Veronica Traumer had been involved with a wealthy man who'd been a co-owner of a major football team, this man was not Tink's father, and had not even been in Veronica's life at the time Tink was born.)

Though Tink took cell phone pictures frequently, you could never take a picture of her, still less a video; she had a phobia about seeing herself on YouTube.

"Don't ever take my picture without my permission," Tink growled. "And don't worry—you won't ever get my permission."

Tink's own pictures were sometimes of people but more often of natural things—misshapen trees, rock formations, massive clouds, derelict houses and buildings. Her pictures were stark and strange and dreamlike and beautiful, and you could never have guessed that the squirmy, smirky little red-haired girl was the creator of such images.

Her major project was a sequence of photos of the nighttime sky taken with a digital camera and superimposed on portraits of people, for a striking effect—"Eternity pushing through Time."

It was one of Tink's night-sky photographs Merissa and Hannah would use for the school yearbook cover, superimposed on miniature portraits of every member of the senior class. And it did have the eerie effect of Eternity pushing through Time.

A terrific cover, everyone said.

Just a little scary, but—terrific.

7.

TINK QUOTE OF THE WEEK

"I'd like to be your friend—but only if you promise not to ever, ever count on me."

8.

"GAMMA GOBLIN"

Tink surprised us, as well as our gym instructor, Ms. Svala, one day, performing on the parallel bars like—almost!—a trained gymnast.

With an air of sudden inspiration, having watched other girls perform, or try to perform, Tink bounded onto the mat between the bars and lifted herself with a look of frowning concentration into a handstand, which she managed to hold for several precarious seconds, her legs and small feet quivering with strain over her head.

For weeks Tink had been sulky and rebellious in gym class—she hated, she said, "physical" things—even more, "organized physical things." It wouldn't have been far-fetched for Tink and Ms. Svala to get along well—they were both high-energy, impatient people—but somehow it never happened, for Tink bridled against authority: "Nothing pisses me like being told what to do. Even when I want to do it."

And nothing annoyed Ms. Svala like girls who resisted her cheery good nature. Girls who, when she called out her high-voltage greeting, only just mumbled in response, or scowled instead of smiling.

"Bloody Gestapo," Tink said. "What if somebody doesn't *want* to be happy?"

So one day when she suddenly took a turn on the parallel bars, as if she'd wakened from a trance, we were taken by surprise, and we clapped as our unpredictable friend swung swift and double-jointed as a monkey; then dropped to the mat, executed several perfect somersaults, leapt up, pivoted on one foot, and somersaulted back—all with a look of intense concentration, biting her lower lip.

Then suddenly—Tink was sweaty, and tired. Wiping her flushed face with the backs of both her hands.

We all wore short white gym shorts and T-shirts, except for Tink, who alone was allowed to wear long sleeves. You could see—you could glimpse—that there were marks—(scars?)—on Tink's wrists.

We whispered together, "Do you think that Tink has cut herself?"

(There was a rumor that, at one of her former schools, which had been a boarding school, Tink Traumer had left suddenly after she tried to "harm herself" in some mysterious way. But now that we were Tink's close friends, we hated such rumors and never listened to them.)

Hannah said, "It could be that Tink has some kind of—I don't know—medical treatment? Like, my uncle goes to the hospital every month for a blood infusion—there's something wrong with his white blood cells and he has to have gamma goblin. . . ."

"Gamma *goblin*?"

We laughed at this. Hannah laughed. What was she trying to say?

Another girl was lifting herself on the parallel bars, on tremulous arms. Unlike Tink, this girl wasn't small-boned and sinewy but of average weight, with a little belly and soft, fleshy thighs—not a gymnast's body, and not very interesting to watch.

Tink was approaching us, lifting her long hair off the back of her neck. Though she pretended to dislike attention, she'd been pleased that we'd applauded her performance—but she didn't like it that we were talking about her in an undertone.

We didn't want to think of Tink having any kind of medical treatment, ever. We wanted to think of her as the girl we'd have liked to have been if we hadn't been born the girls we were.

"Good work, Tink! Next time, we'll take it slower."

Ms. Svala was impressed with Tink, too. But Ms. Svala understood that you couldn't push Tink, you'd always be disappointed if you expected something of her.

9.

A TINK TALE: "BAILING OUT"

There was no reason.

There were many reasons.

There came the razor blade between my fingers.

There came the current like electricity through my arm—through my fingers—directing the blade into the soft, yielding flesh of the inside forearm.

Why doesn't matter.

How requires precision.

Big Moms had hope for me, she said. As she had hope, still, for herself.

Hel-lo! I am Veronica Traumer and this is my little daughter, Katrina. Say hello, Katrina, c'mon, let's see that dazzling smile.

Oh, where is that dazzling smile?

(That goddamned dazzling smile—WHERE IS IT?)

It was a fact: There were secrets in Veronica Traumer's life—and in her daughter's life as well. Rumors of "health issues"—physical? mental?—of which Veronica spoke mysteriously and with an air of stoic melancholy.

Yet the child had a "career"—a high-paying career, in fact.

Though not always able to work, for mysterious reasons.

(Was she away somewhere? Was she living with the estranged/unidentified father?)

(No one knew. No one dared ask Veronica.)

(Though to the child she would speak bitterly. *You! I think you came between us. Not your fault—you didn't ask to be born—your so-called father is not the marrying kind, and he is not the daddy kind, and as for child support—the bastard is definitely NOT THAT KIND.*)

"Trina? *Trina!*"

The doorknob was frantically rattling. Big Moms's perfume penetrated the locked door. I wanted to shout at her, *Go away! Go away! You weren't supposed to come home until tomorrow.*

But I was too weak. And instead lay very still in the luke-warm bathwater as it stained red.

The bathroom door was never unlocked. The door was removed from its hinges—"unhinged"—by Mr. Leo and one of his young assistants. Big Moms was screaming—unless it was a siren screaming. Someone covered me—my skinny, sickly-pale naked body—as I was lifted onto a stretcher and borne away. And now there was a siren—I was inside the siren. Like a wild, high laughter it was, but I don't think that the sound was me. I was fourteen then. I didn't think that I would ever be older, but I am older now, and I promise I will not make that mistake again.

10.

SECRET

It wasn't like Tink had not warned us.

It wasn't like Tink had not prepared us.

We'd known that something was wrong—those last several months of her life, when she seemed always to be missing school, or hadn't much time for her friends, or was "away" somewhere mysterious.

"She's seeing a shrink in Manhattan."

"She's auditioning for a new TV series in L.A."

"She's visiting with her father—somewhere."

(No one knew the smallest particle of any fact about Tink's father—it was the one subject you would never, ever bring up with Tink. So this was pure conjecture.)

It seemed too ordinary to suggest that if Tink stayed out of school as others did, it was for the same reason—she was sick with a bad cold, or flu.

Or she hadn't finished a paper, or hadn't studied enough for an exam. Or, just maybe, she was feeling rebellious, or depressed— "Some days are just not *school days*," as Tink said.

• • •

After Tink d**d, it would be revealed that she'd missed sixteen school days out of approximately seventy in the 2010–2011 school term. The Quaker Heights Day School would release to the press only the fact—(assuming it was a fact)—that Katrina Traumer's absences had all been explained and had been considered *legitimate*.

When Tink missed school, she didn't return our text messages except to say

TINK IS AWAY & TINK WILL RETURN. LOVE YOU.

Mr. Trocchi said mysteriously, as if he had some special connection with Tink or maybe with her glamorous actress-mother, "Tink Traumer is no ordinary student, you know. Her destiny is elsewhere."

"Movies? Hollywood?"

"A play in New York?"

"A new TV series?"

(Though we knew that Tink had "retired" from acting, she'd told us and told us, yet somehow we wanted to believe that our friend might change her mind.)

(Though we want our friends to be just like us, and to not be superior to us, we take pride in having "famous" friends—we even like them a little better if they are "famous," and yet our friends.)

In an undertone, so Mr. Trocchi wouldn't hear, Anita Chang said severely, "Tink Traumer is *suicidal*. Her destiny might be *nowhere*."

• • •

We hated Anita for saying such a thing. We did not—we DID NOT—want to believe that Tink, who was our friend, was *suicidal*.

11.

"SURPRISE, TINK!"

We'd planned a surprise party for Tink.

Is this a good idea?—we weren't absolutely certain.

Tink had spoken admiringly of "wild, crazy surprise" parties on the "set"—(meaning the TV set, we gathered)—and not all of these were birthday parties. Could just be a *party-party*, to surprise somebody you liked who was maybe feeling a little blue.

We always did something for our birthdays, but we'd never yet had any party for Tink, who was new in our lives but who had come to feel like our oldest friend.

The pretense was: Chloe's mother was going to be away, and so Chloe had asked Tink to spend the night with her; the rest of us would be waiting when Tink came in, and we'd surprise her.

We'd made funny cards. Tink had referred to *non-birthday cards* so we made them.

Chloe's mom was divorced; Chloe had no sisters or brothers. So her mother was often involved in her life, and in the case of the surprise party for Tink, Chloe's mother helped plan every step of it and insisted upon preparing most of the food, though we came over to help. (Tink's favorite foods—vegetarian lasagna; ginger carrots and nutmeg spinach; arugula salad tossed with Italian dressing, raisins, and sunflower seeds.) Mrs. Zimmer even baked a cake—devil's food with egg-white frosting spelling out HAPPY NON-BIRTHDAY TINK!

And then, Tink didn't come.

She must have guessed that something was planned that revolved around her, and it wasn't going to be just a night with Chloe but with others. So, she didn't come.

We should have known. Tink hated *fuss*.

Chloe was upset. Mrs. Zimmer was hurt.

Chloe texted Tink and called her—no answer.

"She must have overheard us. Must have guessed something. Maybe she was afraid we were going to play old TV videos of her show. She's *weird*."

"Oh no, it's our fault. With Tink, you can't *presume*."

Nadia said, "I feel so bad. I feel like this was my idea."

Merissa said, "I think it was my idea. I feel terrible."

Hannah said, "Do you think she's angry at us? Some people just don't like surprise parties."

Martine said, "Tink wants to be the one in charge of surprises. Tink doesn't want to be *surprised*."

We gave up texting and calling Tink and decided to have dinner ourselves and to enjoy Tink's non-birthday party without her. Chloe's mother drifted away upstairs with the excuse of a migraine.

Chloe said, "This was all my idea. I can't imagine why I thought it would be a good one."

Merissa said, "The fact is—Tink warned us."

"Warned us how?"

"She's always said, 'I'd like to be your friend—but only if you promise never, ever to count on me.'"

Merissa was right. We just hadn't wanted to remember.

Then, as we were preparing to leave for our homes, at about nine p.m., Chloe's cell phone rang: It was Tink.

"Hey, guys—it's me. Bet you had a great time without me."

"But how did you know?" Chloe was baffled.

"It's a 'surprise' party, right? Don't ask me how I knew."

"Did someone tell you?"

"No! But I could guess, around you guys. I knew something was up and I figured . . ."

Chloe held the phone up for us to hear. We were all talking and laughing at once.

Tink said she was sorry she hadn't been able to come. She'd wanted to, she said. But she hadn't been able to.

We told her it was okay. We understood.

We passed the little phone around. We talked to Tink, and laughed with her, and Tink sounded like her usual self, that low, scratchy, funny voice, and something edgy and sad beneath.

"You could still come over," Chloe said hopefully. "It isn't so late. We have lots of cake. My mother made the most delicious devil's food cake. . . ."

"Oh God. Your mother . . ."

"Mom really wanted to, Tink. She had a great time. She loves to cook, and the dinner turned out really well—vegetarian lasagna. We can save some for you, in fact. Mom was hoping—"

At the other end, Tink began to cry.

"Tell your mother I'm sorry. I'm really s-sorry. I never even thought about your m-mother! It's just that I couldn't come. I wanted to, but I—I couldn't come. I love you guys, but—"

We listened in shocked silence. Tink appeared to be laughing, but it was obvious that she was still crying, too.

Tink asked if she could speak to Chloe's mother, and Chloe said sure, she'd take the phone upstairs to her mom; and when Chloe went upstairs we looked at one another, and we'd stopped laughing. And Hannah said, "I wish there was something we could do to make Tink like herself better."

This was a surprising remark. But we knew Hannah was right. We tried to think. What could we do? What could girlfriends *do*?

"Just be really nice to Tink. If she lets us down, if she's weird sometimes—just ignore it, and love her. *Just love her.*"

12.

THE CURSE

Senior year means doing everything for the final time.

Except Tink's final year with us was our junior year. When no one was prepared for an ending.

We would wonder—did Tink know? *When* did Tink know?

Later it would seem to us that she'd been saying good-bye almost since we'd known her. Out of nowhere she'd come into our lives and, just as mysteriously, now she was leaving.

Our art instructor at school mounted an exhibit of Tink's Night Sky photographs in the school gallery, which was up for the month of March; our local Quaker Heights newspaper published a full-page feature on Tink's work, which included a terse interview with the young student artist.

> **Interviewer:** *What are you trying to say in these photographs?*
> **Katrina Traumer:** *I'm not trying to say anything. Photographs don't say.*
> **Interviewer:** *Let me rephrase my question, then. The "Night*

Sky" sequence seems to suggest that human beings are related somehow to the constellations—to the universe—maybe to God?—but are unaware of that fact. Is this a fair interpretation?

K.T.: *A photograph is like a poem—there should be different interpretations.*

Interviewer: *What is your greatest hope as a photographer?*

K.T.: *To take some good pictures.*

Interviewer: *What is your great challenge as a photographer?*

K.T.: *To take some good pictures.*

Interviewer: *Do you intend to continue studying photography after graduation?*

K.T.: *After graduation? That's too far away to plan.*

Interviewer: *You'd had a quite successful career as a child actor on the TV series* <u>Gramercy Park</u>. *Do you ever anticipate returning to acting?*

K.T.: *No.*

Interviewer: *What was it like to have a career at a time in life when most children are just—children?*

K.T.: *I thought this interview was about my photographs.*

Interviewer: *Yes, of course. But our readers would also be interested in your experiences as Penelope in* <u>Gramercy Park</u>.

K.T.: *But I'm not. I haven't been interested in Penelope since I was nine years old.*

(The interview might have been longer, but the newspaper feature ended abruptly at this point.)

It must have been a sign we hadn't known how to interpret: In April of that year, Tink cut off most of her hair!

Tink's ripply, frizzy, burnt-red hair, which was snarled at the nape of her neck and wasn't always what you'd call super clean—suddenly, one day, was gone.

"Oh, Tink! My God! What have you *done*?"

We'd been invited to Tink's house. An invitation to Tink's house was rare.

(Tink came to our houses often. She'd come to study with us, and stay for dinner—though we'd have to coax her, and our mothers would have to coax her, before she gave in. For often it seemed that Tink's mother was "away," and maybe there was just a housekeeper at Tink's house, or maybe there was no one at all. Tink would not have told us.)

We all came together in Merissa's mom's station wagon to the house at 88 Blue Spruce Way, in which Tink and Veronica Traumer had lived for less than two years. It was a sprawling, showy, "custom-designed contemporary" on a hilly lot above an artificial lake bordered by blue spruce trees as if in a scenic calendar in which no one actually lived.

At the house, Tink opened the door for us. Instead of her signature black leggings, she was wearing jeans and a red GUERRILLA GIRL T-shirt. She was barefoot, and most of her hair was gone.

"Hey, guys! Love ya." Tink had to laugh at the looks on our faces.

We were stunned, staring at Tink's head, which looked so small, and vulnerable, like a small child's head.

Tink had not only cut off her hair with scissors—"without exactly looking to see what I was doing," as Tink explained—but when her mother saw the disaster, she'd taken Tink to a hairstylist in Quaker Heights to "minimize" the damage.

You could say that Tink's hair was both a disaster and, in a weird-punk way, chic. It was shaved at the nape of her neck, a half-inch long except at the crown of her head, where it was an inch long, and fuller. Our girlfriend looked like a punk rocker or maybe a street urchin in a comic strip—hair sticking up in short tufts.

We hugged Tink. We tried to laugh with her. We didn't want to accuse her but—what a surprise this was! It felt like some sort of rebuke.

"Come in! Quick! Big Moms will be downstairs soon enough, and all over my 'girlfriends.'"

Tink led us inside her house. The large white-walled rooms were sparsely furnished, and the tall windows had no curtains or blinds; on the floors were scatter rugs, each colorful, beautiful, probably very expensive, but inadequate to fill the large floor space. After nearly two years, it seemed that Veronica Traumer hadn't quite moved into her new house.

Why had Tink cut her hair, and why without warning?

"Maybe I had brain surgery over the weekend. Or ECT."

"ECT—what's that?"

"Electroconvulsive therapy. Electric shock."

We laughed because Tink laughed, but we didn't know what to think. The loose-fitting T-shirt disguised Tink's thinness, but you could see her bony hips and pelvis in the tight-fitting jeans, and she appeared to be shivering—in fact, the house was over-heated.

"ECT has a bad rep, but it actually *works*. Shocks you out of your narcissistic stupor. Sure, your IQ drops an octave, but— what the hell. You become tractable and, like, *lovable*."

Seeing how perplexed we were, and the horrified look on Nadia's face, Tink said airily, "No. I just got sick of my old hair, and cut it off. Who else is gonna do it, if not me? Also to piss off Big Moms, she's got this obsession with being *feminine*." Tink laughed. "*Femininity* is a weapon, Big Moms says. You bet, it can be lethal in the right hands."

Tink brought us into the kitchen to get Cokes and smoothies from a large Sub-Zero refrigerator. A dark-skinned woman, whom Tink introduced as Valeria, was preparing dinner—the spicy smells were overwhelming.

Tink had invited us each singly—confidentially. *Don't tell anyone else, please, this is a small private party at my house for just special people.*

We'd conferred with one another, of course. It wasn't difficult to determine whom Tink had probably invited.

"See, Big Moms is taking us on a trip next week. We're flying to 'L.A.,' as it's called. And I wanted to make just the perfect impression—just as *feminine* as possible."

We were in an adjacent family room with a large fireplace, a fifty-inch flat-screen TV, floor-to-ceiling plate-glass sliding doors. Even this room, which was more comfortable than the rest of the rooms we'd seen, with Mexican tiles on the floor, bright-colored sofas and chairs and pillows, looked as impersonal as a designer room; you could see that Tink had no favorite place to sit, but wandered around as you would in a hotel lobby, before dropping onto the floor beside a sofa.

Valeria came into the room to bring us appetizers. She laughed when Tink said she was the best cook ever and Big Moms was conspiring to kidnap her, to take her with them.

"Are you really going away, Tink? Where?"

"No. I mean—yes. Maybe."

Tink laughed. She was sprawled on the floor with her thin legs outspread. Her bare feet were like an urchin's. Without her frizzy burnt-red hair to hide behind, Tink looked awkward and exposed. Her face was pale; even her freckles appeared to have faded.

"I mean—there's a preliminary trip. And depending on the outcome of this preliminary trip, there may be a permanent trip—a 'removal.' Depends."

"But—when would this be? We have, like, six weeks before school ends. . . ."

"Who knows? *I'm* not in charge."

We wondered if Veronica Traumer was moving to Los Angeles to make a film. Or work in TV on the West Coast. *Gramercy Park* had finally ceased its long run after a dozen years, and its cast, which had grown older with the seasons, would all be looking for new work.

Tink was a tease: No matter what she told us, seemed to confide in us, if we asked her a direct question she'd deflect it with a joke, or make a sarcastic reply.

We were reminded of Mr. Trocchi's remark. *Tink is no ordinary student. Her destiny is elsewhere.*

How badly we wanted to believe this.

At last, after about a half hour, as Valeria was about to serve dinner—(we were all going to help her bring dishes to the table)—Tink's mother came downstairs, hurrying to meet us.

"Ohhh—girls! How lovely."

We had glimpsed Tink's mother before, and we'd seen photos of the actress Veronica Traumer online, but we'd never seen the woman close up until now.

She was so—*bosomy*. And her face seemed large, like a moon. And her skin seemed to give off a light, as if an actual spotlight shone on her.

If you looked closer, you could see that Veronica was expertly and heavily made up. Her face had none of the delicate bone structure of Tink's face, but you could see an uncanny resemblance around the eyes and the bridge of the nose; otherwise, Veronica's face was fleshy, as if there were no bones beneath. We guessed she'd had "work" on her face—injections, or implants—for her cheeks were full and the skin around her mouth just slightly puffy; her face was amazingly unlined for a woman of her age, which we knew to be over forty.

Veronica's eyes were a dull mud-green, not vivid and striking like Tink's, but glamorously made up with eye shadow and eyeliner. And she wore gold lamé capri pants and a taupe jersey top that showed the impress of her large breasts, and shoes with clattery heels. All this for a weekday evening at home with no guests more important than her daughter's high school classmates.

Her perfume wafted to us and enveloped us like a mildly toxic cloud.

Quickly Veronica's eyes darted about us, from face to face: Did she know us? (She should have known Merissa Carmichael, at least, and maybe Hannah Heller, but she didn't seem to recognize them.) Should we introduce ourselves? Tink had turned sulky and silent and wasn't at all helpful, sprawled on the floor beside the sofa.

"Trina? Where are the rest of your guests?" Veronica smiled uncertainly.

"These are them, Moms."

"But—I thought you were inviting all your new friends from school." Veronica looked perplexed, disappointed. You could see that life with her adolescent daughter was fraught with surprises difficult to interpret. "All your friends from Quaker Heights Day School." Veronica enunciated the formal name of our school as if eager to demonstrate that she knew it.

"I said I was inviting the people I like."

"No boys?"

"You didn't want boys, did you?"

"Well—I'd thought . . ."

"If there are boys, there is sex. You don't want 'sex'—so why d'you want 'boys'? Make sense, Moms."

Tink spoke so impatiently to her mother, we were embarrassed.

Veronica was smiling, or trying to smile. Her hair had been bleached a striking platinum blond, like Merissa's, but it was as synthetic-looking as a mannequin's hair. Her fleshy lips were outlined in deep purple.

"It's just that I'd thought—somehow—you are sixteen years old, after all, aren't you?—and you've mentioned boys, I think. . . ."

"A party with boys would be Friday or Saturday night, not Wednesday. Or maybe you don't know which day of the week this is, since you aren't working right now."

Tink was behaving so rudely, we exchanged glances with one another. Not one of us would have spoken like this to our mothers in the presence of guests; yet Veronica only winced, and smiled in a way to suggest that this was a strategy of hers—smile, *smile*. For after all, Veronica Traumer was a quasi-public figure, accustomed to TV lights and interviews. Accustomed to *performance*.

We saw that she was holding a glass of wine in her fingers, which were glittering with rings. And her fingernails were long and oval and brightly polished.

Since Tink made no move to introduce us, we introduced ourselves to Veronica Traumer: "Chloe"—"Shelby"—"Merissa"—"Nadia"—"Martine"—"Hannah"—"Anita."

We could see that Veronica's gaze moved lightly from each of us to the next and that, though listening, she wasn't going to remember a single name.

In an almost flirtatious voice she said, "How Trina merits such nice girlfriends, I can't imagine. You all look absolutely—nice—and beautiful—and *well-mannered*. Trina must be much nicer to you than she is to her mother."

"Moms, that is so maudlin! Please."

Veronica was sipping wine. She regarded us with a sly smile. "*She's* the prissy one, you know. *She* doesn't approve of her mother's lifestyle." Veronica laughed, a surprisingly high-pitched, girlish giggle.

It was time for Valeria to serve dinner. Hesitantly the Latina housekeeper was standing in the doorway to the kitchen, looking to Veronica, who seemed oblivious of her. Tink was also oblivious of Valeria.

Merissa said, "Excuse me, Tink, but—maybe—Valeria would like to serve dinner? We can help her."

Yet Tink didn't seem to hear. And Veronica didn't seem to hear.

Though daughter and mother were purposely not looking at each other, it was awkwardly clear that they were intensely aware of each other. As Veronica sipped from her wineglass, she stroked her bare, softly fleshy forearm in a way that must have infuriated Tink, who squirmed, trying not to look up at her mother but failing, at last.

"Big Moms has a very banal lifestyle," Tink said, "which she wants to think is chic."

She tried to speak lightly, like a brash young child in a TV sitcom, but her green eyes flashed with hurt.

Veronica laughed. At first it seemed that Tink's joke wasn't an insult to her, but then, with no warning, she lunged toward Tink as Tink sprawled on the floor, and slapped her.

We could not believe it: Veronica slapped Tink's face, so hard that Veronica's numerous bracelets rattled and chimed.

"You vicious little bitch! Why do I put up with you? If you want to die, why don't you? No one will miss you! No wonder your father has *vanished from the face of the earth*."

In her clattering heels, Veronica stalked out of the room. It was a TV moment—wasn't it? We wanted to think that it wasn't exactly real, though Tink's cheek was flaming from the slap and she'd recoiled like a wounded little creature, hiding her face and drawing her knees up to her chest.

Then Tink laughed, and the painful moment was past.

"Big Moms is *melodramatic*. She never learned *nuance*."

13.

TINK SAYS GOOD-BYE

HEY GUYS, GUESS I WON'T BE SEEING YOU FOR A WHILE.
LOVE YOU GUYS BUT FEELING KINDA BURNT OUT. NBD.
TINK

14.

OBITUARY:
KATRINA OLIVIA TRAUMER

Katrina Olivia Traumer, 17, a resident of Quaker Heights, died in her family home at 88 Blue Spruce Way in the early hours of June 11, 2011.

Ms. Traumer, a junior at Quaker Heights Day School, transferred from the Brearley School in Manhattan in the fall of 2010. She had had an early success as an actress, and from the age of six to the age of eleven she'd played the child Penelope in the popular TV series Gramercy Park, in which her mother, Veronica Traumer, also appeared in a leading role. Ms. Traumer's TV credits also include episodes of Medium, Two and a Half Men, Masterpiece Theatre, and Law & Order: Special Victims Unit.

According to the county medical examiner, the cause of death has not yet been determined.

Ms. Traumer is survived by her mother and her grandparents, Margaret and Reardon Traumer of New Britain, Connecticut.

In lieu of flowers, donations may be made to the Humane Society of the United States.

QUAKER HEIGHTS JOURNAL,
June 14, 2011

We were crushed. We were devastated. Tink's obituary was so *ordinary*.

These words, written by someone who'd never known Tink, had nothing to do with the girl we'd known.

And the photograph that ran with the obituary hardly resembled the quirky, beautiful Tink we knew!

We cried together. We hugged one another, and we cried.

We were sick with grief. And we were angry.

Why? Why did you do it, Tink?

She'd sent us each a final text message. That was all.

Classes had ended for the year. Exams had ended. Class Day was past, and graduation was scheduled for the following Monday.

Tink had skipped Class Day, but we hadn't guessed that that meant much—she hated speeches and "formalities" in the school auditorium, where "the air was like ether," she said. Though she'd known that she was probably going to be named as one of the Outstanding Artists of the year, for her Night Sky exhibit, still Tink had snubbed the ceremony, and when her name was called by Headmaster Nichols from the stage, there was an embarrassing silence until Merissa Carmichael rose from her seat and said apologetically, "Tink isn't feeling well and couldn't come to school today. May I accept for her?"

Merissa had carried the crystal plaque with KATRINA TRAUMER engraved on it home with her, thinking to give it to Tink the next time she saw her.

But she never saw Tink again.

There was no funeral, only a private ceremony to which no one we knew was invited. We didn't even know where Tink was buried—or if she was buried.

For all we knew, Veronica had had her cremated.

We wanted to have a memorial service for Tink, but Veronica Traumer never answered our calls or letters. The house at 88 Blue Spruce Way looked vacant, with no vehicle in the driveway. We went—daringly—to ring the doorbell, but no one answered. We wished we'd known Valeria's last name; we might have contacted *her*.

We had a Memory Wall for Tink online. Here we posted photos of Tink and photos by Tink. We posted poems by Emily Dickinson, Walt Whitman, and Robert Frost. Though we knew that Tink would give us hell, we posted photographs of her as little Penelope on *Gramercy Park*, since this had been a part of our friend's life, a life that had intersected with the public for five years, long ago in Tink's life but not so long ago in history.

"There is something more to why Tink did what she did. Something more that hasn't been told."

We thought this might be so, but we had no proof. We wanted to believe that there was more to Tink's d***h than we knew, and that there was more to Tink's life than we'd known.

Whatever we do for Tink, on our Memory Wall, never seems like enough.

But then, Tink hasn't actually vanished. She is *gone* and yet—

It's like striking a match and the flame goes out and still you smell the hot, acrid powder smell and you know there's a fire somewhere even if you can't see it.

III

THE SLUT

1.

"GO FOR IT!"

Oh God. Now he will know.
Now, no turning back.

She backed away. Staggered away.

She was terrified—thrilled—*excited*.

For now he would know that she loved him. He would know, and he would understand, and he would—maybe—call her, and want to see her.

No turning back.

She wondered what Tink would think about what she'd done. For Tink had often nudged Nadia in the ribs—"Go for it, girl!"

And soft-eyed Nadia would say, "Go for—what?"

"What there is to be *gone for*."

That was Tink. She'd tell you to do what you *wanted to do*—the hell with the consequences.

2.

THE BIRTHDAY GIFT

He was opening the present. Unwrapping it, and lifting it from the bubble wrap, carefully . . .

Why, Nadia! This is—so beautiful. . . .

Nadia, I can't accept this. . . .

Nadia, I—want you to know—you are so beautiful, so—special—to me. . . .

Then Mr. Kessler would grip Nadia's head in his hands—his fingers spread in her hair—he would kiss her forehead, gently—her nose—her silly snub nose—her lips . . .

Love you, Nadia! My beautiful girl . . .

"I l-love you too, Mr. Kessler."

Or should she say, softly, "I have always loved you, Mr. Kessler—since I first saw you. . . ."?

It wasn't clear to Nadia where she and Mr. Kessler were. In his car, maybe.

Yes, that was likely. Mr. Kessler was giving her a ride—(home? In this bad weather? This was plausible)—and the mood between them was tender, suspenseful.

Nadia had seen Adrian Kessler driving a Subaru station wagon with colorful bumper stickers: GO GREEN! (front) and I BRAKE FOR BUTTERFLIES (rear). It was not so unlikely that he might give her a ride home in this vehicle.

And if so, it was not unlikely that they might stop—park—somewhere. For Mr. Kessler would want to speak seriously with Nadia, after their conversation in his office the other day, and what had passed between them; and, once Nadia had given him the present, he would know her feelings for him, which were very intense, and very deep.

Except: Nadia wasn't sure that she wanted Mr. Kessler to know who'd given him the present. Just yet.

Yet he was smiling at her, and for the first time *really looking at Nadia Stillinger.* Not as a female student, but as an individual—a young woman.

As gently he closed his fingers in her hair, leaned in to her—closer . . .

Nadia swallowed hard. Her eyelids fluttered. She felt her heart kick like a frightened bird inside her rib cage.

There came a whistle: "Hey—Nad-ja."

Nadia turned, in dread. Seeing that it was—oh God: friends of Colin Brunner.

Football teammates of Colin's. Those loud, mean boys with jeering faces like hawks' beaks—one of them was Rick: what was his name, Rick Metz?

Nadia felt sick. The terrible thing was, Nadia knew him from a party the previous weekend.

It was too late to turn away. To pretend she hadn't heard.

Yet clumsily Nadia turned away. Her face was pounding with

blood; she was sure she must be flushing beet red.

"Nad-ja? Want a ride?"

The boys laughed. Sniggered. There'd been sessions at Quaker Heights Day School since last fall focusing on *harassment, cyberbullying,* how you should report such incidents to the headmaster immediately, but few girls would want to do so—*If you tattle, that will make things worse for you*—so Nadia would try to ignore them, Nadia wished she could stick her fingers in her ears like a small child and ignore them, and now she was walking away from them—trying to walk calmly, her head held up, without haste, without betraying the anxiety she felt—but one of the boys crowded her from behind, pushed against her, giggling: "Hey, babe. Watch it." Another boy jostled him; like ridiculous small children they were hooting with laughter, wrestling one another, nudging Nadia off the walk and into a mound of gritty snow that looked as if dogs had urinated into it.

"L-leave me alone. . . ."

Noisy and laughing, the boys strode on. It wasn't clear if they'd even heard Nadia's pleading voice.

Why had they had to bump against her? Why push her? That was pure meanness.

And they would report back to Colin, for sure.

And on their Facebook pages, for sure.

(Nadia didn't know, because she had not looked.)

(Nadia had heard—something . . . Nasty-cruel, mean and vicious, what they'd posted about *NADIA STILLINGER,* but the fact was, she had not looked.)

"Bastards! I hate you."

Or, no: "Pricks! I hate you."

Prick was a better word. Tink had said guys think with their *pricks*.

Cocks, dicks.

These were all good words that Tink had used.

If you remember that a guy thinks with his prick, essentially you can be protected from him. But if you forget . . .

Nadia had made a mistake, she had forgotten. Or—somehow—after unwisely drinking beer with Colin—(and maybe Colin had put a pill in Nadia's glass when she wasn't looking)—Nadia had just stopped being aware of what Tink would have called her *well-being*.

It was so unfair! It had turned out wrong, and yet—it might have turned out differently.

Just now, when Rick Metz and his friends had jeered at her and pushed her off the path—they might have just smiled at her, and said, *Hi, Nadia!* as they'd say to another girl. They might have treated her politely, or at any rate not meanly. *It was just unfair.*

Because of Colin, and the mistake Nadia guessed she'd made—(she couldn't remember clearly, and no one was going to tell her)—first in Colin's car and then in his basement, it would never be made right. The guys would not even look at her without seeing *Nad-ja! Nad-ja!* She was wearing a new quilted dark-rose jacket from the Gap with a fleecy hood—if the guys had gotten a clear look at her, a fair look, they would have been impressed.

For Nadia Stillinger was pretty—really, quite pretty. Not beautiful, for her face was too full, and the expression on her face too yearning, but she was pretty; it wasn't an exaggeration, as people said, that she had beautiful dark-brown eyes. . . . And she certainly wasn't skinny or anorexic.

But the guys hadn't really looked at her. Colin hadn't really looked at her. *That* was the mistake.

She couldn't tell her girlfriends—Merissa, Hannah, Anita, Martine would be merciless with her. Chloe might be sympathetic—Chloe wasn't quick to judge. But Tink!

The good thing was, when the boys had hassled Nadia, she hadn't dropped Mr. Kessler's gift on the wet pavement out back behind school. In a nightmare scene out of middle school, they might have started kicking it like a soccer ball.

Not that it was breakable—it wasn't.

Wrapped in bubble wrap and hidden in a large, shiny-gilt tote bag from Neiman Marcus, embossed with the initials AJS—Nadia's stepmother's initials. And this tote bag was inside a large grocery bag with paper handles.

Nadia had borrowed her stepmother's glamorous bag for the occasion, reasoning that the gift for Mr. Kessler was so special, she could hardly bring it in a shopping bag to leave for him, nor did she want to jam it into her own ordinary tote bag, let alone into her backpack—where it wouldn't have fit anyway.

Reasoning too that Mr. Kessler would give the bag back to her and she could return it to her stepmother's closet before its absence was detected.

Then again, Amelie had so many nice things, leather handbags from Prada and Louis Vuitton, bags made of brocade with tortoiseshell handles imported from Morocco, it wasn't likely she'd miss the gilt bag immediately.

"Nadia! Hi! What are you doing here?"

Merissa! Nadia wasn't happy to see a friend just now.

Merissa was smiling at Nadia—but strangely, Nadia thought.

She knows. What they've posted about me.

She knows, and feels sorry for me.

"Are you waiting for—is it Mariana? Your housekeeper?—to pick you up?"

Nadia murmured no—well, yes . . .

"If you need a ride, Alex is driving—we're going to a JV meeting downtown—he could swing around and take you home first . . ."

Quickly it had happened in the New Year: Merissa Carmichael and Alex Wren had become a couple, of a sort—at least, they were very good friends and were often seen together; several times, Merissa and Alex had sat together at lunchtime, as Merissa's friends cast curious glances in their direction. Alex was tall and lean and soft-spoken and easier to talk to than boys in their class like Shaun Ryan; it was clear that he liked Merissa, very much. Merissa's friends saw that she was happy in Alex's company, relaxed as she'd never been with Shaun; she smiled and laughed more, and did not seem so stiff and *perfectly poised*.

In fact, Merissa looked healthier lately. She wasn't so very thin—her face was a little fuller.

Nadia felt a little stab of envy. Merissa had a boyfriend, of course—Merissa was likely to have boyfriends, being so beautiful, and slender; Nadia had never felt comfortable with Merissa, who seemed always to be coolly judging her and had never seemed to like her as much as she liked their other friends.

Now Merissa was comfortable enough with Alex to offer

Nadia a ride home in his car. And where were they going together after school? JV—Junior Volunteers?

"Thanks, Merissa—that's really thoughtful. But I don't need a ride."

"You sure? Alex won't mind. Your house isn't far out of our way, maybe ten minutes. . . ."

"No, *thanks*. I'm fine, M'rissa."

Please go away. Please don't interrogate me. Can't you see—I want to be alone.

Nadia was trying to be her usual smiling, slightly breathless self. She was the most *girlish* of the girls of Tink, Inc., the most young-seeming; which endeared her to her friends at times, but at other times exasperated them.

Nadia and Merissa had had at least one good moment together, Nadia remembered, though she doubted that Merissa would remember: when Merissa had fallen down the school stairs and cut her forehead the previous year, and Nadia had spent a little time with her later that day, and Merissa had been in strangely elevated spirits—"Maybe I'll even have a little scar, to remind me to pay attention when I'm running downstairs."

Nadia had thought this was a strange remark. Yet she'd understood it perfectly.

Wanting to say now, *Hey, it looks like you don't have a scar after all.*

But Nadia didn't want to continue this awkward exchange with her friend who was on her way to meet her very nice boyfriend in the student parking lot. She was uneasy with the way Merissa was eyeing the grocery bag, trying to see what was inside it.

"Something for my stepmother," Nadia said, with a roll of her eyes, to indicate a painful subject. "Don't even ask."

Merissa frowned, and didn't ask. The subject of Nadia's *très impossible* stepmother was well known to the girls of Tink, Inc.

Though Amelie wasn't nearly so entertaining, or so monstrous, as Tink's Big Moms.

"You do have a ride home, Nadia? Right?"

"Yes!" Nadia insisted.

"Okay, sweetie—see you tomorrow."

Sweetie. Nadia was moved.

When she'd talked with Mr. Kessler the other day, in the privacy of his office, and told him certain intimate things, she hadn't told him about her friends—the girls of Tink, Inc. Somehow, it was difficult to speak of friendship.

Nadia waited until Merissa was safely out of sight, then continued into the faculty parking lot. Snowflakes had begun to fall, swirling out of a sky of corrugated wintry clouds.

Nadia, what were you thinking!

Were you thinking—at all?

There it was: Mr. Kessler's green Subaru with the bumper sticker that made Nadia smile—I BRAKE FOR BUTTERFLIES.

Now she had to hope that the vehicle wasn't locked.

(Her father was so vigilant about locking his expensive car, a Porsche, he automatically locked the car when it was in the (locked) garage!)

Hoping too that no one was watching her and would wonder what Nadia Stillinger, a senior, was doing alone in the faculty parking lot, *acting suspicious.*

Luckily, it was one of those dark winter days, hardly any sun and snow flurries melting on the pavement, and by four p.m. almost dusk.

Nadia approached Adrian Kessler's vehicle. Saw her gloved hand reach out to touch the handle of the right rear door—it was *unlocked.*

"Oh God. Maybe—better not."

Her heart pumped like a fist. She felt Tink close beside her but could not determine what Tink would advise.

"But maybe—yes? Except . . ."

Here was the problem: Nadia hadn't been sure what was the best way to give the secret gift to Mr. Kessler. For she wanted it to be—well, *secret;* but she wanted Mr. Kessler to know, too.

Nadia had made the accompanying card herself. It was a sort of birthday-Valentine card—(Mr. Kessler had happened to mention in class that his birthday was this week, and it seemed to Nadia that he'd glanced in her direction, smiling)—in the shape of a heart, of red construction paper, with smaller hearts and flowers in silver felt-tip pen, and carefully printed words:

> Mr. Kessler—
> Happy Birthday!
> Dani A.

In Mr. Kessler's science class, in conjunction with the phenomenon of variations and permutations, they'd recently discussed anagrams: Mr. Kessler had entertained the class by jotting onto the blackboard ingenious examples like "the eyes"—"they see"; "butterfly"—"flutter by"; "desperation"—"a rope ends it." Nadia had doodled in her notebook NADIA DANI A.

But would Mr. Kessler see that "Dani A." was an anagram? Would he understand that the name was a secret code—secret between him and Nadia—for *Nadia Stillinger*?

She thought so, yes! For surely Mr. Kessler thought of Nadia as much, or nearly as much, as Nadia thought of him.

She was sure that he would recognize the wriggly shapes and rainbow swirls in the little painting she was giving him—meant to remind him of the PowerPoint slides he'd shown last week in class—many-times-magnified photographs of microscopic creatures called protozoa.

Mr. Kessler was a teacher of science, but his classes were always so *visual*. Nadia felt sad, a stab of loss, that Tink had not seemed to have faith enough in the future, or in her life in the future, to have lived into her senior year at Quaker Heights—if she'd taken Earth and Our Environment with Adrian Kessler, maybe that would have made a difference.

Nadia had hesitated about signing the card. She'd wanted to sign *Love, Dani A.*, but her hand shook so, she could not write *Love*.

Nadia made her decision: She opened the right rear door of her teacher's vehicle and quickly set the glittery faux-gold bag inside, on the backseat.

Then she turned blindly away.

Then she was running through a scrim of slow-falling snow. She was too anxious and too excited to return to the school building to call her father's housekeeper—the last thing she wanted was to encounter another friend, or one of her teachers. It seemed that every time they turned around, the girls of Tink, Inc. ran into Mrs. Jameson, who all but clutched at their arms, regarding them with searching, "sympathetic" eyes—*If ever you want to speak with me, in private, about your friend—about how you are dealing with the memory of—your friend . . . Please know that I am available at virtually any time.*

Nadia had had several conferences with Mrs. Jameson. She knew that others had, too.

Yet it never seemed to be enough.

The fear was, another girl would harm herself in the wake of Tink Traumer, who'd been such a charismatic and enigmatic personality.

As Tink would have observed, *Imagine the ugly publicity for QHD if there's a Tink copycat!*

Nadia made another decision: to walk home.

It was rare for QHD students to walk home, for part of the walk was along a busy state highway.

Mostly, QHD students were picked up by their parents, or by friends' parents. There were school buses, but it wasn't cool to ride them.

Coolest of all was to have a boyfriend like Alex Wren, who could drive you. Or maybe coolest of all was to have your own car and drive yourself.

It was about a mile and a half to the Stillinger house on Wheatsheaf Lane, in a residential neighborhood called High Brook Farms.

She had a fear of being shouted at, if she walked along the road. Colin Brunner and his crude friends. *Nad-ja! Naaad-ja! How's about a ride . . .*

That terrible, ugly word they'd posted: *S**t.*

S**t, like d***h. You did not want to acknowledge such words if you could avoid them.

And Mr. Kessler might be driving on Post Road also, and see his student trudging along the side of the road in swirling snowflakes. . . .

If Mr. Kessler pulled the green Subaru over to the side of the road, to invite Nadia to climb inside . . .

Nadia swallowed hard. She was having trouble believing that she'd actually left the gift for Mr. Kessler in the back of his car.

It was a very special gift, in fact. Probably expensive.

He would know what it meant. He would know how Nadia Stillinger loved him.

And how clear her life, now. It had never been Colin Brunner she'd "loved"—all that had been a mistake. All along, it had been Adrian Kessler whom she loved, and would die for.

Oh God. Now—he will know.

Now, no turning back.

3.

THE GATHERING STORM

Nadia walked quickly. Soon she was out of breath.

Unlike the other girls of Tink, Inc., Nadia wasn't an athlete. She wasn't very *physical*, if she could avoid it.

Something was going to happen, she thought—she *knew*—like a gathering storm you could see in the sky above the Atlantic Ocean, off Nantucket Island: massive, bruise-colored clouds threaded with rays of red sunshine like veins of blood.

Beautiful! But scary, too.

Most of August they spent in the beautiful old dark-shingled house overlooking the ocean, on Nantucket. This was Nadia's mother's house, or had been. Nadia felt *so bad*—she could not truly remember her mother in the house. She'd been too young for true memories, and even photographs of her mother were scarce—Nadia's father had hidden them all away, maybe.

Or worse.

So—what was happening was like a gathering storm. Though you could see it in the sky, you *could not prevent it.*

But you could run from it! You could run for shelter.

"Tink, I wish you were here. I need your advice."

Nadia told herself Mr. Kessler would understand. Tink was gone, but Mr. Kessler was here and he would provide *shelter*.

In his office, Adrian Kessler had told Nadia certain things. He had shared with Nadia Stillinger certain things. He had not told anyone else—any other of his students, Nadia was sure.

He'd touched her wrist, lightly. The skin still tingled!

Through Nadia's body—the tips of her breasts, between her legs where she was uncomfortable sometimes, and could find no comfortable way of sitting; in the region of her heart, which was so suffused with sadness, sometimes—but more often with warmth, hope, *excitement*.

He had touched her all these places.

Not *literally*—but emotionally.

Of course, Nadia had told Mr. Kessler—things. She'd shared with him certain facts about her life that none of her friends knew, and even Tink had not known.

Knowing that Mr. Kessler would *understand*.

Nadia, of course—you must have guessed—I love you.

But I will have to wait for you to grow up.

You're just a girl—sixteen—but in another four years, you will be twenty. And I will be . . .

Nadia had discovered that Mr. Kessler was twenty-seven just this week. And so in four years, he would be just thirty-one.

This was—*old*. But not *really old*, of course.

If he waited for her. If he promised.

Nadia's father was fifty-one. Now, that was *old!*

Nadia's father's new wife, Amelie, was twenty-nine. Nadia's aunt Harriet, who was her father's older sister, teased Mr.

Stillinger when the new young wife was out of the room—*Is there some equation between you getting older and them getting younger? Where will it end?*—but Mr. Stillinger hadn't seen any joke in this.

Nor did Nadia, overhearing, think it was the least bit funny.

The night before, Nadia had exhausted herself trying to figure out how to give the gift to Mr. Kessler. Lying awake in her bed, squirmy and itchy and feeling a sensation like red ants crawling over her body—her *flabby waist and hips* she hated—and between her legs, the scratchy hairs she hated—thinking of how Amelie saw an *aesthetician* who did *Persian waxing*, a cosmetic procedure Nadia didn't altogether understand, but knew that it was de rigueur if you wanted to wear a very minimal bikini.

When Nadia first heard about this, she'd texted her friend Chloe Zimmer: A.S. IS SO GROSS DON'T EVEN ASK.

Between Nadia and Chloe text messages flew back and forth about their S-Ms—(private code for *stepmother*)—since each of the girls had a stepmother.

Though Chloe, at least, didn't have to live with *hers*. Just had to see *the b***h*—(Chloe's abbreviation, funnily expressed as a sort of sneeze)—every third weekend when she went to stay with her father and his "new family" in Westchester County, New York; for Chloe's parents had *joint custody* of her, which made Chloe feel like a dog shuttled back and forth between households.

"What about your mother, Nadia?" Chloe had asked; and Nadia had said with a bright little smile that she hadn't exactly lived with her mother—or even seen much of her mother—since she'd been five years old.

Chloe seemed embarrassed for having asked the question. "Wow! That must be hard."

Nadia shrugged, saying, "I guess it was. When I was little."

Nadia had a secret about her mother she didn't intend ever to reveal, not even to Chloe. Nor had she told Tink.

Nadia had learned from a previous school in Connecticut, where she'd believed she had good friends, that you must never tell anything really crucial about yourself, not even to a close friend.

Nor did friends appreciate *whiners*. Nadia Stillinger was not ever a *whiner*!

And Tink herself had said, *Some secrets are toxic. Not to be shared.*

Nadia worried, possibly she'd already told Chloe too much. And Hannah, and Martine—texting them about Mr. Kessler. Mostly Nadia's text messages were playful and joking about "Mr. K.," but once she'd texted them about the "special looks" that her science teacher gave her over the heads of other students; and the "special help" he'd given her with her lab notebook, so she'd managed to get an A-minus.

Nadia hadn't (yet) told them about the intense conversation in Mr. Kessler's office. How Mr. Kessler had looked at her with such sympathy, and how he'd touched her wrist.

Lightly reproving, he'd said, *You're a very intelligent girl, Nadia. You must have faith in yourself.*

Nor had she told them how she felt about Mr. Kessler—*Love him so. Love him more than anyone in the world. I would die for him. I am serious!*

If Mr. Kessler had a diseased kidney, for instance, Nadia

would *donate a kidney* to him—anonymously.

Or, *Dani A.* would be the donor.

But she hadn't told Chloe. She would not tell anyone.

Just Adrian Kessler—when he called her, after opening the present; when he realized that *Dani A.* was *Nadia Stillinger*.

If only she hadn't made that terrible mistake with Colin Brunner!

(Colin hadn't even been nice to her, really. Just smiling at her so her heart melted—it was that silly! She was such an idiot!—and whatever they'd given her to drink, or slipped into her drink, made her thoughts weird and perforated so it was like carrying water in a sieve to *try to think* with the loud hammering music, and the guys' laughter, and Colin saying, *Nadja? Nad-j-ia? Don't pass out so fast, hey, Nadjjja!*)

If only she'd realized that the person she loved was Adrian Kessler and that he was a superior man—kindly, intelligent, idealistic.

The way Mr. Kessler spoke about global warming! The way he spoke about the future of the planet!

She was shivering, walking in the January wind. The Gap jacket was fleece-lined and she had the hood up, but still she was cold, for the jacket came only to her waist.

Shouldn't have bought straight-leg jeans. That was a mistake. The other girls could wear these, like Merissa, and Anita Chang.

Nothing more uncomfortable than tight jeans, waistband, crotch, knees. She'd been trying to diet—starving herself, practically—but it didn't seem to do any good. She'd eaten—how many?—four, or five—oh God, maybe six—of those little fruit-flavored Dannon yogurts instead of a real lunch that day.

Hannah said you could make yourself seriously sick, eating so crazy.

Nadia said, wanting to laugh, *No Big Deal!*

That was Tink, in Nadia's head. Sometimes she wanted Tink gone from her head, but then she'd be stricken with such a sense of loneliness, like when her mother *vanished*, she knew that she could not ever give up Tink.

And Tink had promised never to give *her* up.

Maybe not in actual words. Tink hadn't been sentimental. But there had passed an understanding between them, Nadia knew.

Feeling now a little sickish. Like—a storm at sea, rushing to land.

Just could not think. Since Tink had d**d. She'd tried to tell Mrs. Jameson how sometimes a buzz of mad hornets were thinking for her.

Maybe medication? Antianxiety, antidepressants?

Nadia was scared of meds. She seemed to remember that her mother had taken meds. Or meds had been prescribed for her mother. *How many is too many? How few is not enough?*

She'd been crushed when Mr. Kessler had scolded her.

In class! Everyone listening!

But then, she'd known what this meant. The special connection between them, that he cared for her, and wanted to help her.

Nadia's way of behaving in public—particularly in school—was annoying to some people, she knew. But she didn't know how else to behave!

If you're beautiful, skinny, smart—you can *be yourself.*

If not, you have to *make people like you.*

Since grade school in Connecticut—(in that confused interlude after Nadia's mother had gone away and there was a new "mom," Mr. Stillinger's *second wife,* of whom no one ever spoke now, especially not in Amelie's presence)—Nadia had cultivated a way of capturing attention as she'd had as a small child, more naturally: widening her eyes—parting her lips—expressing surprise, even awe—curiosity, wonderment; seeming so helpless; in fact, she *was helpless,* and most adults were immediately sympathetic.

Her father, for instance. It was very hard for Mr. Stillinger to discipline his daughter, who might burst into tears at the slightest criticism.

In school, often Nadia was restless, squirmy—too nervous to sit still. If attention didn't focus on her, where *was she?* Frequently she waved her hand to answer a teacher's question without exactly knowing what she meant to say. Sometimes she interrupted other students while they were speaking, blurting out answers before the teacher called her name—"Now, Nadia, *settle down.*"

But Nadia's teachers rarely scolded her. They didn't have the heart. In any group of students Nadia was the most childlike and *yearning to be loved,* and *so sweet*—and apologetic as soon as she realized she'd behaved rudely, clamping her hand over her mouth in embarrassment.

"Ohhh—I'm *sorry.*"

And—"Did I interrupt? I didn't *mean to.*"

The surprise was that Nadia often gave correct answers—*intelligent answers*—though you wouldn't expect so, judging from just looking at her.

Tink had liked her, but why? The girls of Tink, Inc., were *so cool*—why'd Tink care for silly, fat Nadia Stillinger?

She'd almost wanted to ask Tink that question—except Tink would've been embarrassed.

Because I don't see what you see, when you look in the mirror. I see some other Nadia, who's my friend. Got it?

It had been shocking to Nadia when at the start of the new term Mr. Kessler, who was usually so polite, funny, and mild-mannered, had spoken sharply to her in front of the class. Nadia hadn't even been aware that she had interrupted another girl who was answering a question—she'd been too excited, enthusiastic. Mr. Kessler had interrupted *her*—"Nadia, *please!* Wait and speak in turn."

Nadia had been crushed, obliterated. The rest of the class hour passed in a haze of shame and barely withheld tears. When the bell rang, the science teacher relented, seeing Nadia's crestfallen face. As she tried to slink past him, Mr. Kessler said, with a forgiving frown, "I realize that you're very enthusiastic about our class, Nadia, but others are, too. You don't seem aware of interrupting other people, and your behavior might be confused with rudeness."

Rudeness!

"Ohh! I'm sorry, Mr. Kessler."

"You seem to become overexcited. Can you count to five?—to ten?—before you fling up your hand?"

"Oh, yes. Yes—I will."

Nadia's heart was suffused with warmth, with *love*.

The way the handsome young science teacher had looked at

her—his hazel eyes, his reproachful-yet-teasing smile.

I will. I will!

I will earn your respect.

Part of Nadia's anxiety about being noticed, and being liked, had to do with the fact that her father had moved to Quaker Heights only three years before, in the middle of Nadia's freshman year in high school. She'd had friends—(she wanted to think)—at her old school, but here in Quaker Heights, New Jersey, she knew no one. Friendships among the most popular girls had already been established since grade school, if not day care; even their mothers knew one another, it was so *unfair*. Boys were different: Boys liked new girls if they were pretty and vivacious, funny and flirty and not serious—and, with her straight-cut bangs that fell to her eyebrows, and snub nose, and warm brown eyes, Nadia Stillinger was *cute*.

What Nadia's stepmother, Amelie, called *charmant*.

Nadia's stepmother Amelie, with her French accent and tinkling laughter, was certainly *charmant!* When Nadia was in the young Mrs. Stillinger's company, just walking into one of the upscale stores at the Quaker Heights Mall, or climbing out of Amelie's white Mercedes coupe, was an adventure—people could look nowhere else but at Amelie, who carried herself as if she were perpetually on camera.

The former Amelie LaSoeur had been a fashion model—(or so she described herself)—with a mane of ashy blond hair, six feet tall in high-heeled leather boots, tight-fitting designer jeans, and an ocelot-fur jacket from Bergdorf Goodman. Amelie had a face that glared like something on a billboard.

"*Charmant*, Nadia—you must try harder. You have a pretty

face—or will—when your cheeks are not so—what is it?" Amelie spoke in French-accented English and laughed with the most delicious sort of cruelty, the kind that pretends to be helpful. "Like one of those—what is it—cheepmonks."

Of course, anyone who overheard this remark, including Nadia's father, laughed in delight at Amelie's so-*charmant* mispronunciation: *cheepmonks* instead of *chipmunks.*

Cheeks like a *cheepmonk's:* meaning *fat.*

Of course red-faced Nadia laughed, to show that she wasn't *hurt.*

Or if she was, Nadia laughed all the harder.

Tink had said to just hang in there, a stepmother is not a bloody *mother.*

You can grow up and move away and escape a stepmother as you can't a bloody *mother.*

Nadia had climbed a hill into High Ridge County Park. She'd been talking to herself, anxious and shivering and yet sweating inside her clothes. Amelie sometimes crinkled her nose in Nadia's wake, complaining, Une jeune fille *must bathe. If she is to sweat like a little piggy, she must bathe soon.*

The mangled English made Amelie's remarks funny. Even Nadia's father laughed, when otherwise he'd have felt disgust for his slovenly fat daughter.

Nadia was leaning against a railing. Staring down at the fast-running Lenape River, which was about thirty feet below her.

This was a narrow but deep and allegedly treacherous river that cut through the hilly countryside north of the village of Quaker Heights. Near shore, Canadian geese in a flotilla were paddling in the cold water and communicating with one another in short, honking cries.

"Oh, Tink. I think that I did something really, really stupid. I think that I . . ."

Nadia was pressing against the railing, staring down. She felt bitterly how unfair it was that Colin Brunner's friends had not taken time to notice her attractive new jacket; they'd never really noticed how attractive she was.

How unfair, Nadia had no mother: only just a stepmother.

Like a girl in a Grimm's fairy tale.

There came a thin, uplifted cry, or call—somewhere behind Nadia in the woods.

Nadia turned, startled. She'd assumed that she was alone.

She could see no one. The woodchip paths were covered in a fine dusting of snow and were deserted.

Yet again—there was the thin, plaintive cry.

"H-hello? Is someone there?"

Nadia's heart beat strangely. It was a sensation she'd felt several times since Tink had left them, but usually in her sleep: in a dream.

Now Nadia was wide awake. Her wakefulness hurt her, like an overpowering light shone into her eyes.

"Is it—Tink? *Tink?*"

Nadia swallowed hard. She stared eagerly toward the woods—a deciduous woods mostly, and the tall, straight trees barren of leaves.

"Tink? Hey, Tink?—Is it you? I wish . . ."

This was ridiculous, Nadia knew. Yet her heart continued to beat so strangely, as if she were in the presence of—someone, or something.

She'd been leaning too heavily on the railing, that was it. She'd been half wanting the railing to collapse beneath her weight. There was something about heights that entranced Nadia: frightened her, yet compelled her. Tink knew this.

Tink had once confided in her friends that she had a phobia about heights—just coming near to the edge of a roof or a precipice, or standing on a balcony, she would feel a swooning urge to throw herself off.

But Tink had said she would never do this.

Why?

Too bloody messy. Too public.

Tink had been joking, of course.

Most of Tink's mordant remarks were jokes. Of course.

There was a stirring in the underbrush about twelve feet from Nadia. A small furry shape appeared—a cat—staring toward Nadia with widened tawny eyes.

Was this a wildcat—a lynx? Its fur was a beautiful bristling silver laced with black stripes and spots.

Nadia stepped away from the railing slowly, not wanting to frighten the cat. It might have been a feral cat, staring at Nadia from out of the underbrush. Its throat quivered, Nadia heard a soft mewing sound.

It's Tink. She has come to me.

Nadia was shivering so hard that her teeth chattered. She saw that the cat had no collar and its haunches were very thin. Again came the plaintive mewing cry.

Fascinated by the cat in the underbrush, which was looking so purposefully at her, Nadia approached the animal with an extended hand. Softly she murmured, "Kitty! Kitty-kitty-kitty . . . Are you lost? Are you hungry? Poor beautiful kitty . . ."

The cat hesitated as Nadia approached. It seemed to Nadia that the little cat yearned to come forward, to sniff at her extended fingers and rub against her ankles—but fear held her back.

"I wish you would come home with me, kitty. Please, kitty . . ."

The cat shrank backward. Its ears were laid back and its tail twitched nervously. Its throat quivered again, and this time Nadia heard a sharp hiss.

"Oh, kitty! I'm not going to hurt you—I promise."

But the cat turned now and ran away gracelessly through the underbrush. Nadia took a few quick steps after it, calling, "Kitty-kitty!"

In an instant the cat had vanished. Nadia's breath steamed in the cold air. Soon it would be late afternoon, and dusk—she had better hurry home before she was thoroughly exhausted and chilled.

She would walk quickly now. She was anxious to get home.

She was thinking, *Tink sent a sign to me. Tink did not want me to harm myself in the river.*

She was thinking of her stepmother Amelie's lynx jacket. Beautiful fur, exquisite markings, and so soft . . . Nadia hadn't quite realized, when she'd first seen her young stepmother's fur jacket, that many people are disgusted by fur coats; that many people are morally revolted by the practice of skinning beautiful creatures for their fur. And wasn't lynx an endangered species in the United States? But Amelie had a ready excuse: Her lynx jacket, which Nadia's father had given her, was *vintage*, not new.

Amelie had picked it out for herself from a chic boutique in Tribeca.

The poor cat! Nadia vowed she would return to High Ridge Park the next day to leave food for her.

Just thinking of the cat that had mewed to her, Nadia was feeling better. More hopeful, somehow.

It was childish to think that Tink had sent the little cat to her—Nadia knew. And yet.

Thinking, *Maybe it wasn't a mistake. Maybe Mr. Kessler will understand. Maybe*—Nadia didn't dare to think, *Maybe my father won't miss the painting.*

By the time Nadia returned home to the two-story fieldstone-and-glass house at 6 Wheatsheaf Lane, which always looked as if no one lived in it, the wintry sky had darkened almost to night, and the slow-falling snow wasn't melting so quickly.

Unlike her friends, whose parents—mothers, in any case—were vigilant about their daughters' whereabouts at all times, Nadia wasn't concerned that her father or stepmother would have wondered where she was since she'd failed to come home from school at her usual hour.

Neither Nadia's father or stepmother would be home, she knew. This was a consolation!

Even Merissa Carmichael, who sometimes complained of her mother's *excessive vigilance*, now that her father had moved permanently out of their lives, really took comfort in knowing that a parent cared about her, if perhaps excessively. Cell phones had to be forbidden at Quaker Heights, otherwise mothers would be calling their children constantly through the day; as Anita Chang joked, she couldn't go to the restroom without her mom checking on her. Nadia thought it was ironic that all of the girls of Tink, Inc., were so *watched over* by their mothers—except for Nadia, and, when she'd been among them, Tink herself.

It was marveled how, if you invited Tink to come to dinner at the last minute, even to stay overnight, she was very casual about checking with her mother, who might or might not have been home in any case.

No lights were evident in the Stillinger house, from Wheatsheaf Lane. In the little cul-de-sac in which the Stillingers lived, two other large fieldstone houses, looking like architects' models, were also mostly unlit except at the rear, where the housekeeper would be preparing a meal in the kitchen.

Nadia's father was CFO at a pharmaceutical company with headquarters in Quaker Heights, New Jersey; previously, he'd been a financial officer at a pharmaceutical company in Hartford, Connecticut. And before that—but Nadia's memory shut down. *Not healthy to dwell on the past! Nobody likes a whiner.*

Even when Mr. Stillinger wasn't traveling, when he was at the New Jersey headquarters, most evenings he worked late at his office. And today was a day when Amelie was *in the city*—that is, New York City.

This was a relief! Nadia could eat a meal alone, a nice meal prepared by Mariana, and she could check text messages as she ate, or anxiously scan Facebook and incoming emails—no need to talk.

When would Mr. Kessler discover the present in his car, open it and discover the painting—and the card?

How soon—hours? minutes?—before he realized that *Dani A.* had to be *Nadia Stillinger*?

By now, nearly five p.m., Mr. Kessler had probably left school. Often Nadia had seen him, when girls' chorus practice was breaking up, crossing the parking lot with several other teachers—frequently, in fact, with a new, young math teacher in the middle school whose name sounded like a TV name—Lula Lovett.

Nadia called out a cheery hello to Mariana, in the kitchen. Nadia was always cheery and upbeat in the housekeeper's presence, but she didn't want to linger in the kitchen for even a minute; she was too excited and distracted to do anything more than take from the refrigerator a container of strawberry yogurt and from a drawer a spoon with which to eat it.

Thinking, *Oh dear God, he will call me soon—maybe. Or— email.*

Or—maybe not until tomorrow, after class.

4.

"LEFT WITHOUT SAYING GOOD-BYE"

Suddenly she'd known. It had come to her—unmistakably.

Which was why she'd gone to see Mr. Kessler in his office—she had to be certain.

"Why, hello, Nadia! I wasn't sure that anyone was waiting here. . . ."

The expression on Mr. Kessler's face. An avidity, an alertness, and something like alarm in his eyes fixed on her face.

And when Nadia scrambled to her feet, clumsy, laughing, as she'd been sitting on the floor outside Mr. Kessler's office for—how long?—at least forty minutes, she would have lost her balance and fallen back down except Mr. Kessler instinctively reached out to grab Nadia's hand, to steady her.

"Hey! Gotcha."

He'd laughed. And Nadia had laughed, blushing and breathless as if she'd run up a flight of steep steps.

He was relatively new to Quaker Heights Day School. Nadia would calculate that he'd joined the faculty in the year that she'd transferred to the school—though she hadn't taken a course with the science teacher until her senior year.

There were several science teachers on the high school faculty: biology, physics, chemistry, Earth and Our Environment.

Adrian Kessler was the youngest and had quickly acquired a reputation for being demanding.

At QHD, where classes were smaller than in public schools, and personalities were prominent, it came to be quickly known that Mr. Kessler, though you might trade witticisms with him, laugh and joke with him, was one of the *less persuadable* teachers.

Athletes who'd seemed to be favorites of Mr. Kessler's in class, with a habit of slighting schoolwork on the eve of big games, soon discovered that Mr. Kessler was a man of principle. He listened to excuses, smiled sympathetically, and seemed to agree, but then quietly restated his position: Grading in his courses was "blind"—all that mattered was the work itself, not whose work it was.

"In the world, you'll be judged by what you *do*, not what you *are*."

(But was this so? Not all Quaker Heights students believed this, for there was evidence among their families and acquaintances that who you *are* was often more important than what you *did*. But it was hopeless to argue with the idealistic young Adrian Kessler.)

Calling the roll on the first day of class, Mr. Kessler had managed somehow to be very funny, making little jokes of students' names, and of "Nadia Stillinger" he'd invented "Nadia Stillfinger," which had seemed to Nadia thrillingly funny—though afterward, when she tried to recapitulate it to friends, the joke was very mild, indeed.

Mr. Kessler had also demonstrated a "modest feat" of memory at the conclusion of the class by recalling, student by student, up and down the aisles, their first and last names. Though he hadn't known them before calling the roll, already he'd affixed names to faces. Again he'd made them laugh, though they were also impressed.

And then, how thrilling it had been—how strangely tender, even intimate—when Mr. Kessler not only recalled "Nadia Stillinger" but "Stillfinger."

"In our high-tech age, we must not become overdependent on our machines to 'remember' for us. The brain is like any muscle—if it isn't exercised, it will atrophy."

Some of the work students would be doing in Earth and Our Environment would involve memorization: activating parts of the brain otherwise dormant. Earth and Our Environment was a science course for non-science college majors, but even students enrolled in AP Physics had enrolled in it, for Adrian Kessler had master's degrees in both biology and neuroscience.

Nadia felt a little stir of dread, for she wasn't at all gifted in science, still less in math; yet Mr. Kessler seemed reassuring. She liked it that the teacher's warm hazel eyes crinkled at the corners with good humor. You could see he liked to *tease*.

No one in Nadia's family seemed ever to *tease* her—though she'd noticed how, in other families, teasing was a principal mode of communication.

Especially parents and children. Dads and their daughters.

Nadia's father seemed confused by her—as if she was getting too big, too *old*. He'd looked away with a little knife blade of a frown between his eyebrows when at last—hesitantly—Nadia had worn her new bathing suit on the beach at Nantucket. (How self-conscious she had been! She wondered if Amelie had been deliberately misleading, assuring her that she looked "terrific" in the two-piece knit suit.)

Nadia had been trying hard—very hard—to lose weight. Over the summer she'd gained weight out of anxiety—overeating, especially soft, creamy-sweet things like yogurt and smoothies—in the wake of *what had happened to Tink*; at her heaviest she'd weighed 119 pounds—*horrible!* (Nadia was just five feet four inches tall.)

By the start of the fall term she'd managed to get her weight down to 111, which was still high—her goal was *ninety-eight*, which she knew to be Merissa Carmichael's weight, or at least it had been Merissa's weight months ago.

Every girl Nadia knew obsessed about her weight except Merissa Carmichael, who appeared to be naturally thin. And Tink, of course—Tink had once remarked that her goal was to gain weight, not lose it.

In her least favorite class, PE, Nadia was required to change clothes in the girls' locker room, and she grew sullen and resentful, trying practically to hide inside her locker. She saw girls' eyes moving onto her—her breasts, her wiggly buttocks and thighs—with expressions part envy and part scorn.

This past August in Nantucket, in her new swimsuit but hiding inside an oversized shirt out of which only her pale, fleshy thighs seemed to emerge like something bloated, Nadia had felt plenty of eyes on her—men's eyes—old men's eyes, for *God's sake*—and she'd never been so mortified as when she'd overheard a (male, middle-aged) friend of her father's remark to him, on the veranda of their oceanfront cottage, *Your daughter is getting to be quite a Renoir, eh? And she's only, what, in middle school?*

Nadia had wanted to run away, humiliated. She knew very well who Renoir was—what sort of fat, flabby, bovine females the French artist had painted—and she knew what an insult it was, to be mistaken for being in middle school when she was *seventeen* and about to start her senior year of high school!

Her manner, her little-girl breathiness. Her whispery voice and quick, tinkling laughter—these were ways to appear younger than her age.

She'd hate herself, Nadia guessed. If she had to observe herself.

Smiling too much. Tink had noticed.

High school boys weren't so attracted to Nadia as older guys out of school, and adult men. Strangers' eyes moving onto her body made her feel both uncomfortable and thrilled.

Text messages sometimes came to Nadia's cell phone from boys she didn't know, or hardly knew—she read with surprise, shock—embarrassment—and quickly deleted. Some of the IDs were clearly fraudulent, bringing Nadia the kind of messages a girl learns to quickly delete without reading.

BABY TITS. ASS.

BLOW. GO DOWN. FUCK ME.

Nadia laughed nervously—as if the guy or guys who'd sent it might be observing her. Quickly she sent these ugly words into the tiny trash-can icon on her cell phone.

If a friend asked Nadia about one of these messages, she said, giggling, "Oh, just nothing!" Or "Gross!"

Lots of girls received these *sexts*. It was nothing personal, really.

Never would Nadia tell or report *sexting*. Worse than being a *whiner* was being a *snitch*.

And anyway—how could you know who'd sent it, let alone prove it? Girls who had reported nasty sexts or mean online postings had been punished by guys ganging together against them, sending a flood of obscene messages and even threats of murder.

HOW'D YOU LIKE YOUR SLUT HEAD CUT OFF & SENT TO DADDY IN A BOX.

(This was a notorious message a Quaker Heights girl had received the previous year in a case that was still pending. Nadia Stillinger wanted nothing like *that*.)

Really beautiful girls like Merissa Carmichael were not treated this way. And girls like Tink—who were tough, and funny about sex.

Nadia accepted this, for her own father winced at the sight of her. She would not ever be beautiful, she would always be one to be elbowed aside, pushed off the sidewalk, or her head gripped in a drunk boy's big hands, forced to b**w him in a toilet stall, or in the front seat of his car, if she wanted a ride back to her house.

It had to do with Tink, she'd thought. After Tink, Nadia had sort of lost control, for a while.

Except now, with Mr. Kessler. Now Nadia had fallen in love for the first time.

She would not ever be beautiful, Nadia knew. Amelie had all but told her, you have to be born with *high cheekbones* to be beautiful, and Nadia's face was as soft-looking as a rubber doll's.

Maybe you take after your maman, Amelie said. *You surely do not take after your* papa.

Nadia was ashamed to ask Amelie if she knew anything much about Nadia's mother—if Nadia's father had ever shown her photographs, for instance.

Of course, that was ridiculous. Nadia's father would never have spoken of her mother to Amelie, or to the previous wife, let alone shown them photographs of her.

Nadia's mother's name was never mentioned in any of the houses in which Nadia had lived with her father.

Years ago, when she'd been a little girl, Nadia had asked her father where Mommy had gone, and her father had said, *Gone, Nadia. And she didn't say good-bye to me—or to you.*

Still, Nadia knew her mother's name. Even if it was a name banished from the household—*Esther.*

This was a beautiful name, Nadia thought. An unusual name, out of the Bible maybe—"Esther."

Sometimes Nadia spoke her mother's name aloud. Sometimes she whispered.

More often, she called her mother *Mommy.*

And this, too, she whispered when she was sure no one would hear her—"Mommy."

"Guys don't like you if you're smarter than they are. But if you're too much dumber than they are, you're a *bimbo.*"

Nadia laughed uneasily at her friend's remark. She knew what a *bimbo* was—if her stepmother Amelie hadn't been so chic and so shrewd, with her flashy good looks, she'd be a *bimbo.* And the fat, fleshy, doughy-faced females in the paintings of Renoir, lots of them nude, looking steamy-warm as if they'd just climbed out of a hot bath—for sure, these were *bimbos*.

Nadia said, "It's scary to try for just-between. Not too smart, and not too dumb." She'd laughed, and her friends had laughed, but was it funny? Hannah and Chloe were popular senior girls who had friends who were boys but not boyfriends—too much was expected of a girl, especially senior year, if you had an actual boyfriend.

Nadia had been naive, or frankly stupid, imagining that Colin Brunner, one of the popular football players, whose father was a New Jersey state senator, would be her *boyfriend*.

He'd laughed in her face, practically.

Nadia's in-box was jammed with SLUT SLUT SLUT SLUT SLUT but she'd scarcely noticed. Quickly she'd clicked delete.

Now she was turning her attention to her schoolwork.

Nadia was excited about Mr. Kessler's course, Earth and Our Environment. She'd looked ahead in the textbook and online, and especially she'd been intrigued by the material about animals adapting behavior to environment—the pictures of South American jaguars, African leopards and elephants and giraffes made her smile, they were such beautiful creatures. Ecosystems—biomes—biospheres—the roles of living things in ecosystems—these were concepts Nadia could understand, and maybe she could talk intelligently to her father about them, since her father had majored in biology at Harvard before switching to a business major.

When Mr. Kessler showed the class illustrations of the Earth as a single organism with countless diverse parts, as part of his PowerPoint presentation, Nadia felt reassured, somehow. As if it were revealed that there was a place for her after all. The idea of the Earth as a single organism made her feel safe.

"And how do we know the Earth is a single organism?" Mr. Kessler asked the class in his genial fashion, as if they were just having a conversation together.

Before one of the brighter students, like Virgil Nagy, could answer, Nadia's hand leapt into the air.

"It has a single name—Earth?"

"Well—yes. . . . But entities are not names, you know, Nadia—you would be you, if you were not Nadia Stillfinger."

This was sweetly funny; this was a gentle sort of teasing. Nadia guessed that she'd said something stupid—as usual—but Mr. Kessler was deflecting it, so that the class would not laugh at her.

Other hands had lifted around her, but Nadia plunged on, stubbornly: "Because it has a single—*atmosphere*? So things can *breathe*?"

A much smarter answer!

Because he respects me. And he looks at—ME.
Because he can see into my soul and he does not laugh then.

Soon it happened that Nadia was doing very well in Earth and Our Environment—her highest grade!

Where usually, in the past, science and math had been Nadia's weakest grades.

Where usually, when class discussion became abstract or intellectual, Nadia held back for fear of making a fool of herself, she now leapt in excitedly, competing with the really smart students when Mr. Kessler directed discussion to what he called "hypotheticals."

For instance—global warming.

"The future can't be exactly predicted—of course—but certain characteristics of the future can be predicted, extrapolating from the present, and past history, and projecting into the future. There are parts of the world that are clearly drying up—and other parts, along coastlines, that are flooding—eroding away. Environmental scientists have studied masses of data and have, overall, come to disturbing conclusions. So, your generation will inhabit this future that is evolving—which scientists are hoping we can remedy, or slow down, through global legislation. Can you think of ways in which the environment is not local—or national—but global?"

Discussion was lively. The most informed student was Virgil Nagy. Virgil spoke in a rapid nasal voice, rattling off statistics about temperatures worldwide and "carbon footprints," and for a while just he and Mr. Kessler were talking; then another student asked about the future—and Mr. Kessler said, frowning, "All we know about the future is that it doesn't exist—and never will. The future is the present time, perceived from the past."

Urgently Nadia's hand waved in the air. Her fingernails gleamed a pale coral pink and, though slightly bitten, prettily caught the eye like fluttering butterflies.

"Isn't there a future, *somehow*? People talk about it all the time and make predictions."

Mr. Kessler said, "What I mean is, there is no future—just as there is no past. These are abstract ways of speaking, not to be taken literally. There is only a continuous present. We exist only *now*."

This was a blunt statement, meant to be provocative, maybe. It was like Mr. Kessler to provoke students into discussions, even upsetting them sometimes.

"Mr. Kessler, what about a time machine?"

"Well, Nadia, you tell us. What about a time machine?"

Nadia squirmed happily at her desk, which was in the third row, near the windows. There was a buzzing in her ears, but it was a benign, glowing sort of buzz—honeybees in the sun, not hornets.

"Like, in movies and things, there's these time machines—scientists do experiments—sending somebody into the future, and . . ."

Virgil Nagy, on the far side of the room, laughed scornfully. Without troubling to raise his hand, he said, "Sci-fi is not *science*. It's *made up*."

"But—can't there be a time machine, Mr. Kessler?"

Nadia sounded anxious. As if the possibility of a *time machine*, or a *future*, had some personal meaning to her and wasn't just a discussion topic for science class.

"Nadia, I'm glad you brought up this just-slightly-digressive-but-relevant subject. I knew I could depend on you."

This was a casual, harmless remark—(wasn't it?)—a teacher meaning to be kind, encouraging, cheery, and upbeat. It didn't signal a special, secret meaning—(did it?). But Nadia sat entranced at her desk, staring at Mr. Kessler as if memorizing not only the teacher's words but every molecule of his being.

I love him. He is the one. Not—

—anyone else.

In his affable, smiling way Mr. Kessler was explaining to the class that in science fiction—"science *fiction*—Virgil is quite right about the distinction between science and fiction"—individuals can travel into the past or the future through some sort of ingenious machinery. "But unfortunately, in the universe there is no place where there could be a past—and the future hasn't happened yet, so the possibility of going there is palpably absurd."

Palpably absurd! This was the sort of phrase Adrian Kessler often uttered, a repudiation of a commonly held belief, but in so genial a way, you didn't feel insulted if it was a belief of yours.

Which was why many of Adrian Kessler's students liked him, very much—and others, who resented the comparatively low grades he gave them, disliked him.

"Because 'past' and 'future' are notional concepts—they are ideas, not realities or entities. Of course we all plan for the future and remember the past—but our relationship to each is very subjective, and tenuous. 'Past' isn't a place like Antarctica—you can't travel there."

Virgil Nagy said, sneering, "There is no *there*—there."

Gordy Squires said, objecting, "But there are *potentials*—like seeds, genes, fetuses. They exist in the present but come into being in the future."

"That's true, Gordy. But still there is no future *in existence*. The future has to evolve out of what we have now—the present."

"But if you shoot an arrow, it flies to its target—in the future. . . ."

"An arrow flying to its target is *always in the present*."

Mr. Kessler went to the green board to make chalk figures,

which Nadia copied in her notebook, hoping she might understand them afterward. Something about the way Mr. Kessler spoke about this subject—*arrow, target, flying, always in the present*—filled her with a nervous sort of anticipation, as if some profound truth were about to be revealed, which would illuminate *her*.

Instead the bell rang. No fifty minutes passed so swiftly as Nadia's fourth-period science class!

And there were too many people waiting to talk with Mr. Kessler—one of them, Nadia saw with dislike, was Sasha Coleman, who seemed always to be lingering after Mr. Kessler's class to ask him some transparently made-up question and to lean close to him, displaying her slender legs in lime-green tights beneath a chic, very short leather skirt.

So Nadia took up her backpack and left the room with the others, indifferent to which of her classes was next.

She was basking in the glow of Mr. Kessler's warm gaze. She was basking in the glow of Mr. Kessler's words, intimate as a caress, in front of the entire class—*I knew I could depend on you.*

Soon then modified to *Nadia, I knew I could depend on you.*

Virgil Nagy fell into step with Nadia. Since she'd become one of the more serious students in Mr. Kessler's class, Virgil seemed to be noticing her for the first time, though they'd been in numerous classes together and had in fact each transferred to Quaker Heights at about the same time.

It was flattering, in a way, that a boy like Virgil would want to walk with Nadia—boys who were attracted to Nadia Stillinger were not usually what you'd call *brainy*.

Except it was hard to talk with Virgil, who loomed over

Nadia like a giraffe. He had to be nearly six feet.

"You always seem so happy, Nadja. What's your secret?"

Happy! This was a surprise.

It was like Virgil to speak in this awkward way, which seemed just slightly bullying. Unwittingly he repelled girls he hoped might like him, and repelled boys even more—the word for Virgil among even nice guys was *geek*.

Nadia supposed that Virgil was just shy and socially uneasy like she herself. But she had learned to be, she believed, *charmant*. Virgil, with his slightly grayish teeth, which were crooked in front if you looked closely, and his habit of staring into your face, hadn't a clue.

"Actually, my name is 'Nad-ia'—not 'Nadja.'"

"Oh—sure. Sorry."

Virgil was crestfallen. A flush rose into his long, mournful, bloodhound face.

Virgil was said to be foreign-born—from Budapest. He spoke with an accent and seemed always about to stammer. His father was rumored to be separated from the family and taught at somewhere prestigious, like MIT or Harvard. His mother taught math at the local public high school. But no one really knew much about Virgil, except he was *super bright/a super geek*. He was respected without being liked, though everyone would have said he was a *nice guy*—except for being *a pain in the ass* if you were in classes with him, since he invariably got the highest grades and his long, lanky arm was always flailing in the air.

Virgil was almost stammering now. Wanting to intrigue Nadia by saying something further about the future—time machines—as if these were subjects Nadia really cared about, while really wanting, she sensed, to ask her something more personal.

"Of course I know your name is 'Nad-i-a'—I'm sorry to mangle it."

Nadia relented, laughing. It wasn't in her nature to feel superior to anyone.

"Actually, 'Nadia' is a name I hate. 'Nadia' just isn't *me*."

Nadia had never admitted this to anyone before. The words had just come out.

"It isn't? Who is it, then?" Virgil spoke in his annoying riddlesome way, baring his gums in a geeky grin. "Well—what name would you prefer?"

"I—I don't know."

"'Virgil' is a weird name, too. Nobody is named 'Virgil.'"

"Well—where you're from . . ."

"Not there, either. It's weird there, too."

Virgil paused, frowning. You could sense that Nadia's casual remark had somehow offended him. "What makes you think I wasn't born *here*? In America?"

"Were you?"

"Legally speaking, yes."

Virgil spoke sharply. Nadia hadn't the slightest idea what he meant, but she knew that no one who'd been born in the United States in any normal way would speak of being born in *America*.

"A name that's an anagram of my name is 'Dani A.' I'd like 'Dani'—or maybe 'Adriana.' That's a beautiful name."

A moment before Nadia wouldn't have thought of "Adriana." Though she'd worked out "Dani A." a few weeks ago, after Mr. Kessler discussed anagrams in class.

"Dani—Adriana—they're both nice names. But I like Nadia, too."

It was at this point that Virgil drew a deep breath and asked Nadia if she'd like to study with him sometime—"If you need h-help with, like, algebra"—and Nadia said quickly, "Thanks, Virgil, but I—I don't think so. Or maybe just not right now . . ."

"Sure! Just let me know, Nadia. I mean, Adriana. Anytime."

Virgil tried to speak lightly, but Nadia could see that he felt rebuffed.

How embarrassing this was! She knew that, as she hurried from him without a backward glance, he was gazing after her with reproachful dark bloodhound eyes.

Within seconds she'd forgotten Virgil. She'd intended to meet up with Chloe at their lockers, but soon she'd forgotten Chloe, too. Her heart was suffused with an almost suffocating warmth.

Knew I could depend on you, Nadia.

Only you.

Soon it happened that Nadia was talking about Mr. Kessler all the time.

Beginning to see her friends exchanging knowing glances—Chloe, Hannah, Merissa. And a sort of amused/jeering expression in Brooke Kramer's face: "Kessler? He's gay."

"G-gay? Who says so?"

Brooke shrugged. Her smartphone was vibrating inside her pocket, and surreptitiously she drew it out to peer at the caller ID—of course you could smuggle a cell phone in if you were careful.

"Mr. Kessler is not gay—I'm sure. And if he is, it's his business, right? For all we know, he's married."

"He isn't wearing a wedding ring."

"So?"

"There's something, like, wrong with his eyes—isn't there? He looks at you with, like, his right eye—but the left eye isn't in the same place. . . ."

Nadia hadn't noticed anything unusual about her teacher's eyes except that his gaze on her was *kindly, thoughtful, respectful, sweet*. And *affectionate*.

In her dreamy-distracted state, Nadia missed girls' chorus rehearsal, canceled a trip to the Quaker Heights Mall with Chloe and Anita, failed to complete a thousand-word critical essay on F. Scott Fitzgerald's *The Great Gatsby* for English, did poorly on a major math exam. She'd been negligent about applying to colleges and universities, though this was the major, obsessive topic of conversation among virtually everyone at Quaker Heights—it didn't seem real to Nadia; she was *a senior* and she was *graduating from high school* in a few months—one more thing not to think about.

(After all, Tink wasn't going to college. Where would Tink have applied, if she were still among them? You could not imagine Tink Traumer cravenly making out dozens of application forms, writing "personal essays" and self-hyping résumés. Maybe an art school, or a photography school—but knowing Tink, maybe not.)

When Nadia missed a dental appointment arranged for her by Amelie, her stepmother said curtly, "*Très bien*. If the *jeune fille* does not *regarde* her teeth, why should I? From now on you will schedule your own appointments, *s'il vous plaît*."

Senior year was not going well. Just the words *senior year* made Nadia's heart shrink.

Often she was desperate to avoid Colin Brunner and his friends—except Colin had so many friends. Not just guys on the team but others guys and girls, too.

Looking at Nadia Stillinger like she was a—s**t.

Luckily for Nadia there were other "incidents" among Quaker Heights seniors—other girls singled out as "s**ts" on Facebook. So maybe, in time, the guys would forget about Nadia as she was trying to forget about them.

Hannah and Chloe had said to Nadia, in a concerted way that signaled how the girls of Tink, Inc., had probably been talking about Nadia behind her back, "Nadia? You can report them, you know. Remember Mrs. Jameson told us, there's a Harassment Hotline. . . ."

"R-report who? I d-don't know what you mean. . . ."

"Those assholes—Colin Brunner and his friends. If—"

"I—I don't know what you mean. Good-bye!"

Blushing furiously, Nadia ducked her head and walked away.

No one brought up the subject again. At least, not to Nadia's face.

And what people said about her behind her back—she wasn't going to think about.

For she had, now, something very different to think about.

Someone very different.

She knew his teaching schedule. She knew when he arrived at school, usually—and when he left.

She knew his not-new-but-in-decent-condition Subaru.

She knew his office hours, which were three thirty p.m. to four thirty p.m.

It was a coincidence, Nadia believed: When she went to see

Mr. Kessler, on an afternoon in January, Tink had been gone exactly six months on that day.

Mr. Kessler preferred it if students made appointments to see him. He'd said that repeatedly since the start of the school year. Still, Nadia decided on impulse to "drop by" his office. Otherwise, making an appointment seemed *too deliberate*.

As if she had something crucial on her mind. As if seeing her science teacher was something she'd been planning, lying in bed at night.

It was 3:48 p.m. Someone was in Mr. Kessler's office, which was disappointing but no surprise. Nadia slid to the floor to sit, to wait patiently.

Mr. Kessler's office was in an older, dark-brick building on campus. Younger faulty had their offices here. Nadia knew the building well; she'd prowled this corridor a few times, just out of curiosity, to see where *Adrian Kessler's* office was.

It was beginning to be upsetting to her that the student lingered so long in her teacher's office—a tall blond soccer player/senior who wasn't even Mr. Kessler's student at the present time—(judging from what Nadia could barely overhear)—but was taking AP Chemistry with another science teacher on the faculty. Much of what the girl was saying to Mr. Kessler seemed to be fretful complaining about this teacher and anxiety about where she should apply to college.

The girl had to be seventeen years old at least. And an athlete. Yet her voice was breathy and whining, *girlish*.

That really annoyed Nadia! The girl sounded like *her*.

There was a nearby bench where Nadia might have sat, but she preferred the floor. For here she was partly visible to her teacher if he happened to glance in the direction of the open doorway—if he saw Nadia waiting, maybe he'd try to terminate his conference with the tall blond girl more quickly.

So anxious! Nadia stared at her watch, seeing the seconds fly past. And over in Weldon Hall, Mrs. Conway was wondering where Nadia Stillinger was—Mrs. Conway was offering a tutorial for students like Nadia who needed a little extra help with their writing.

It isn't like Nadia to just not show up. Think she's sick?

By now, maybe Nadia's classmates weren't saying this. Maybe they had an idea where Nadia might be hanging out.

Oh, this was bad luck! Several girls—Chloe, Martine, a girl named Chrissie—happened to come along the corridor at this time and saw Nadia sitting on the floor, in front of Mr. Kessler's office. A quick exchange of glances among them—Nadia wasn't imagining this.

"Hi, Nadia! Why're you sitting on the *floor*?"

It was cruel of Martine to tease Nadia by threatening to knock on Mr. Kessler's part-opened door to draw attention to Nadia out in the hall—Nadia begged in a whisper, "No! Please don't!"

Martine laughed, but Chloe and Chrissie saw the distress in Nadia's face and pulled Martine away.

They know, then. How I feel about Mr. Kessler.

She hoped that her friends wouldn't talk—and laugh—about her.

Most of all she dreaded something cruel and stupid posted online, where everyone could see it—including her teachers.

Including Mr. Kessler.

I will kill myself. By now, I should have.

Except I am not brave like Tink.

At last, at 4:23 p.m., the tall blond soccer player left Mr. Kessler's office, swaggering with her backpack and nearly stumbling over Nadia with a sneering look—"Excuse me!"

Nadia knew the girl just a little—Sylvie. Nadia saw with satisfaction that Sylvie's face was blemished at her hairline.

"Nadia! Hello. I didn't think that anyone was waiting to see me."

Clumsily Nadia scrambled to get to her feet. When she nearly lost her balance, Mr. Kessler instinctively reached out to grab her hand and steady her.

The warmth of Mr. Kessler's hands! Nadia felt faint. . . .

She saw that Mr. Kessler had shut up his laptop to take home. He'd switched off the little lamp on his desk. Now he switched the light back on and said, with a welcome smile, "Well, Nadia—have a seat. What can I do for you?"

Tell me that you love me. That I am not fat, and ugly, and stupid—and my father is embarrassed by me.

Mr. Kessler's office was a small space he shared with another young teacher. Bookshelves were made of an inexpensive metal and were crammed with mostly paperbacks. On the wall above Mr. Kessler's aluminum desk was a dazzling photograph of Earth as a biosphere, and on his desk were several small photographs in frames. Nadia's heart clenched with worry, that one of these photos was of a girlfriend.

She said, trying not to stammer, "I—I was wondering, Mr. Kessler—about time—like, you said there is no future and there is no—past. . . ."

"Well, yes. Those are ways of speaking rather than

entities—things. For instance, this is a pencil—you can see it, touch it, use it. But 'past'—'future'—are what we call *abstractions*. They are a kind of shorthand vocabulary."

Eagerly Nadia nodded. In her classes, she often nodded without knowing what her teacher was saying, really—though she felt the truth, the *plausibility*, of her teachers' statements. And so her nodding wasn't phony or hypocritical but genuine.

"But—if there could be a time machine—"

"We've gone over that, Nadia. There can't be anything like a sci-fi 'time machine.'"

"But then—maybe—if there could be"—words came to Nadia heedlessly, wildly—"something like—a hypnotist—"

"A hypnotist? I don't understand, Nadia."

"Well, I mean—someone to hypnotize you—to take you back to the past—in your memory. In the memory cells in the—brain? Like, you could be hypnotized, to remember? And what you remembered from long ago would be the past."

Nadia spoke with such pleading, and the expression in her eyes was so yearning, the smile faded from Mr. Kessler's lips. He seemed to be looking at his girl-student as if he'd never really seen her before.

"Why, yes, Nadia. I suppose you're right. You could—theoretically—be hypnotized and remember the past. And you could be—theoretically—*in the past*, then. Or so it would seem."

"I'm sorry—I guess I'm really stupid. I mean—science is hard for me—almost as hard as algebra. Because you have to know something *real*, you can't just be making things up the way you do in English, discussing a book, or in art. But the idea of a time machine—hypnotizing—"

Mr. Kessler made a gesture to slow Nadia down—she'd been speaking rapidly. "Now, Nadia—please don't be hypercritical of yourself. You're a very intelligent girl even if you aren't always entirely articulate about your thoughts. You must have faith in yourself."

Very intelligent girl.

Have faith in yourself.

Nadia couldn't believe what she was hearing. She was sure that none of her other teachers, though they were all very nice, thoughtful men and women, had ever spoken so encouragingly to her.

"Then—the past isn't gone, exactly? It's in the brain? Some part of the brain?"

"What you're saying is very interesting, Nadia. I've never thought of it that way—though perhaps others have, and have written about it. Neuroscientists have found that deeply imprinted memories are recorded in parts of the brain, and these cells can be activated electronically. Of course, it would probably be difficult to locate the right part of the brain, and it might be dangerous."

"Oh—dangerous? Why?"

"Because there are things we have all forgotten—suppressed. And there might be good reasons why."

"But—but—if it would make you happy, then—it would be worth it, wouldn't it?—to be hypnotized, and to risk the danger."

Nadia spoke so urgently, again Mr. Kessler paused, smiling uncertainly.

In his classes—in most classes at Quaker Heights—teachers were warmly engaging, direct, and friendly, but there was an invisible border no one crossed, which involved the intensity with which teachers and students communicated. The tone of their discourse was invariably light, even playful; where there was earnestness, there was also a degree of detachment. But here was Nadia Stillinger gazing at her teacher with such a look of raw, childlike need—her teacher was made to feel uneasy about how to respond.

"What is there about the past, Nadia, that so intrigues you?"

Nadia was dabbing at her eyes with a tissue. Worse, her nose was running.

She heard herself laughing—her nervous little-girl laugh.

"I—I—I—c-can't . . . I d-don't want to t-t-talk about myself. . . ."

"What is it, Nadia? Has something—happened?"

Nadia was wiping her eyes and at the same time trying to smile. Her mind seemed to be working slowly—oh, she felt clumsy!—like hauling herself out of a pool, suddenly heavy after the magical buoyancy of water.

Nadia remembered a girl at her previous school in Connecticut remarking in PE class, at the school pool, *Swimming's a whole lot easier if you're kind of—like—*fat. The girl hadn't been trying to insult Nadia, but clearly she was speaking of Nadia's example; she'd only been stating an obvious fact.

He knows about Tink. Must know.

But maybe not that Tink was my best friend.

"The reason I was emotional before—it comes over me at

221

times I can't predict. There was somebody in my family who died . . . last month."

"Nadia, I'm sorry. Who was it?"

"My g-grandmother . . ."

This was true. Nadia's grandmother—her father's mother—had died just after Christmas. Nadia had never been encouraged to be close to this grandmother, who'd been in a nursing home for years, and, it was said, hadn't been able to recognize even her son for a long time; but the fact that the white-haired elderly woman had *died*, and had *gone away*, as her mother had done when Nadia was six, had been upsetting to her.

Like Mommy. And not saying good-bye.

Like Tink. No good-bye.

In fact, Tink had texted her closest friends on the eve of her d***h. But she hadn't said a personal good-bye to anyone, and that was hard to accept.

Since her grandmother had died, Nadia had been thinking about her mother as she hadn't for some time. And (maybe) dreaming of her.

Waking with tears on her face, and a sharp, cramped sensation in her chest, as of irrevocable loss. Wanting to protest, *But Nadia Stillinger is too silly—shallow—to feel anything deep. This is wrong.*

Nadia knew the importance of maintaining an air of breathy girlishness. Lowered eyes, slightly parted lips, quickened breath—even her frowning father might give in and feel sorry for her, and not scold her as she deserved.

Tink had told Nadia not to smile so much.

Nadia had been shocked, that anyone would say such a thing.

Because if you're female and you smile, it just means that you want to please whoever it is you're smiling at.

A person with her own sense of dignity and self-worth only smiles *when she wants to*. That was why Tink rarely smiled when she was being photographed. And when she met people, Tink might smile, or not smile, according to how she felt.

But Nadia wasn't Tink. Nadia so wished that Tink might have taken Mr. Kessler's course; Tink might be alive now.

It had long been a secret that Nadia's mother had *died*. In fact, Nadia's father had never exactly revealed this fact to her—Nadia had learned, almost incidentally, from her aunt Harriet, who was her father's sister but seemed to have felt an allegiance and loyalty to Nadia's mother. *No one will tell you anything directly in this family, Nadia dear—and you don't dare ask.*

Mr. Kessler didn't seem to know anything about Nadia Stillinger's family life, which was a relief to her. Most of her teachers and certainly the headmaster knew that Roger Stillinger was a Very Important Executive with a Very Important Pharmaceutical Company; Nadia supposed that many of her classmates knew, too. (Of course, most of Nadia's classmates were from affluent homes, as Quaker Heights, New Jersey, was one of the most affluent communities in the United States.)

But no one seemed to know that Nadia's biological mother had died ten years ago when they'd lived in Connecticut; and that Mr. Stillinger had acquired not one but two young, attractive wives—stepmothers for Nadia—in that brief interim.

Mr. Kessler was asking Nadia about her grandmother. And Nadia was telling him what wasn't exactly true—how much she'd loved her grandmother—but was true about her mother.

If Nadia shut her eyes tight, she could (almost) see her mother again.

She could (almost) hear Mommy's voice again.

. . . Mommy is feeling so tired, but Mommy loves you. Mommy hopes that . . . you will remember her with love and forgiveness.

"Excuse me, Nadia? Are you all right?"

Nadia's eyes snapped open. She hadn't slept well the night before—that was the problem.

"Oh, Mr. Kessler—I'm sorry. I guess I—like—I don't know—" Nadia laughed, embarrassed. "Something came over me, like a light going dim. Maybe I'm—hungry . . ."

Breakfast was just too early for Nadia—her stomach felt queasy in the morning. And neither of Nadia's stepmothers had had anything more for breakfast than black coffee, since they, too, were "dieting."

By lunchtime, Nadia was ravenous. But she rarely ate an actual lunch at school with her friends—everyone was dieting, to a degree. Their favorite drink was Diet Coke, and their favorite foods were tiny fruit yogurts, which they ate with excruciating slowness, leaving the fruit-jam untouched at the bottom of the container.

By dinnertime, Nadia often felt "sickish"—"bloated"—from a succession of Diet Cokes and so didn't much mind when her father didn't arrive home for dinner and her stepmother was "out, with friends."

Mariana prepared a real dinner for Nadia, which Nadia

sometimes ate, or picked at. Mostly she brought delicious snacks upstairs to her room and ate while texting, checking email, doing homework, or watching TV. Weird how you could be kind of hungry yet bloated-feeling, even sickish.

Nadia didn't weigh herself every day. Only days—mornings—when she felt that her tummy had *gone down* a bit in the night.

Her goal was ninety-eight pounds. How thrilled she would be, how proud, and how beautiful.

Mr. Kessler was saying thoughtfully that he didn't really recommend hypnosis as a means of "retrieving" the past.

"Is this an idea someone has suggested to you? Someone in your family, for instance?"

Nadia shook her head emphatically *no*.

Her father would be furious at the idea. She could not bear thinking how he would respond.

Of course, Nadia would never dare mention it, but she'd thought—maybe—she might try to save money, and someday, if she could find a hypnotist who didn't live too far away, she might ask the hypnotist to take her back *in time*: to when she was six years old.

"When powerful memories surface, Nadia, as in nightmares, the individual can be unprepared—engulfed. War veterans sometimes suffer from amnesia, for good reasons."

Post-traumatic stress disorder. Nadia knew these words but had never supposed that such a condition might apply to her.

Mr. Kessler asked Nadia when she'd first lost someone or something close to her, and Nadia said, "My mom's parrot," in a way that struck them both as funny, and they both laughed.

This was a relief, though strange: to laugh!

It was strange, too, that Nadia never called her mother "Mom"—only "Mommy."

But the story she would tell Mr. Kessler, as it quickly evolved, was of "Mom's parrot"—a signal that they could both relax, and smile.

"My mom had an African gray parrot. Jasper. He was prickly and cranky and wouldn't let anyone else near him except my mom—and even my mom, he'd peck sometimes if he was in a bad mood. He was very smart, actually—he could say a few words like 'hello,' 'good-bye,' 'how–are–ya,' 'shh!' and 'Jasper hon-gy.' He was a beautiful bird, and he lived to be pretty old, I guess—my mom had gotten him when she was a girl. 'Jasper and I grew up together,' Mom would say." Nadia paused: This was so amazing! She had not remembered that remark of her mother's ever in the past.

"Yes, African gray parrots are extremely intelligent. They may be on a level with primates like chimpanzees. Crows, too, are highly intelligent—more intelligent than dogs, cats, horses, even pigs."

Mr. Kessler seemed relieved to discuss a scientific principle.

His teacherly manner was a warm protective coat he could slip on with ease.

"Jasper was too smart for his own good, people said. He squawked at people he didn't want to come near, like—some-times—my father." Nadia laughed; this seemed like an amusing fact. Talk of any pet is usually amusing—(isn't it?)—though Nadia heard herself say, with a grim smile, "Jasper picked at his breast until he was almost bald there. And he'd pick until he began to bleed. And Mom said, 'Oh, we shouldn't go away so much and leave Jasper, he's lonely—he's so smart, he knows what it is to be lonely.'"

This, too, Nadia had not remembered until now. It was strange how her mother's voice was present to her, in the protective solitude of Mr. Kessler's office.

The teacher was speaking of ways of human reasoning, which they would be taking up soon in class: innovation, cognition, programmed behavior/instinct. Most animal and bird species were programmed genetically, but there was "quasi-reasoning" in certain primates, like chimps, who could solve simple problems in ways that human beings might solve them, like using instruments—sticks—which could make their arms longer. But a dog, a cat, a horse, a pig—these animals were not so highly evolved in intelligence.

Nadia protested, "Dogs and cats are sometimes pretty smart. They can communicate with you—what they say has *meaning.*"

"Yes, but their sounds are not *linguistic.* They don't speak *language*, and the meaning you infer from their sounds isn't the sort of meaning that belongs to language."

"Sometimes an animal will sense what you think, or what you feel—more than a person. They can communicate better than some people, who don't feel much of anything and don't care."

Nadia was becoming emotional again, she had no idea why. Her nose was running, her eyes were blurred with tears; she knew that she was making Mr. Kessler uncomfortable but couldn't bring herself to leave the safety of his little office.

"My m-mom went away, somewhere. My father won't say where."

Because she left us without saying good-bye. Not to me, and not to you.

"Did she, Nadia! That's very unusual."

Mr. Kessler spoke cautiously, like a man venturing out onto ice he isn't certain is frozen solid.

"In the fall, it was. When I was starting first grade. I had to take first grade over again. I guess I was—kind of—*sick*."

This was true. Nadia's mother had gone away in September. That was easy to remember, because it was the start of school. And so the excitement about school that everyone felt was painful to Nadia, for it was too intense and too filled with hope—that whatever had gone wrong would be made right again.

From time to time Nadia's mother had gone away from their home, and it was never explained. Nor was Nadia told *where*.

Nadia would wake up, and someone would tell her—her father, or a housekeeper—*Your mother has gone away for just a little while. But she will be back.*

Except finally, the last time. No one had said, *She will be back*.

They'd lived in Connecticut then, in a place of rolling hills, large shingled houses on large lots. Sometimes waking in the house on Wheatsheaf Lane, Nadia had to think hard to realize that she wasn't in another house, at another time.

"I'm very sorry to hear that, Nadia. I wish that I . . ."

Nadia was crying. Instinctively Mr. Kessler touched the back of Nadia's hand, to comfort her. His fingers closed around her hand.

Nadia dared not move. Thinking, *I love you, Mr. Kessler— more than anyone in the world.*

Briskly Mr. Kessler released Nadia's hand and got to his feet, apologizing to her—he had an appointment at five p.m. in the village. He was asking Nadia if she'd spoken with Mrs. Jameson, and Nadia murmured yes.

Impossible to concentrate on homework that night.

Nadia's brain seethed with replays of her (secret) conversation with Mr. Kessler.

And his fingers closing on her fingers—not once but twice. Nadia could not recall anyone, since her mother, having held her hand in such a way.

Though she knew she should resist, Nadia texted to Chloe.

CAN U KEEP A SECRET

Chloe texted back—

YES

Nadia texted back—

SOMETHING HAPPENED TODAY

Chloe texted back—

TO U TODAY?

Nadia texted back—

U WLDNT GUESS WHAT MR. K SD TO ME TODAY

Chloe texted back—

WHAT

Nadia texted back—

IT'S A SECRET SORRY—CANT SAY

U CAN GUESS THO

Chloe texted back—

CAN'T GUESS!!!

CAN KEEP A SECRET

Nadia texted—

LOVE MR. K—I WOULD DIE FOR MR. K—

I THINK HE KNOWS

Chloe texted—

HOW DOES HE KNOW, DID U TELL HIM???

Back and forth like Ping-Pong the texts flew, until Nadia felt so light-headed she had to turn her cell phone off for the night.

Soon then Chloe forwarded the text messages to Hannah, because she knew that Hannah was concerned about Nadia; Hannah forwarded the messages to Merissa, Martine, and Chrissie; Martine and Chrissie forwarded to several other girls, of whom one was Brooke Kramer, who forwarded them to twenty-three individuals, all of them seniors at Quaker Heights, both boys and girls.

5.

IMPROVISATION

"No one will miss it."

The little painting hung in a guest-room suite that was rarely used, at the rear of the Stillinger house. Nadia was sure that neither her father nor her stepmother had entered that part of the house for weeks, perhaps months.

Mr. Stillinger collected artwork: paintings, photographs, lithographs, prints. Nadia had overheard her father say that art was an excellent investment if you chose carefully.

Never buy second-rate art; it soon becomes third-rate. But first-rate art increases in value—and it's beautiful to look at.

In the living room there were several large canvases that looked like angry scrawled graffiti; there was a tall, narrow canvas all vertical, drippy black lines; there was a painting of the back of a person's head, shiny-haired as if shellacked. In the dining room, its impact doubled by a facing mirror, was a nude by a famous British painter depicting a lumpy, fattish, dough-colored, middle-aged man with a mashed face—Nadia could hardly bring herself to look at this, *so ugly!* In the front hall there was a Chagall lithograph, depicting what looked like magical scenes—this made Nadia smile.

Visitors to the Stillinger house, led into the interior by Mr. Stillinger or by the new, young wife Amelie, would stare at the artwork illuminated by recessed lights in the ceiling and say, *Oh! This is—beautiful,* or *Oh! this is—unusual.* Always the tone was admiring, respectful. For everywhere in Mr. Stillinger's house there was much to admire, as well as the large, custom-designed house itself.

Nadia would have most liked to give Mr. Kessler the Chagall lithograph—its airy, floating figures and swathes of color suggested the biosphere pictures he'd shown the class. But she knew better: The Chagall, prominently displayed, would be missed *immediately,* even if she substituted another artwork in its place.

There were less conspicuous works of art in Mr. Stillinger's home office, as he called the large walnut-paneled room, including stark black-and-white photographs of ancient Greek statuary, which made Nadia feel uneasy, as if even the headless figures were staring at her with Olympian contempt. In the hallways and in the guest suite at the rear of the house, which was rarely used, there were small watercolors and oil paintings, which no one ever saw. Nadia switched on a light in the guest bedroom— "Here it is! *Protozoa.*"

Nadia was excited, thrilled—she'd found the perfect gift for a science teacher with a love of biology.

It was a relatively small painting—framed, under glass— measuring about fifteen inches by twenty inches—not too bulky or heavy, and very beautiful, Nadia thought. Though it was abstract, its floating deep-rose figures and swirly lines reminded her of Mr. Kessler's PowerPoint slides of microorganisms called protozoa.

For all Nadia knew, maybe the painting was of protozoa—or some other microorganism.

Nadia lifted the painting from the wall. What a surprise—it weighed only a few pounds. She could easily bring it to school.

She would wrap it first, carefully, in bubble wrap.

The artist's name was just legible, in black paint at the left-hand bottom of the canvas—*Kandinsky*. On the back of the painting was more information—*Improvisation 1912. Wassily Kandinsky*.

Nadia knew that Kandinsky had to be a real artist—otherwise her father wouldn't have purchased the painting. But she'd never heard the name before and couldn't recall her father saying much about this painting in her presence.

Nadia smiled. Here was the perfect gift to give to Mr. Kessler: a serious work of art by a Russian-sounding artist, of whom maybe he'd heard, and it looked like certain of his PowerPoint slides that he had remarked were *beautiful—like art*.

"Single-celled forms of life"—Mr. Kessler had spoken with a kind of reverence of the squiggly little ovoid figures he'd called protozoa. Nadia had stared in wonder at Mr. Kessler's pointer as he'd explained what was known of the *origins of life*—the *building blocks of life*.

It was important to know, Mr. Kessler told the class, that an individual human being was comprised of an infinite number of microorganisms, including bacteria—friendly bacteria. We could not exist as *physical beings* without these invisible organisms within us.

"But sometimes they kill us, don't they, Mr. Kessler?" Virgil Nagy had to show his superior knowledge.

Nadia laid the painting carefully on a chair and searched for a replacement, making sure that the substitute artwork was approximately the same size as the Kandinsky painting and not so very different from it—at least to Nadia's eye.

This other small artwork wasn't a painting but a pastel drawing of a green landscape, which Nadia took from the guest bathroom. There were several pastel drawings in the bathroom, and maybe this one wouldn't be missed, since not even Mariana came into the guest suite on a regular basis.

Stealthily Nadia carried *Improvisation* upstairs to her room—though no one was around to observe her.

From one of Amelie's closets, Nadia took the shiny gilt tote bag—reasoning also that Amelie wouldn't notice it was missing. The expensive bag from Neiman Marcus had been fashionable at one time, but Nadia hadn't seen Amelie using it for at least a year.

That night, Nadia made the birthday card for Mr. Kessler and worked on the little note to him.

She'd experimented with several notes but decided that the simplest was best:

> Mr. Kessler—
> Happy Birthday!
> Davi A.

"*He* will appreciate it. *He* will understand."

There was no way that Nadia could sign her own name.

It just wasn't possible.

"It will be our secret. Between us."

And so the next day Nadia brought the painting to Quaker Heights Day School in her stepmother's bag inside a grocery bag.

"What's in the bag?" Martine Hesse was curious.

Nadia murmured something about her stepmother. She had to "deliver something" for her stepmother to a woman friend.

"I don't know," Nadia said stiffly, moving away. "You'd have to ask my stepmother."

School passed in a trance of oblivion. Even Mr. Kessler's class seemed to take place at a little distance from Nadia, like a dream into which she'd wandered. After their intense conversation of the previous afternoon, Mr. Kessler seemed almost to be avoiding Nadia, though when she raised her hand, he called on her to answer a question about the meaning of *cognition*.

After school, Nadia waited until the parking lot was near deserted before bringing the gift to Mr. Kessler's Subaru and leaving it in the backseat.

And hurrying away, she was suffused with excitement, and dread—*Oh God. Now he will know.*

No turning back.

"Kitty? Where are you . . ."

The next morning Nadia returned to High Ridge Park. It seemed urgent to her—a desperate matter—that she find the beautiful lost lynx-cat and feed her. If she could, bring her home.

It seemed to her that Tink would want this. Maybe, in fact, Tink had directed this.

Mewing at Nadia, to alert her to danger.

Mewing at Nadia, to make her realize that she was not alone.

Nadia had brought a can of tuna fish, all she could find in the house that might be suitable for a cat.

Nadia's father had never had pets. On principle, he did not approve of pets—*All they do is shed, smell up the house, scratch the furniture, and they can't be trusted in a household with expensive art.*

Pleadingly Nadia called, "Kitty? Kitty? Oh please—kitty . . ."

She was shivering with cold, and with excitement—her teeth chattered and her heartbeat was so *fast.* Never had she come to High Ridge Park—or any park, for that matter—alone; it wasn't like Nadia to be outdoors, to walk in the woods along dirt trails, to peer into the underbrush searching for a little lost cat. Every school morning, Mariana drove Nadia to school. Most afternoons, she came to pick Nadia up, unless Nadia had a ride home with friends.

Nadia? You don't want me to drive you this morning? No?

You can walk? Can you? So far?

Nadia had laughed, saying it wasn't *far.*

Nadia hoped the housekeeper didn't notice how unusually edgy and excited she was. Or, if Mariana happened to go into the guest wing, that *Improvisation* was missing.

In the woods Nadia tramped, calling, "Kitty-kitty!" and peering into the underbrush. She'd been unable to sleep the previous night for more than a few minutes at a time. Repeatedly she'd switched on her bedside lamp to check her cell phone to see if—maybe—Mr. Kessler might have texted her by now.

He had never texted her before. He had never emailed her.

It did not occur to Nadia that Mr. Kessler didn't have her cell phone number, nor was he likely to send her an email, for in the exigency of the situation she was not thinking clearly.

Yet she could envision his message to her.

"DANI A."—WHAT A BEAUTIFUL SURPRISE!

THANK YOU, THANK YOU, THANK YOU, DEAR "DANI A."

PLEASE COME TO SEE ME IN MY OFFICE AS YOU DID YESTERDAY.

I WILL THANK YOU IN PERSON.

Or maybe Mr. Kessler would write PLEASE CALL ME, NADIA. AS SOON AS YOU RECEIVE THIS MESSAGE. MY CELL IS . . .

But there were no new calls or messages.

Compulsively Nadia checked, and rechecked—sliding open the little panel at the bottom of the iPhone screen to unlock.

But no one had texted her.

But Nadia wouldn't think of this just now. In High Ridge Park in the snow-crusted grass she searched for the lynx-cat to feed her—and save her life. And maybe, if there was a way that her father wouldn't know about it, bring the little cat home with her to live.

"Kitty? Don't be afraid of me! Kitty—please . . ."

Finally, it was getting too late: Nadia had to leave, to half walk, half run to school to arrive just as the first bell, for homeroom, was ringing.

"Nadia? Hi . . ."

Whoever it was—a girl, a girlfriend, someone in Mr. Kessler's science class—Nadia didn't know, too distracted to glance back.

She breathlessly entered Mr. Kessler's classroom in a haze of anticipation, dread—looking quickly to Mr. Kessler, who wasn't in his usual position by his desk, but in a corner of the room with his back to the students, speaking on his cell phone.

Usually, Mr. Kessler talked with students before class, but this morning he appeared to be distracted. Even his necktie was slightly askew.

Nadia knew something was wrong: Mr. Kessler didn't glance over at her.

After he shut the cell phone, Mr. Kessler seemed to rouse himself, smiling wanly at students gathered around his desk. Nadia wasn't one of these; she took her seat numbly.

Something is wrong, wrong, wrong.

Class began. Mr. Kessler spoke. The subject was—(Nadia couldn't concentrate: What was the subject?)—and Mr. Kessler glanced about the room as often he did, pushing his glasses against the bridge of his nose, except he was frowning now, and did seem distracted.

He wasn't looking at *her.* He wasn't acknowledging *her.*

He only glanced at Nadia once or twice, as he glanced at others in the class. But there was *nothing special* in his eyes. There was *nothing special* he was trying to convey to her, an indication of the secret bond between them.

Nadia was beginning to feel faint. She'd forgotten to bring anything in her backpack to eat between classes—she'd been too distracted that morning in her desperation to get to High Ridge Park.

Now she could barely remember High Ridge Park.

He doesn't know it was me. He must think it's from someone else—"Dani A."

Nadia sat rigid in her seat, scarcely aware of the classroom that surrounded her. She heard laughter—good-natured laughter. So Mr. Kessler was joking. She had no idea what he and the others were saying. It was like the morning after the night that her mother had *gone away*—she'd heard voices but had no idea what the words meant.

Mr. Kessler didn't call on Nadia Stillfinger that day.

He doesn't know. He doesn't care. He doesn't love me.

The bell rang. Nadia stumbled to her feet, snatched up her backpack, and left without a backward glance.

So hungry!

In a girls' restroom far from the senior corridor, where she wasn't so likely to encounter anyone she knew, Nadia hid in one of the stalls to eat—try to eat—the canned tuna she'd brought for the little lost cat. Clumsily she managed to open the can with an opener she'd brought from home, but the strong fishy smell was unappetizing—though Nadia was faint with hunger, she couldn't eat more than a mouthful.

Making sure that no one was in the lavatory to see, she tossed the can and its smelly contents in the trash.

How bizarre it would seem, to girls entering the restroom! Such a strong smell of canned tuna fish! If Nadia hadn't been so miserable, she'd have laughed.

The remainder of the long day passed in a blur. Fifth period, sixth period, seventh . . . Nadia was so distracted with worry about Mr. Kessler and the painting she scarcely noticed people glancing at her curiously—some of them, rudely.

Boys? Boys she knew? Or—boys she didn't know, but who

seemed to know her?

A guy named Hawkeye—that was his nickname, a friend of Rick Metz's, standing in front of Nadia, blocking her way on the stairs, she wasn't sure why.

Her natural response was to smile back—to say *Hi!*

But no, better not. Hawkeye was not a friend.

The guys' smiles were not friendly smiles but bared-teeth smiles like the smiles of robots in video games.

Felt too sickish to go to girls' chorus rehearsal—this was the third time in a row Nadia was skipping practice. Hannah texted her WHERE R U? but Nadia shut up her phone without replying.

And on her way out of school, on the walk behind school where, almost twenty-four hours before, she'd stood pondering whether to leave the gift for Mr. Kessler in his Subaru, Nadia saw several senior guys looking at her and slyly smiling—"Hiya, Nad-ee—how's it going?"

Nadia turned quickly away. A blush rose into her face.

Walking quickly away. Blindly.

Not hearing a derisory chanting in her wake—*How'd Nad-ee like suckee my cock?*

Nadia didn't hear this. Rude laughter drowned out whatever she might have heard, except she was walking so quickly away and without a backward glance.

Did not hear the chanting after her—*Slut-tee Nad-ee. Hey-hey, slut-tee Nad-ee like suckee?*

Did not hear. Not any of it.

· · ·

240

Just to help me sleep, honey. Sleep, sleep, sleep is the most wonderful gift you can give another.

It isn't that Mommy doesn't love you. Mommy loves you.

But Mommy is so very tired now, honey.

If you love Mommy, please do not wake Mommy. Please promise!

Nadia had promised. Nadia had wanted to sleep curled in Mommy's arms on Mommy's bed beneath the beautiful hand-sewn quilt from Mommy's mother that looked like apple blossoms, but Mommy had sent Nadia away this time, for Mommy was *so very tired, and needing to sleep.*

Nadia had promised, and so she did not wake Mommy up, and in the morning of the next day—or was it the next day—or another day—the housekeeper came to take Nadia away because Mr. Stillinger was just returning from Bangkok and his plane had been delayed for several hours. And still, Nadia did not break the promise she'd made to Mommy, she had never broken the promise she'd made to Mommy, nor did she confide in any-one the promise she'd made to Mommy; and soon, she forgot the promise she'd made to Mommy, for it was safest that way.

In this wintry time of the year when Mommy *went away.*

"Nadia, where the hell have you been? Are you always so damned *late?*"

Amelie spoke so harshly to Nadia, her eyes glared with such undisguised dislike, Nadia was stunned. She'd just entered the house—as usual, through the kitchen—though noting, absent-mindedly, that there was something wrong in the kitchen, something *not right*—only a single light burning above the sink, and—where was Mariana?—having been preoccupied with a growing sense of shame, misery that Mr. Kessler didn't care for her really—(unless there was some mistake, some misunderstanding, and Mr. Kessler really did care for her but knew he must not show his feelings in public)—when her stepmother came rushing into the kitchen, furious as Nadia had never seen her.

"There's an emergency situation here! There's been a theft here! Your precious Mariana—always pretending to be so goddamned *nice!*—has been stealing from us! I've asked her to leave our employ."

Nadia stared at Amelie, uncomprehending.

Mariana? Stealing? And had she been—fired?

"Don't look for her—she's gone. She's been stealing from us, and she denies it—lying to my face. Your father will deal with her; I can't. And she won't be paid for this week!"

In her fury, Nadia's stepmother no longer spoke with her *charmant* French accent. How confusing this was!

Numbly Nadia set her backpack on the counter. Numbly moving her fingers, fumbling with the zipper of her quilted dark-rose jacket as her stepmother raged:

"Imagine! Stealing right out of my closet! And I'm sure she's taken jewelry of mine, too—a pair of earrings I've been missing for months, and it never occurred to me that Mariana might have taken them—and my Dior scarf, remember, when we came back from Nantucket—"

Horror washed over Nadia. Her heart began beating so hard, she felt she might faint.

"What—did Mariana t-take?"

"My beautiful bag! The gold bag—it was one of my favorites.

I went to look for it and couldn't find it anywhere, and I asked Mariana, and the way she looked at me—I can detect guilt when I see it—and subterfuge—and of course she denied it, she said she has never taken anything from any house she has worked in, ever. And she kept denying it, that's what makes me furious. I can see that someone like Mariana, who has so little, might be dazzled by such a bag, and thinking that I haven't been using it lately, thinking, 'Maybe Mrs. Stillinger won't miss it,' but I'm not that naive."

Nadia was feeling faint. And she was feeling sick to her stomach.

"I—I—took the bag. Not Mariana . . ."

"*You?* You did not. You're covering for Mariana, I can see it in your face."

"No—I'm not c-covering for Mariana. I—took your bag . . . I'm so sorry, I didn't think you would c-care. . . ."

"Believe me, *ma petite amie*, your room was the first place I searched—and the bag isn't there. And I can see in your face, you're lying now."

"Amelie, no—I did take your bag. It wasn't Mariana—please believe me."

"Where is it, then?"

"I—I don't know. . . ."

"You took the bag, but don't know where it is?"

"I'm not s-sure. . . ."

"Well, if you took it, and you don't have it, where did you see it last? Where did you leave it?"

Nadia stood frozen, staring at the floor. Her brain seemed to dip, whirl, sink.

"I—I d-don't remember. . . . But maybe I can get it back. . . ."

"You 'don't remember' where you left it—but 'maybe you can get it back'?" Amelie laughed harshly. Nadia could see that her usually composed and *très chic* stepmother would have liked to seize her shoulders and give her a very hard shake.

"Just, it wasn't Mariana. Please don't fire Mariana. I—I'm so sorry. . . ."

"No. I don't believe you. You and precious Mariana—I hear you laughing together in the kitchen, and when I come in, you both go *silent*. Well, she's no saint—she's no more a mother to you than—than—anyone else." Amelie began to stammer, so angry. Before Nadia could plead with her further, she turned and stalked out of the kitchen. Nadia stood forlorn and abashed, not daring to follow.

Upstairs in her room Nadia sank onto her bed. Her backpack fell to the floor; her cell phone tumbled out and she made no move to pick it up. A gathering roar of angry hornets in her brain. She was trying to remember—what? Trying to hear—whose words?

Sleep, sleep, sleep is the most wonderful gift.

It isn't that Mommy doesn't love you.

Mommy loves you. . . .

6.

SHAME

"Nadia? What on earth are you trying to tell us?"

Nadia tried to speak—but could not. Nor could she bear to look at her father's face, contorted with incredulity and anger.

Summoned by his hysterical wife, Mr. Stillinger had driven home from work early. He hadn't believed the situation to be the emergency Amelie called it until on a sudden impulse he searched the house to see if any of his own valuable possessions were missing—and soon discovered that the Kandinsky painting was gone.

"Whoever stole my painting was trying to be clever—covering her tracks by putting another work of art in its place. But only an idiot would confuse a pastel drawing by Prendergast with an oil painting by *Kandinsky*."

"But why—why would Mariana take a *painting*? And why that painting?" Amelie was still determined to believe that Mariana was the thief.

"Well—she isn't very bright. Obviously! She's just barely a 'legal' alien—she isn't educated. Maybe she thought she could sell it—somehow. Still, it doesn't seem like something our housekeeper would take, like your Neiman Marcus bag." Mr. Stillinger's fingers were twitching as if he'd have liked to get hold of someone. "We'd better call the police and report it now."

And so, Nadia had no choice except to tell her father what she'd done.

Provoking the red-faced man to turn his fury on *her*.

Nadia tried to summon the right words, stammering and faltering. That she'd wanted to give a *gift* to her science teacher, Mr. Kessler—that she'd taken a painting that resembled a photograph of protozoa. Mr. Stillinger stared at his daughter, shaking his head in disbelief.

"You couldn't have thought of this theft on your own, Nadia! Who is this science teacher? Did he put you up to it?"

"No! Oh, no. Mr. Kessler doesn't even know. . . ."

"I'll call him. I'll call him first, and then I'll call the police. This isn't petty theft, this is grand theft. Do you know how much that painting is worth, Nadia?"

"N-no . . ."

"At least three million dollars."

"Th-three million dollars?"

"Wassily Kandinsky is a major artist of the twentieth century! What were you thinking?"

Nadia could barely think, there was such a roaring in her ears. Her father was looking at her with such *hatred*, she wanted to hide her face and run from the room.

"I—I wasn't t-thinking. . . . I didn't think you would miss it, and Mr. Kessler would—appreciate it. . . . He likes beautiful things."

"Oh, he does, does he—like 'beautiful things'?"

"He has photographs of the Earth as a biosphere. And colored plates of single-celled organisms, and the human brain. . . ."

"And you took Amelie's bag, to put the painting in? To give to him? Why on earth?"

"I—d-don't know. . . ."

Because the bag looks like gold. Because the bag is beautiful too and was discarded in the closet with other expensive things and no one ever saw it.

And the painting on the wall—no one ever saw.

Because I love Mr. Kessler and wanted him to know. And I don't love you.

Nadia begged, "Please don't call anyone, Daddy. Please! Especially not the police—*please!*"

"You don't seem to understand, Nadia. This Kress—Kressler—received stolen goods from you, a minor. This isn't a misdemeanor, this is a felony. The man must have encouraged you—urged you on—you wouldn't have thought of such a thing yourself. You're just a girl—a very young, naive, impressionable girl. But it isn't like you to be dishonest, in any way—that, I would swear to. You agree, Amelie?"

Glowering, Amelie, taken by surprise, had no choice but to agree.

"This man—this science teacher—has had a corrupting influence on you. I will certainly call *him*, and I will call the *headmaster* at that fancy school of yours—the tuition and fees we pay, we might as well be sending you to Princeton!"

It had long been a household contention that Quaker Heights Day School was an expensive school, even more expensive than the Quincy Academy in Connecticut. Yet Mr. Stillinger would not consider allowing his daughter to enroll at the public school, though it had an excellent reputation. Nadia had had no choice about which school to attend, since her father had been transferred to Quaker Heights, but she was made to feel guilty about the situation.

"Oh, Daddy, please—don't call anyone! It's all my fault, not Mr. Kessler's fault at all. He doesn't even know that I—that I'm the one—I didn't s-sign my n-name—exactly. . . ."

"Didn't sign your *name*—exactly? What are you trying to say?"

"I l-left the painting in Amelie's bag in the back of his car—with a card—but I signed the card with another n-name. . . ."

"You didn't even sign your *name*? You gave away a three-million-dollar painting by Wassily Kandinsky to your *science teacher*? Without even telling him who you are? Whose painting it is?"

"I—I had a reason. . . . I'm so sorry! I'm so very sorry! Just let me call him, Daddy—I can explain—please don't call him, or the headmaster—it might get Mr. Kessler in trouble, and he's such a wonderful man. . . ."

Nadia saw that her father was both furious and thrilled—Mr. Stillinger had a penchant for strife, combat, and litigation. He had not ascended the highly competitive hierarchy of the corporate world by being reasonable and forgiving of wrongs committed against him.

Always it had seemed to Nadia, as far back as she could recall, when her mother was still alive, that her father had taken a kind of grim satisfaction in "wrongs" committed against him—whatever action he took then was *justified*.

"It was Mr. Kessler's birthday this week, so I thought I would give him something. And I wanted it to be s-special. . . ."

"His *birthday*? How on earth did you know that?"

"He mentioned it in class."

"Mentioned in class—his *birthday*? What kind of arrogant behavior is that? Telling adolescents—susceptible adolescents—that it's his *birthday*? So his students will bring him *presents*? This is outrageous."

"Oh, no, Daddy—you're misinterpreting it. Mr. Kessler only just happened to mention his birthday, I can't remember why—he's always talking about personal things if they are 'representative' and relate to scientific ideas somehow. It's the way all our teachers teach, they're not arrogant, they're *friendly*. . . ."

"Yes, I'm sure they are very *friendly*. Did everyone bring him presents?"

"N-no . . ."

"And why did you, if no one else did?"

Nadia's brain seemed to stop dead. She knew that she should be very careful what she said, that her indignant father was avid to seize her words and misuse them for his own purpose, yet she continued, stammering, "He—talked to me about death. . . . I was feeling kind of bad about M-Mommy . . . This is the time of year she went away . . . though I didn't tell him much. And I guess I started to cry, and—we were in his office, after school—and Mr. Kessler *touched my hand*—and it made me feel better right away."

"This man, this adult—Kressle—*touched your hand*? In his office, after school?"

"Just for a minute. Just to make me feel better. It was only just what anyone would do, who was n-nice. . . ."

"Nadia, let me see if I get this. The science teacher of yours called you into his office after school, when no one else was around—"

"Daddy, no! Mr. Kessler didn't call me in, I just—went in. I went to see him during his office hour. . . ."

"And was anyone else around?"

Nadia recalled the girls who'd laughed at her. And Colin Brunner's friends who'd laughed at her.

"Y-yes. Some people. It was after school. . . ."

"And was the office door open or closed?"

"Open! The office door was open."

Nadia couldn't recall if this was so or not. In her romantic replaying of the scene, Mr. Kessler's office door was *shut*.

"So an adult man, a stranger, encouraged you to talk about your private life, your family life, including your deceased mother; he provoked you into crying; and then, to comfort you, he *touched your hand*? And where else did he touch you?"

"Nowhere, Daddy. J-just my hand, for a m-minute . . ."

"And this romantic encounter prompted you to leave a birthday gift for the man, whom obviously you adore, worth somewhere in the vicinity of three million dollars? Nadia, this is preposterous behavior! Even for you, so immature for your age! How did he encourage you?"

"Mr. Kessler didn't encourage me—I mean, to give him any-thing. He was just nice to me and—I guess—I like him, a lot. Please don't call Mr. Nichols, our headmaster—it might get Mr. Kessler into trouble, and none of this is his fault at all. . . ."

"Yes. Exactly. It might get Mr. Kressler in trouble—that is exactly what I intend to do."

Nadia's father stormed out of the room. Nadia stood paralyzed, looking after him.

Amelie said, disgusted: "And now I suppose I have to call Mariana! *I* have to apologize to Mariana!" Her streaked-blond hair was in her face, and there were frown lines in her usually smooth forehead. "You! Deceitful Nadia! *You* are to blame."

Nadia murmured an apology, how many times she had murmured, *Sorry, I am so sorry,* deeply shamed and mortified and remorseful, but as she moved to edge past Amelie, the distraught woman struck out at her in sheer frustration, cuffing her on the side of the face with the back of her hand.

"You! *Trompeuse! Et grosse!* For shame!"

Tink. Where are you . . .

Tell me what to do, Tink.

I feel so bad. I have made such mistakes.

Despite Nadia's pleas, Mr. Stillinger called Quaker Heights Day School as he'd threatened, Nadia would learn later.

Though it was well past school hours, after eight p.m., Mr. Stillinger managed to speak with Mr. Nichols.

And Mr. Nichols called Adrian Kessler.

And Adrian Kessler was astonished to learn that his student Nadia Stillinger was the mysterious "Dani A." who'd left a framed painting for him in a woman's gilt tote bag in the rear of his Subaru—"My God, you mean the painting is *real*? A *real* *Kandinsky*?"

He'd discovered it in the rear of his station wagon and brought it home, of course. At the moment it was on a table in his living room, propped up against a lamp.

It was a strange, dreamlike, abstract painting—reminding him of something familiar, though he couldn't have said what.

"An original work of art? The girl left for—*me*?"

This was astonishing. Adrian had thought, as he told Mr. Nichols, that a friend at school—one of his colleagues—had left him the painting as some sort of birthday joke. The name "Dani A." meant nothing to him—he'd been utterly baffled. Of course he'd assumed that it was just a reproduction, though a very good reproduction, in what looked like an expensive frame. And of course he'd heard of Wassily Kandinsky, but he wasn't sure that he could identify a Kandinsky painting.

Yes, he assured Mr. Nichols—he'd made inquiries. He'd spent hours calling friends and acquaintances to see if one of them had played the prank on him—he'd asked friends if they could identify "Dani A." He'd thought that the card to "Mr. Kessler" had been a trick to make him think that it had to be from a student—somehow, he hadn't thought that it could be a student, though probably, in retrospect, he should have suspected that.

"I guess I thought it was a joke that would be explained soon—like on my birthday. Which is tomorrow."

Adrian laughed uneasily. Headmaster Nichols, an older man with a penchant for hypervigilance regarding parental complaints about his faculty, had been listening in ominous silence.

"Nadia Stillinger. Maybe I should have guessed. . . ."

"Why do you say that, Adrian?"

"Because Nadia is—has been—talking to me quite a bit after class lately. She's a bright girl, but very insecure. Physically she's mature, but in other ways she's very young."

"Is this girl attractive?"

"Attractive? I—really can't say."

Adrian didn't want to say yes. And he didn't want to say no.

"How would you characterize your relationship with her?"

"Relationship? Why—nothing out of the ordinary."

"Just the sort of relationship a teacher would have with any student?"

"Y-yes." Strictly speaking, this was probably not true. But Adrian swallowed hard and resisted the impulse to explain further.

"Then why did the girl give you a birthday present, Adrian—worth three million dollars?"

Three million dollars! Adrian was astonished.

Thinking what a story this would be, related to his friends. And on his twenty-seventh birthday, which would have been, otherwise, a not very exceptional birthday.

"I—don't know, Mr. Nichols. I think that Nadia is a little excitable—impressionable."

"In what way excitable, impressionable?"

"She tends to be a little more emotional than most students. She seems always"—he hesitated, not wanting to say *breathless, yearning*. Not wanting to say *pleading, adoring*—"very intense about whatever she's talking about, as if it had a personal meaning to her. Scientific ideas, for instance. . . ."

Mr. Nichols spoke in a neutral voice, as if he were making no judgment, only just stating facts: "Personally, I don't know

Nadia. I certainly know of Roger Stillinger, her father, but I've never had the pleasure of meeting him. I seem to remember a quite glamorous young woman—the girl's stepmother?—bringing her to school for an interview, before her application was accepted; and this young woman, Mrs. Stillinger, has come to a few PTA meetings, I think. Nadia's father is CFO at Univers Pharmaceutical. I make it a point to know such things. And he's very upset, as you can imagine. He demanded that I call you at once and tell you to bring his painting back to him, and the bag it came in, immediately—or he has threatened to call the Quaker Heights police."

Adrian Kessler, who'd been standing in a doorway, felt his knees grow weak. He fumbled for a chair and sat.

"Call the *police*? Did you say—*police*? Mr. Nichols, I didn't steal the painting—the girl left it in my car—she didn't even give it to me, certainly I wouldn't have accepted it. And I didn't even know who'd given it to me until a minute ago, when you called—how could this possibly be my fault?"

"No one is saying it's your fault, Adrian, in any way. But people can file complaints with the police without evidence. Mr. Stillinger is angry and suspicious. He spoke very aggressively—he may have been drinking. He claims that you must have exerted 'undue influence' on his daughter, and that you've been seeing her after school in your office, to discuss 'personal' matters."

"No. This all wrong. Give me Mr. Stillinger's address, please, Mr. Nichols, and I'll return the painting right now."

"And the bag. The gold bag it came in. Don't forget that."

• • •

Shame! Nadia hid away in her room, wanting to die.

Her face was still smarting from Amelie's slap. Her eyes welled with tears of hurt and indignation.

Her father had called Headmaster Nichols. In a sniggering voice outside her shut door, Amelie had told her that her teacher was "returning" the painting—as if Mr. Kessler had been the one to have taken it.

Oh! Oh God. Poor Mr. Kessler, humiliated.

Because of her, humiliated.

He would hate her now. He would never feel kindly toward her again.

Anxiously Nadia waited. Every few minutes she checked her iPhone to see if there might be a message from Mr. Kessler, but of course there was not.

Then, at 9:12 p.m., she saw headlights turn into the driveway outside. On the lighted front walk there was a man hurrying— Mr. Kessler?—Nadia wouldn't have recognized her teacher wearing sweatpants and a nylon parka, carrying the gaudy gilt tote bag with an object inside.

How unfairly Mr. Kessler was being treated. Nadia could imagine what harsh, insulting, unjust things her father had said to Mr. Nichols about him.

Nadia hoped that Mr. Kessler wouldn't bring the silly little birthday card to show her father, too.

What a reckless thing she'd done! Yet at the time it hadn't seemed reckless at all but a sweet, intimate, playful gesture—if only Mr. Kessler had known who "Dani A." was.

Nadia heard voices downstairs. Her father's voice, and another voice she had to suppose was Mr. Kessler's, not so loud.

She stood in the doorway of her room, listening without daring to breathe, but she couldn't hear distinct words.

She wondered—would Mr. Kessler ask to speak with her? Her father would never allow it.

Amelie hadn't apologized for slapping Nadia. She'd seemed to have forgotten immediately.

No one had ever struck Nadia before. Not even her father on those occasions when he'd been in a rage at her. *Only a brute will strike a child*—Nadia had heard this somewhere.

Nadia remembered how Tink's mother had slapped *her*.

You'd have expected, from Tink's brash manner, that she'd have reacted more assertively against her mother, but she hadn't. Poor Tink had pressed her hand against her stinging cheek in silence, just as Nadia had done.

Nadia wondered if, after Tink had *gone away*, her mother even remembered having slapped her in front of her friends.

Nadia ventured into the corridor, to the top of the stairs. Her father had commanded her to "stay in your room," but she had to hear what was being said downstairs.

. . . claims you touched her. Talked of "personal things" in your office.

. . . claims you "comforted" her, after you made her cry. In your office, after school. When no one else was around.

. . . claims you drew her into talking about her mother. Which is none of your goddamned business. Taking advantage of a naive, immature, impressionable girl.

Mr. Stillinger's deep, angry voice. And there came Mr. Kessler's less forceful voice protesting, *No . . . no . . . not like that.*

Nadia listened anxiously. She hadn't been able to eat much

that day—she was light-headed, dizzy. Biting at her thumbnail and seeing the bloody cuticle.

. . . misunderstanding, Mr. Stillinger. Believe me. Nothing like that.

Cautiously Nadia descended the stairs. The adults were standing in a room that opened off the foyer, that Amelie called a "drawing room"; no one was seated. Mr. Kessler hadn't even been invited to remove his nylon parka. On a table was the Kandinsky painting, which had been unwrapped and no doubt carefully inspected by Mr. Stillinger. Also on the table was the gilt bag, which looked cheaply glamorous now, like something you might purchase in an airport store, though it had originally cost seven hundred dollars.

How strange it was to Nadia to see Mr. Kessler in her house—in gray sweatpants, parka, and running shoes. His hair was disheveled, and he seemed so *young*—many years younger than her dominating father, and younger than Amelie. Though Mr. Kessler was the tallest person in the room, Mr. Stillinger outweighed him by many pounds.

As Nadia moved to the doorway, her father's eyes shifted to her with a look of pained surprise and disgust.

"Nadia! Haven't you caused enough trouble? I've told you—*stay out of this*. The painting has been returned—the situation is under control. Mr. Kressle is about to leave, but this isn't the last he will hear from me. I intend to file a formal complaint with the headmaster, and if Nichols doesn't cooperate, by which I mean a disciplinary hearing, I will file a report with the police. Touching a distraught girl—provoking her to tears, and to personal disclosures—will not go unnoticed."

Mr. Kessler protested, "Mr. Stillinger, I explained to you—*I did not*—"

"My daughter doesn't lie, sir. It will be her word against yours."

Mr. Stillinger's eyes glared in his flushed face. Even his ears were reddened. In calmer circumstances Nadia would have sensed that, though her father spoke threateningly, it was possible that he wasn't entirely serious—he liked to intimidate, and to frighten, but it wasn't like him to pursue an issue once he'd won and had forced others to capitulate to him. His intention was to assert his dominance over his daughter's much-admired science teacher, and humiliate the man. He enjoyed, too, playing the bully in the presence of his young wife.

But Nadia was too upset to register this. She pleaded, "Daddy, no! Mr. Kessler did not touch me—not my hand and not *anywhere*. He *did not*. He *did not* cause me to cry—I was crying before I went to see him. None of it was his fault—it was my own crazy idea to give him a birthday present. It won't be my word against his—and you can't make me testify against him."

Adrian Kessler turned to stare at Nadia. He was trying to smile but looking agitated as Nadia had never seen him.

"Why, Nadia . . ."

"I'm so sorry, Mr. Kessler! I n-never meant to—I wasn't thinking . . ."

Nadia's father turned to her angrily. "Turn around and go back upstairs, Nadia. Immediately."

Mr. Kessler objected, "Don't speak to Nadia like that, please, Mr. Stillinger. She's upset, she's been under a good deal of strain—this isn't the way to handle the situation."

"And who are you? What business is this of yours? You can leave our house now, Mr. Tressle. Just—leave."

"Mr. Stillinger—"

"You've caused enough disturbance in this household for the time being—taking advantage of an unstable adolescent girl. Please—just leave the premises."

"I don't think you should frighten your daughter as you are doing, Mr. Stillinger. You don't need to raise your voice to her. Nadia may have acted impulsively and immaturely, but she didn't do anything really serious, and your precious painting is back with you unharmed."

"If you don't leave immediately, Mr. Tressle, I will call the police. Or I will eject you bodily. Which do you prefer?"

"Are you threatening me? Are you threatening Nadia? If—"

"Get the hell out of my house, you pathetic—prep school teacher!"

Mr. Stillinger pushed at Mr. Kessler's chest, forcing him backward. Both men were panting, and for a moment it looked as if Mr. Kessler might push back at Mr. Stillinger—then the younger man thought better of what he was doing, and backed away.

"If they hurt you, Nadia—tell me. They have no right to terrify you or harm you—"

"Out! Get the hell out! You—child molester! *Pervert!*"

Mr. Kessler left. Nadia ran to the front door of the house to follow him, but Mr. Stillinger gripped her arm to pull her back.

"Mr. Kessler—take me with you! Please—take me with you! I don't want to stay here with them. Mr. Kessler! Please . . ."

Mr. Stillinger yanked Nadia back, as if she were a limp cloth doll. And Amelie, cursing under her breath, slammed the front door.

Through the buzzing in her head Nadia could hear Mr. Kessler's station wagon kick into life and depart.

Red taillights diminishing into the darkness, beyond Wheatsheaf Lane.

Nadia was unresisting now. She was not even crying now. Her furious father and her furious stepmother were saying terrible things to her, spitting terrible words at her. Nadia scarcely heard, and scarcely cared. She was suffused with shame; they could not hurt her further. In a few minutes they would banish her upstairs to bed—as if she were a small child. As if she were six years old, defenseless. They would deprive her of her cell phone and of her laptop. They would punish her, for they were ashamed of her, and hated her. And Nadia had not the spirit to resist. She had not the strength to tell them, *I don't love you—you can't hurt me. I wish I was with Mommy. I wish that Mommy had taken me with her—that's where I belong.*

7.

"SUSPENDED"

SHE TEXTED HIM—KESSLER! SAID SHE'D DO ORAL SEX WITH HIM—IF HE SHOWED HER HOW.

SHE LEFT HIM A BIRTHDAY PRESENT—CANDY-FLAVORED CONDOMS IN A GOLD LAMÉ BAG LIKE FROM ARMANI.

SHE SENT HIM NUDE PICTURES OF HERSELF ON HER CELL PHONE—FAT.

WHAT A SLUT! AND STUPID! AND A SENIOR—THINK SHE'D KNOW BETTER, IT'S LIKE PATH-ET-IC.

Posted on a website called QWAKERDEPPS were nude photos of a female with fat, bulging breasts and thighs like hams and Nadia Stillinger's head on her body; and a comical muscleman, also nude, with a small penis and Adrian Kessler's head on his body.

"Gross! This is disgusting."

"Is that real? It looks phony."

"Who cares?"

• • •

Nadia Stillinger wasn't in school. Nadia Stillinger didn't respond to text messages or to calls from her friends.

Merissa Carmichael was so upset, she went to speak with Mrs. Jameson in her office. "We have to stop this. We have to help Nadia. She's not a slut—she's the very opposite. I don't know anything about her giving a birthday present to Mr. Kessler—but I do know that Nadia is very emotional, and that since Tink Traumer died, she hasn't been—Well, I guess"—Merissa began to break down, as Mrs. Jameson listened sympathetically—"I guess none of us have been doing too well. But Nadia especially."

Mrs. Jameson said yes, Merissa was right, the postings were obscene and cruel and would come down immediately, she would see to it. And how was Nadia? Would Nadia like to speak with Mrs. Jameson, too?

Merissa said, wiping at her eyes, "I don't know. I don't know Nadia all that well, actually. I just know we have to stop this—cyberbullying. We have to help her before it's too late."

So sleepy! Sleep like a heavy embrace.

She was sinking beneath the surface of the dark, choppy water; she would not keep herself afloat by the exertions of her arms and legs. Her mother's spirit hovered near. Nadia pulled the covers over her head. *Nadia, it isn't time. Nadia dear, it isn't your time. Go back, Nadia—to your friends.*

8.

THE PLEA

COME BACK, NADIA! WE MISS YOU.

Nadia's friends texted her and called her. And Merissa came to Nadia's house to speak to her in person, to encourage her to return to classes.

Nadia insisted she'd been planning to return. Soon.

"Not 'soon'—tomorrow. Come to school tomorrow."

Nadia felt a clutch of panic. "Maybe—next Monday."

"No. Tomorrow."

"But—I don't think I—I'm ready. . . ."

"Don't be ridiculous, Nadia. What would Tink say?"

"I don't know—what would Tink say?"

"Tink would say, 'Don't be ridiculous, dude.'"

And when Nadia returned to school, and saw that a stranger named Mrs. Rappaport was teaching Mr. Kessler's fourth-period science class, she was shocked, and she was suffused with a new sort of shame; she'd known that Mr. Kessler was still "suspended," yet it had not seemed quite real to her, until she'd entered his classroom.

Virgil Nagy looked at her, with his awkward smile.

"Nad-ia! Welcome back."

"Thanks."

Nadia would have liked to slink into the room invisibly. But she knew that everyone was watching her and that there was no way she could be invisible—(this was like a dream of being naked in public!)—so she made her way to her desk by the window with whatever measure of dignity she could summon and a radiant blind smile, knowing that a blush was rising into her face for all to see. She would have stumbled over a boy's long legs carelessly crossed in the aisle, except at the last minute she stepped over them nimbly.

"And you are—?"

The substitute teacher frowned at Nadia in a pretense of not knowing who she was. *Mean,* Nadia thought.

"Nadia Stillinger."

"Oh yes. Nadia Stillinger." Frowning, Mrs. Rappaport made a mark in a little notebook. "You've been absent quite a while."

Was this a statement of fact, or an accusation? Nadia, blushing, decided to say nothing at all.

After a while, the stares of her classmates eased. With Nadia so blatantly in the room, at her desk, there was really nothing to *see.*

Nadia thought, *Maybe it isn't so important. Nasty things on the internet. Maybe—like TV cartoons.*

After class Virgil Nagy walked with Nadia. You would not have known the scandal attached to Nadia Stillinger, judging by the way Virgil spoke to her. "Mrs. Rappaport isn't anything like Mr. Kessler, is she? She couldn't even pronounce 'proprio-ception.'" (Virgil laughed: He'd been the one to "help out" the embarrassed teacher.) "We're all tired of her getting things wrong and repeating the few things she does know. Some of us are thinking of signing a petition to get Mr. Kessler back *soon*."

"A petition? That's a great idea."

Nadia was excited: She would ask her friends to help circulate a petition to all the students at Quaker Heights, not just those in Mr. Kessler's classes.

Almost immediately Nadia realized how *complicated* and *complex* things were at school—apart from a few glances, snig-gers, and pitying smiles, no one was really so very concerned with Nadia Stillinger any longer.

And public opinion seemed definitely to have swung to Adrian Kessler's side. That was clear.

Merissa said, "The next thing you must do, Nadia, is make an appointment with Mr. Nichols. Not just send him emails—go to talk to him. And to the disciplinary committee—maybe even the trustees when they have a meeting."

"Talk to the trustees! I could never do that."

"To get Mr. Kessler exonerated and reinstated, you will have to."

"I just don't think that I—I—"

"I thought you liked Mr. Kessler! Isn't that what this is all about?"

"Y-yes, but . . ."

"You must help him, then. Only you can help him, really."

"Only me? I—I never thought of that. . . ."

"Only you got him in trouble," Merissa said wickedly, "so only you can get him out of trouble. What would Tink say?"

It happened that Headmaster Nichols had convened a quasi-emergency meeting of the board of trustees and the disciplinary committee, to discuss the issue of Adrian Kessler. This was fifteen days after the "incident" had come to light, with Mr. Stillinger's angry telephone call to the headmaster.

Nadia had asked to be allowed to attend the meeting, to address the committee and the trustees.

She was terrified of speaking to these strangers! She could not believe that such a thing would happen, by her own volition: Like a responsible adult, she'd actually made an appointment to see Mr. Nichols.

Is this how life is? Nadia wondered. *You don't just think about things and get anxious about them; you do something.*

She could not trust herself to speak spontaneously. She spent hours composing her remarks.

On the eve of the meeting, Nadia was sick with apprehension.

It would be easy, she thought, to just not show up at the meeting, which was in the headmaster's office at school. Or she could send an email to Mr. Nichols's secretary saying that she was sick—she wasn't coming to school that day.

"I can't. I can't do this."

There was a deathly silence in her room. At a distance, wind was blowing in tall trees, like barrels being rolled across a pavement.

Elsewhere in the Stillinger house there was silence, too: Both Mr. Stillinger and Amelie were out for the evening, together.

There came a shivery presence in Nadia's room. She knew, without turning, that Tink had entered.

Was Tink disgusted with her? Nadia wouldn't have blamed her.

Nadia said in a faint, whining child's voice, "See, I can't. I just c-can't. I c-can't talk to these people."

And Tink said, *You will do it, dude.*

"No, Tink! I can't. I just—can't. . . ."

And Tink said, *Yes, you can, and you will, dude. No turning back.*

One hundred eighty-six students! The names included a number of students who hadn't yet had a course with Adrian Kessler but who had taken up his cause in the wake of the suspension.

Mr. Nichols's secretary led Nadia and Merissa into the oak-paneled room, in which twenty men and women sat around a heavy oval table. Several faculty members on the disciplinary committee were known to Nadia, but all of the trustees were strangers. It seemed significant to Nadia that she and Merissa were introduced to the room but that no one was introduced to them, for their time at the meeting would be brief.

Nichols wasn't the chair of the meeting, it seemed. The chair was a gentlemanly white-haired alum (class of '56) who wore a glinting school pin in his lapel. His manner was bemused and curious but not unfriendly.

"Girls, welcome! Tell us why you are here."

Nadia was trembling. She and Merissa were both wearing Quaker Heights Day School uniforms—a dark blue wool school jumper over a white turtleneck sweater, with the heraldic insignia of the school over their right breasts: a lion, against crossed staves.

Nadia had suggested the uniforms. Merissa asked where she'd gotten such a great idea, and Nadia said proudly, "It's something Tink would do. You know—dressing funny."

Nadia had written her own statement. At first her voice quavered as she read it, then gained strength as she continued.

"I have come here today to appeal to you to exonerate Mr. Adrian Kessler from any purported wrongdoing or 'unprofessional behavior' and to reinstate him as an instructor at this school. I know that many cruel and crude and inaccurate things have been said about him, and about me, but Mr. Kessler is entirely innocent of anything you might have heard. He had nothing to do with the fact that I left a gift for him in his car, which he knew nothing about; he returned the gift to my father as soon as he was notified whose it was. He did not ever speak improperly with me. He was always kind, considerate, thoughtful, and professional. I am so sorry—my mistake was to act without thinking, and to give one of my teachers an expensive present that wasn't mine to give. And to give it anonymously. I would not ever do such a thing now. Mr. Kessler had no idea who'd left the gift for him and was totally surprised! I know that my father, Roger Stillinger, has filed a formal complaint about Mr. Kessler, but that's because my father is angry at me. He wants to punish me by punishing Mr. Kessler. But I am hoping that you will see that this has all been exaggerated."

Nadia paused, breathing quickly. After her initial panic she'd begun—almost—to relax; it was clear that everyone at the table, including Headmaster Nichols, was listening intently to her, and respectfully—several were even nodding sympathetically.

Then Merissa spoke, presenting the petition to the meeting—(it was passed around the oak table, examined and admired)—and telling of how Adrian Kessler had been a wonderfully encouraging teacher to her: He'd inspired her to write an essay that had won a prize in a national competition sponsored by *Scientific American*, and that had been posted on the magazine's website for a month; moreover, Mr. Kessler had encouraged her to apply for early admission at Brown, and she'd been accepted weeks ago—"I will always be grateful to Mr. Kessler."

Early admission at Brown! *That* was greeted with unanimous approval.

It seemed that both Nadia Stillinger and Merissa Carmichael had made a strong impression on the adults. They were thanked for their testimonies by the courtly chair of the board and escorted from the room, and in the morning a notice was issued by the headmaster's office that Adrian Kessler had been taken off his suspension and would resume his teaching duties the following day.

Pretty damn good, guys!
Couldna done better myself.

9.

THISTLE

She would call the little lost lynx-cat Thistle.

She knew her father would disapprove. Her father would disapprove *strongly*.

She'd mentioned this to Tink.

And Tink had said, *So? Don't tell him.*

"Don't tell him? My father? He'll discover the cat, and—"

Maybe. But maybe not.

"Unless I could hide her. The house is so big, and Daddy is never home much. . . ."

Nadia laughed. This was a very wicked idea!

But not so wicked as stealing her father's painting. Or anything of her father's.

That, she vowed she would never do again.

Or, if she did, she would never, ever behave so carelessly as to get caught.

When Nadia returned to High Ridge Park, she brought with her not only a can of tuna fish but a cardboard box with a few strategically positioned airholes in it.

She hadn't told any of her friends about the beautiful little lynx-cat that had mewed at her in the woods. Not even Merissa.

Nadia believed that if she persevered, she would rediscover the lynx-cat.

Or Tink would send the cat to her.

"Kitty? Oh kitty-kitty . . ."

In the wake of the meeting in Headmaster Nichols's office the day before, Nadia was feeling very good. It did not seem real to her—and yet, it was real—that a decisive action of her own had had such an immediate and positive effect: Mr. Kessler had returned to teaching!

Merissa, too, was thrilled—though she had had much more experience with things going well for her, as Nadia knew.

"The Perfect One—it must be wonderful to be *you*."

Nadia had spoken without guile or irony to her friend, who'd stared at her for a moment as if suspecting that Nadia must be joking—then laughed and said, with a droll little grin, "Oh, yes—it's wonderful. I have to pinch myself to make sure that I'm real."

Strange how Merissa Carmichael was now, as if overnight, Nadia Stillinger's closest friend. The girls guessed that Tink had had something to do with this, but—what?

In the vicinity of the path above the river, and the steep fall to the water thirty feet below, Nadia searched for Thistle.

Cupping her hands to her mouth, calling, "Kitty-kitty-kitty!"

And after a while, maybe forty minutes, maybe an hour—there came a faint mewing sound, from deeper in the woods.

Quickly, Nadia turned, calling, "Kitty-kitty!" and hearing the mewing until at last there was a movement in the underbrush, and there, the little lost cat with the silvery brindle markings and glassy-green eyes.

10.

"NOT GOING ANYWHERE"

Winter was ending: Rivulets of icy water ran glittering in the sun, as banks of soiled snow melted. A sharp wind blew last year's leaves scuttling along the pavement like scraps of tin, and overhead the sky looked like a giant flame was pushing against a cloud barrier and about to burst into flame.

Nadia seized her friends' hands. Excitedly they cried, "What?"

"It's Tink. She's here."

"Tink? Where?"

They turned—they looked up—they were desperate to see Tink, knowing that she was close, teasing.

"Tink? Tink!"

"Tink—are you here?"

But there was silence. Except for the wind, and leaves blown across the pavement—silence.

"It's like Tink not to come when you want her."

They laughed nervously. Their fingers, gripping one another's fingers, had gone icy cold.

"Tink is a *bitch*."

"Tink is *so bitchy*."

They laughed. They listened. They heard nothing.

The house at 88 Blue Spruce Way had been sold. Veronica Traumer had moved away—to L.A., it was believed.

On the internet, Veronica Traumer continued to exist in a sequence of glamour photographs, of which virtually none resembled the others. The actress's exciting news was that she'd just signed a contract for another *Lifetime* daytime series, in which she would play the female lead.

There was very little about Veronica Traumer's daughter, Katrina, except notations that the "seventeen-year-old former child actress" had died in June 2011. On the Wikipedia website was the additional information that Katrina Traumer, a "long-time leukemia patient," had died of "complications" involving that disease.

Leukemia! None of Tink's friends had ever heard that she had had *leukemia*.

"Tink would have told us if she'd had leukemia. We would have known!"

"Well—maybe. But—you know Tink."

"But—if Tink did have leukemia, then—"

"This Wikipedia page says it's 'uncorroborated.' We can't believe it."

"I think that Tink had a bone marrow transplant when she was a little girl. I *think* she'd mentioned that once—in the way that Tink alluded to things, you know? So you didn't know if they were true or not—or maybe they'd happened to that little girl Penelope she played on television, and not to her."

"Bone marrow. We could have donated bone marrow to

her. . . . They look for donors, don't they?"

"Maybe that's what she was asking me. 'A favor.' Oh God! And I didn't realize."

Merissa was stricken. She pressed her hands to her face, in sudden horror.

"I mean—she'd started to ask. Then she changed her mind."

Hannah clutched Merissa's hand. All the girls stood close to Merissa, who was trembling.

"It would explain so much, wouldn't it—if Tink had been sick. If she'd had operations, and was tired of being sick. And so that's why she—why she did what she did. To spare herself more pain and also to spare other people who loved her . . ."

"But Tink would never have said a word; she didn't want anyone to feel sorry for her."

"She didn't want anyone to really *know* her. That wasn't fair."

"Look. We don't know. And if we tried to ask Tink's mother, we wouldn't know if she was telling the truth."

"Tink's mother probably made it up herself—that Tink was sick. That that was how she d-died—of a sickness that no one could cure—not something Tink did because she wanted to. That way Big Moms could have sympathy for losing her daughter, instead of people hating her because she was a lousy mother."

Nadia spoke with surprising vehemence. Since the incident with Mr. Kessler, and the cyberbullying, she was much less passive and compliant than she'd been; at times, you could discern an edge to her voice that was reminiscent of Tink's voice when Tink was in a combative mood.

"You have to be a match, don't you? To donate bone marrow?

It must be like—a blood type? Not just anybody could donate bone marrow to anybody else. . . ."

"Tink wouldn't have wanted to ask. She'd have thought it was just too—too much to ask."

"*I'd* have done it. She didn't give me a chance!"

"I'd have done it. . . ."

The girls of Tink, Inc., joined hands to comfort one another.

"I feel so terrible about this! So kind of—lost . . ."

"Look, we can't be sure. Like it said, the Wikipedia entry is 'uncorroborated.'"

"I wish we could know. . . ."

"Well—we won't know."

"Like about Tink's father—'the Amazing Vanishing Man'— whoever he was, we won't know."

Overhead the sky was losing its light. The glowering red sun behind the clouds had begun to fade. A faint rustle of leaves across the pavement and then silence, and if Tink had been hovering near, now she had departed.

Except that night a dream came to each of us, swift as a flash of light across a wall.

And there was Tink, peering at us from a short distance, as if across an abyss, an expression of reproach on her face—(her face had a fever-tint, a smoldering glow)—it seemed that she was pissed as hell that we'd been speculating about her health behind her back—(her health was her own bloody business)—but she was forgiving, too.

Not going anywhere.
Not for a long time.
You guys would screw up totally if I did.
Just be cool—okay?

Also by Joyce Carol Oates

Matt and his big mouth are accused of threatening to blow up Rocky River High School; Only Ursula, a.k.a. Ugly Girl, really knows what Matt said that day, and is the only one who can help save him. . . . But will she?

Franky knows that something about the disappearance of her mother is terribly wrong— if only she can open her eyes to the truth.

Darren Flynn has the perfect life until the day that a rumor about his teacher—a rumor that involves Darren—spirals out of control. . . . Who can Darren trust now?

Jenna blames herself for the accident that killed her mother—but could her unexpected friendship with a boy named Crow help Jenna face the memories she's fought so hard to erase?

HARPER TEEN
An Imprint of HarperCollinsPublishers
www.epicreads.com